# ANGEL RADIO

A.M. Blaushild

Published by
HARMONY INK PRESS

5032 Capital Circle SW, Suite 2, PMB# 279, Tallahassee, FL 32305-7886 USA
publisher@harmonyinkpress.com • http://harmonyinkpress.com

This is a work of fiction. Names, characters, places, and incidents either are the product of author imagination or are used fictitiously, and any resemblance to actual persons, living or dead, business establishments, events, or locales is entirely coincidental.

Angel Radio
© 2015 A. M. Blaushild.

Cover Art
© 2015 Stef Masciandaro.
http://www.stefmasc.com/
Cover content is for illustrative purposes only and any person depicted on the cover is a model.

All rights reserved. This book is licensed to the original purchaser only. Duplication or distribution via any means is illegal and a violation of international copyright law, subject to criminal prosecution and upon conviction, fines, and/or imprisonment. Any eBook format cannot be legally loaned or given to others. No part of this book may be reproduced or transmitted in any form or by any means, electronic or mechanical, including photocopying, recording, or by any information storage and retrieval system, without the written permission of the Publisher, except where permitted by law. To request permission and all other inquiries, contact Harmony Ink Press, 5032 Capital Circle SW, Suite 2, PMB# 279, Tallahassee, FL 32305-7886, USA, or publisher@harmonyinkpress.com.

ISBN: 978-1-63476-278-6
Digital ISBN: 978-1-63476-280-9
Library of Congress Control Number: 2015906700
First Edition December 2015

Printed in the United States of America
∞
This paper meets the requirements of
ANSI/NISO Z39.48-1992 (Permanence of Paper).

Though I know it pains you to hear this,
You truly are a darling,
Clementine.

(I'm really sorry for making that joke)

# ANGEL RADIO

# 0

EVERYTHING HAPPENED fast, so much so that it never felt like it was even happening at all. It was a neat week of happenings, and then that was it. I was alone. The world was over.

The first day began drearily, a routine morning of filler schoolwork as we approached the end of the year. But somewhere between lunch and gym, someone must have checked their phone, because soon there was only one thing on everyone's mind: aliens. Or angels. It was hard to tell. No matter what they were, they were here and they weren't human.

There were photos and videos all over the web. They floated in the skies, above forests and cities. No one was sure what should be done about them.

It was all so wild. You hear, all your life, that we're probably not alone in the universe. But even when you read the stats that we're likely going to find aliens within your lifetime, it never seems real. It's just like a fun piece of trivia. You think there's other life out there? Cool. Good for you.

So when it happened, it happened… exactly as one might expect, actually. Speculation, conspiracies, riots, and general mayhem. And yet, calm. I mean, this was probably the biggest event in human history, but what could you do about it? Leave the studying to the scientists, the curiosity to the brave, and the rest to those with the will; all the rest of us could do was watch and wait. And sleep.

I went to bed early. No matter how exciting something is, it gets boring after a few hours to just stare at the same photos and videos. My dreams were empty. My life hadn't really changed.

Day two was when it turned bad. The angels started moving. They had never done much more than sit gently, and each seemed to carry a pearlescent hue. I suppose, while their appearance was rather unexpected, little could be found that was disheartening about them.

Each pulsated, softly, like they might carry a heart somewhere below those feathers.

Then they began to move. And while there was still that faint air of peace about them, and that tendency to pulsate, they were suddenly unholy creatures to my eyes, so wrong and so awful. They had eyes; this was always known, always observable. But when they opened all at once, multicolored orbs that were only broken by patches of feathers, I had to avert my eyes from my laptop's screen. There was something *knowing* about their bodies, something awful.

To see a video of a woman—who had just the other day been the first person videotaped touching one—ripped to shreds in a brutal display seemed unsurprising to me. There were religious types who had been, cautiously, considering these angels to be true messengers of God. Their ideas were forced to quickly change, though some still stuck to the idea: the angels didn't kill everyone who came to them. Some were spared. Some were not.

People offered themselves to the angels' judgments, circling them and waiting to be chosen. Some would die. Some would not.

I'm from Brattleboro, a small town in the corner of Vermont with a population of about twelve thousand, and we had one angel watching over us. It had found its perch on the stone of the library roof, and whenever I walked past I averted my eyes.

Ken Stark was the first to die in our town. He was nice. Bookish and pale. Paler in death. I had watched it all, the angel swooping with those great wings, and then Ken Stark was nevermore.

And thus, day two ended in fear. We hugged each other and we cried, the radio and TV blasting all night long, listening even in our sleep for updates.

Day three brought hope. All good things happen in threes. The angels didn't move much but to kill. People started ignoring them. Life went on, sort of. We adapted. I was still going to school, even with the absence of many teachers and students. I didn't really know why. I guess I needed something to take up the day.

The world came together by the third day. Most nations didn't enjoy having so many of their citizens killed and didn't mind putting away past troubles if it meant ridding the world of these monsters. Suddenly, everything had to happen at dangerous speeds. Plans of military strategy were developed with a desperately minimal attention to detail, the hope being that anything would be better than nothing in terms of a response.

The news was supplied with boundless reels of identical footage from the front lines—a concept that had lost much of its meaning as the enemy could be found everywhere. Casualties rolled in, separated into civilians and soldiers. Angels could die, it was discovered. They could bleed. There was still hope. Success was hard, but we looked past that as much as we could.

The fourth and fifth days were one and the same. There was no turn of date, just blood and death. And the news was perpetually on, bringing us fear and comfort. It seemed every time we killed one of them, two more would appear.

I quit school on the fifth day. There were more angels in town now. Three of them. The library angel rarely moved, but the new ones roamed like parade floats. They followed the streets, pacing them out over and over again. When they turned the corner, doors slammed and blinds dropped. I watched them and I waited. They were always looking at you, no matter where they faced. They radiated knowledge.

We had little left to cling to, and I found myself the calmest in my family. My mother and father were no longer working, staying at home and trying to keep themselves busy with hobbies. I watched with scorn. It wasn't that I had no fear. I just didn't *want* to fear, and be as weak as they were. Each night, no matter how distant I tried to be, I would sit with them by the television and eat dinner. On the second night, my mother had cried the most. By the fifth, my father and I had joined.

I'm adopted. Or, I was adopted. My parents died in a house fire when I was seven, and I spent a number of days living in the woods before I was found and the authorities realized I hadn't burned to death. I settled into my foster family fine, and truthfully, I don't have much memory of my life before them. It's a crazy sort of past, I know, but it's always been a strange piece of trivia to me, something I can tell strangers to gather a little bit of sympathy. I don't think very much of it these days.

I never felt more separate from my family than in those last few days. I loved them, right, I loved my parents, but I don't think it was until the last few days that I gathered the strength to tell them this. On the fifth night, we ate pancakes for dinner with all the lights on, five candles on the table, and the television playing on mute. We tried to talk, but a weary nervousness had overtaken all of our interactions lately. My mind was full of desperate thoughts, for the right moment to tell my parents I loved them. It sounds ridiculous, but it was my reality.

By the end of dinner, I felt sick and ashamed. I waited until I was on the stairs, heading to bed early at eight, to shout an "I love you."

They didn't acknowledge it was the first time I had said this. My mother simply said, "I love you too," and that was it.

All I did over those few days was paint. But the angels were hard figures to work off of. I couldn't quite decipher their bodies. Sometimes I'd take my sketchbook and try to draw them from afar—but I had no talent for such formless creatures.

On the sixth day, the day we were created, we lost it all. The angels, slow as they were, as hovering and vast as they could be, began to kill without discrimination. And they never stopped. It lasted all morning and all day and all night. First the major cities, the thick populations taking the longest.

It was almost a perfect wave of south to north, of west to east—the angels in the surrounding towns would only move when the ones in the city had finished their work. The major news networks died off pretty fast. Their cameras were still locked in place, and for a few moments we stared at the bloodied desks, bodies slumped down in the gathering pool of red. A shuffling movement at the edge of the screen reminded us of the slim angel that had crept in to kill them. It had gently avoided damaging the equipment.

We turned to national radio, and when that faded out, we kept to the Internet. But even that began to depopulate. And finally, when our local radio station fizzled out and there was just static....

Well. We were scared. Too scared. It was almost midnight, and we sat in the living room. My mother had a book in her hands, her thumb holding her place as she watched the door. My father sat next to her on the couch, breathing heavily. My mother kept shushing him, whispering to him to keep quiet. There was no way to tell if an angel was coming. There was merely the feeling of dread and the idea of rightness that *of course* we would die tonight. I sat in a chair across from my parents, sketching our cat, and the whole time I was thinking to myself, *This seems to be it.*

But then our bird clock tweeted the call of a summer tanager, and I didn't really realize it at first, but I was lying on the floor quite suddenly and staring up at the wall—and it was twelve twenty. All I could think was *That's odd.*

Then I got up, and I realized my clothes were wet with blood. And I was still alive.

The seventh day had come, and I was all alone.

THE ANGEL left like it had arrived: without me noticing and without a sound. The TV and radio were still on, blasting their white noise as loud as they could.

I was alone in every possible sense of the word.

Almost, but not quite.

I found myself on the floor again. I was in a cloudy state, one not helped by the constant movement of my head. When I began to regain my senses, my body was at an incline, my head being held above the ground by someone's hands.

And then I looked up, and there were eyes there. I had been thinking of eyes a lot—I mean, the angels were covered in them. But these eyes were unlike any I had ever seen. They were dark brown and utterly beautiful.

To sound quite stupid, I'd have to compare them to the bark of a tree, the sort that only seems to grow above murky ponds full of mud and frogs' eggs. The sort of pond you'd swim in as a kid, and come back to every year, no matter how gross it was. The sort of pond you could belong to, and the sort of tree you might try to carve your name into, one year, but completely fail to leave a mark on.

That sort of pond. That sort of tree. Those sorts of eyes.

I blamed my dreamy state for my fascination with his eyes. After all, there was a face there, a jaw and a neck and a nose and a mouth and eyebrows and ears and hair and all that. Skin like the night, face pulled into a look of blank curiosity.

But all I could think about were his eyes. They hung in my mind, almost disembodied figures that haunted my thoughts as I passed in and out of consciousness. By the time I was fully awake, the boy was gone.

But his eyes, his eyes were embedded into my being.

Forever, I'd wager.

# 1

TIME PASSES like any other thing—eventually.

In your typical postworld world, everything would be a desert for some reason, all the houses hollow caskets, and dust storms would rage across the nation.

For me, there were plants and silence. In only a few weeks, it became clear Earth would reclaim its own remarkably fast. In time Brattleboro would become the wilderness it was first carved from.

I left my house. I couldn't afford to look back. But it was so hard to even glance forward that I left myself stuck squarely in the present.

I moved into the school without really thinking about it. I camped in the art department, collecting blankets and pillows from nearby houses and building a sort of nest in the corner of the ceramics classroom. I used the drawing room as my own personal studio, covering its walls in hasty original works. Whenever I got frustrated I would grab a can of spray paint and just color the halls of the school. One day I was so upset, I trashed a classroom entirely, flipping over tables and kicking holes in the wall.

School was a place I hated, but it also was somewhere I could always feel safe. I had spent a good portion of my life in this building. I knew the kids from each class, the teachers from each department. I knew the security guards by face and the principal by name.

So yeah, when I was done trashing that classroom in a desperate fit of anger and sadness, I spent a couple of hours cleaning it up again. Putting all the desks even, taping paper over the holes in the wall, and even writing the date on the board.

I feared I was going a bit mad.

I took to reading textbooks, and sometimes I'd just cry after reading one, just because there was no one else left in the world who could explain a concept to me. I'd cry over a lot of stupid things, actually. When I was cooking canned food over a fire, I'd cry because I was the only person on earth capable of making fire. Or I'd cry whenever I petted a stray dog, because I was the only person left in the world to pet dogs. There was no one left to appreciate art. I was never going to see a dolphin again. No one would ever teach me calculus.

I excused my excessive behavior because, really, what else was I supposed to do with my time?

Every day was like a day in the middle of summer vacation, where you wake up late and go to bed whenever, spending the whole day doing just one thing. I spent most of my days painting, practicing for a gallery show I'd never hold, for an art school I would never get into. But it was all I was good at. I painted a lot of buildings, trees, and all my favorite things like that, but I also began to practice humans. I painted people I knew and people I could barely remember. Sometimes the finished project was nothing more than a glorified sketch. I would paint the teachers, and I'd paint the students, and I'd put my canvases at their desks, only to destroy them moments later.

At one point I spent a day reading the Bible, if only to understand the angels a bit better. Very little was relevant, for certainly my angels were not these messengers of God. Only two verses really stood out to me.

Ezek. 10:12—And their whole body, and their backs, and their hands, and their wings, and the wheels, were full of eyes on every side, even the wheels that they four had.

And…

Isa. 6:2—Above him stood the Seraphim; each had six wings; with two he covered his face, and with two he covered his feet, and with two he flew.

These angels, they were something like that. Great bodies covered in eyes and wings and eyes and wings and eyes and eyes and eyes. A never-ending sphere, hovering without use of its many wings. And when it did use its wings, I could hear it from streets away, and the breeze would toss my hair.

Since everyone had died, the three angels in town had paid no mind to me. The library angel continued its perching and watching; its feet were like hoofed claws gripping on to the roof and gazing over the streets like a gargoyle. The other two simply floated along, tracing out every road in town on repeat. I avoided them like the plague, naturally;

but on the rare occasions when I did accidentally stumble into one of them, it would ignore me.

The two patrollers looked like opposite twins. One had creamy feathers with dappled brown spots; the other was black as a crow with a few streaks of tawny orange. Their bodies were identical, though, sort of oval shaped, with eyes in every crevice. Their eyes were almost all human looking. In a fit of delusion I had once thought I recognized a few of them. The inhuman ones varied greatly, some simply with rings around the pupil, others pure colored, or seemingly inverse human eyes.

The library angel was different. It had more of a shape to it, ringed legs like a forest and two human hands. It sat like a dog, with two of its wings circling its feet, two more wide-open, and two more covering its face. The eyes on its wings faced every direction. I tried not to look at it, clinging to the childlike belief that if you can't see something, it can't see you.

I tried to name them once, beyond their physical features. But I couldn't do it without feeling *wrong* about the whole affair, and so I tossed out my list—of Drzendril and Gabriel, of Czoca and Joriphiel, of Cvac, Lucifer, and of Miasmiel and Michael. Some names were out of books, but others were from my own mind.

When I wasn't avoiding the angels, I was looting random buildings in search of something to fill my time. Domestic animals can't survive too long in the wild, but I had made it my personal quest to free them all. It was better that they die outside and become something else's food than to just decompose in a house.

They all made me feel pretty sad too, like they were all waiting for their owners to feed them and love them again. A couple had taken to following me around and begging for food, and I'd just pet them a bit and walk on.

I had raided all the stores downtown, of course. Tried on all the clothes I would never buy, drank warm beer till I puked, and choked on a cigarette or two. I raided an electronics store and played with all the battery-powered toys. I took an expensive car, crashed it, and then took another one. And crashed that one too. I explored the two or three mansions we had in town, relishing in indoor pools and lavish décor, dreaming about parties I would never have been invited to.

My favorite possession had to be my radio from the wilderness and camping shop. Battery powered, solar powered, and hand-crank powered, it was unstoppable. And only bringing me static, of course. But it was that static that lulled me to sleep each night, and it was that static that haunted my dreams.

I had claimed each street for my own. Elliot Street was all neon spray paint, flowers, and swirls all around, while Flat Street was for moping, fire, skulls, and random words in black paint. I took the whole town, and I tried to fill it as much as possible with whatever I could.

I ran naked in the streets whenever it rained. I washed my body in concrete potholes and my hair under gutters, and then I'd jump in the river and do it all over again.

At least I had food to spare. The first few days I had tried to eat all the perishables I could, and several months in, I was down to the canned foods. But there was a lot of canned food. Plenty in the stores, more in the warehouse and enough in every person's house. I had lighters and matches to spare, and certainly enough wood to burn.

I wished I was living in a desolate desert future, fighting others for food to survive, instead of this empty forest town full of everything I could need. At least it'd be interesting.

I talked mostly to the animals, and once or twice, to the angels. I yelled at the angels, I cried at the angels, I threw rocks at them, and spat at them, and they'd just continue to float on their usual routes.

I was now thoroughly convinced that boy with beautiful eyes had been a hallucination. I had been in so much shock, I had dreamed him up; that had to be it. But I still would climb to the roof of the stone church and look down on the streets, waiting in vain for something to move.

And at night I'd curl up in my nest of blankets, and I'd put the radio on full blast, waiting and waiting and waiting.

IT WAS another morning, and I was once again too lazy to figure out the date. In an attempt to cling to the old ways, I took an ancient laptop from one of the computer carts. Or really, I took the entire cart. Each battery only lasted a couple hours, and it wouldn't be long before I had used them all up.

Living like this really made me wish I hadn't studied painting. If I had taken a keen interest in mechanics, I could maybe figure a way to get electricity. It'd be nice to have working lights again.

The Internet was long gone at this point, but the laptop still played Minesweeper and solitaire. I played them until I was sick of them, but I continued on anyway.

I had also started to write. I had a handwritten journal, one I was having trouble maintaining. My entry for yesterday, for example, read:

*Another day. Windy. Found a couple cute dogs. Almost crossed paths with the tawny angel. Maybe I should try to name it again. I've read more about angel names. Lots of—iels. Lots of weird sounds. One of them must fit. Painted Samson Greenberg from physics class. Slept.*

Writing wasn't really my forte. I guess I had a desire to record all I had done, like if someone found it in the future, but of course there was no one left. Maybe friendly aliens would find it many years from now, and they could study the last days of humanity from it. I don't know.

I liked to imagine myself as a movie character, music swelling as I struggled to survive by myself. The audience cries with me, feeling empathy. Suddenly, almost out of nowhere, the mysterious boy with beautiful eyes sweeps in. He kills the library angel with a few stabs, and bravely grabs my hand. We run together as the tawny and dusty angels follow close, and then we turn around and reveal our weapons, destroying the last two angels easily. Then the boy takes me away to the last stronghold of humanity; everything is okay. The film ends on a triumphant note, hopeful of the human race's will to survive.

This is not a movie, though.

Personally, I'd even accept demons tearing up the earth and Satan ascending to take on God for the final battle or whatever if it meant those damn angels would leave. Maybe I'd fit in with the demons. At least they'd be someone to talk with.

After fiddling on the computer until I became bored, I decided to head out for a walk. I brought my radio with me, holding it by the handle with its volume on full blast. I felt like I needed a totem of humanity whenever I wandered the woods, or else it'd be like society never existed.

The great mountain Wantastiquet overlooked the town, and I had it in my heart that I wanted to climb it. I mean, it was an appealing thought. But honestly I didn't care much either way. I just needed something to do, and if pretending this mountain mattered to me helped, wonderful.

My bucket list was simple and, ultimately, uninspired. And lately it had become impossible. I couldn't go on a safari anymore or find love or travel Italy. My new bucket list was simply to keep on living. Climb a mountain or two. Find something meaningful in this half life.

It was a breezy September day, the nights getting shorter and the days getting colder. The leaves had yet to turn, but last year's colors still lined the forest trail. Not even crunchy anymore, they sounded like paper on my shoes.

I'm not weak willed, but I did cry. Not a heavy thing, not a pathetic thing, just sort of a solitary thing. I was alone. I was alone, and it would sink in for what felt like the first time every couple of hours.

I was feeling lame, even more so because I felt bad about wallowing. I was ashamed to be so miserable, and then angry with myself that I felt bad about being depressed. Like what? I was supposed to be happy about being the last human alive?

Arguing with myself wasn't going to get me anywhere, and neither was angst.

I had a mountain to climb.

A few hours later, I sat on the rocks that marked the top. They weren't technically the highest point, but they did mark the best overlook of the town. From here I couldn't easily tell it was empty. I could almost pretend I was just a school kid, coming up here to hang out on the weekend. Eating a lunch of nonperishable sweets. Probably off to do homework in a few hours.

The radio interrupted my daydreams. It snapped my attention and what felt like my neck, as I spun around to watch it carefully.

Static has a very particular quality to it. Steady and a mix between repetitive and nonrepetitive. So to hear anything else, even the slightest change in sound, was deafeningly different.

I can't sum up what it did to me. It stopped my heart and quickened it at the same time. My head grew crazy, and I almost thought I had finally snapped.

But no—

# ANGEL RADIO

Voices. Voices in the static, incomprehensible sounds and noises, meaningless and empty, but bringing me hope all the same.

I lifted the radio into the air, antenna as high as it could go. I stood on my toes, then ran into the woods in search of the highest point, and eventually I heard it.

"—*rible... any... I... it's possib.... And that en... io.*"

Then there was a sort of high-pitched and short-lived whine, the kind old TVs make when they turn off, and the static became uniform again. But it was enough for me.

There were voices out there. *People* out there. I had heard at least two voices—a man and a woman. And surely this couldn't be their only broadcast—perhaps the first, but they were probably trying to signal other survivors. They probably weren't going to give up now, and neither was I.

Can you follow a radio signal to its tower? I think you can. And even if you can't, I really didn't care. There were other people out there. I was going to pack my bags and leave the library angel, the tawny streaked angel, and the dusty spotted angel behind for good. Leave old memories behind and make some new ones.

I started laughing as I made my way down the mountain. I almost ran down, sliding on the leaves and nearly slamming into several trees. I didn't care. I was laughing for the first time in a long time. I found the tawny angel in the street and danced around it, unafraid. I sang a song to it.

I left my studio without touching my paintings. Maybe years from now I would return here with other humans, and I could give them a tour of my personal art gallery.

I had no idea where I was heading, truthfully, but I was too excited to care. I started on my way, over the hill and across the bridge and past the roundabout, until finally I was out of town and on the highway.

It was going to be a long walk. But I had a feeling I could handle it.

# 2

THE FIRST time I heard a full broadcast, uninterrupted, was a few miles down the road.

I realized about an hour in that I should have just taken someone's car and driven until I ran out of gas, but I didn't want to bother with it. Plus the thought of having to drag a corpse out of a car before being able to drive anywhere disgusted me.

Sort of lazy, yes, but I did most literally have all the time in the world. I didn't even have to worry about food or water, since most of the cars were filled with food rations and first aid kits. I took what I needed, including a particularly good hiking backpack to carry all my stuff.

Any corpses, whether on the ground or leaning out car windows, had rotted almost entirely away by now. They still smelled putrid in harsh sunlight, even if they were mostly bone.

Oddly enough, there weren't that many bodies. There had been nearly none back in town, and out here, their numbers were even fewer. Where did everyone go? Did the angels eat them?

Two days in I stopped in the town of Windsor. It wasn't that special of a place, similar to the one I had come from—an old riverside town in the forest. I didn't rest long.

But it was there, inside the old church that I was sleeping in for the night's rain, that I heard the broadcast.

It started with a change in the signal. I was half-asleep when I heard it, eyes closed and on the brink of exhaustion. But then there was a sharp noise, and I frantically leapt for the dial.

*"...Ello. Good morning. This is Emil speaking. Your host, now and forever."* I had long imagined a human voice, but my dreams couldn't start to compare to the reality that was coming from the radio in front of me. *"We have a special report for you today, dear listener,*

on a favorite sort of angel—the angel sort of angel! I mean the watching sort, to be more specific."

"The Watchers," a woman corrected. She yawned. "You must've seen them. Big. Weird. Lots of eyes. Lots of feathers. Not much more to say."

"Surely...?" Emil started to ask but dropped it.

"I don't know. I've seen them, but not, like, enough to really get a read on them. I've never seen them out in the sky when it's raining, and they seem to like traveling in groups. And they have sort of weird, fleshy skin. Wonder what's up with that? Has anyone actually touched one before? If you, or anyone you love, has touched a Watcher angel, please contact us. I want to know. We want to know."

"Naomi, stay on topic," said another woman.

"Right, right, right. I don't have much more to say. I haven't really been taking notes here. I tried to draw one, though, but that proved too hard. Too many layers. Um." She sounded confused. "I guess if you wanted to kill one, it wouldn't be too hard to just stab them in one of their eyes. Kind of an obvious flaw in their design."

Silence.

"That's all I have."

"Oh. Thank you," Emil said. "That was very... helpful. And now, Ada with the weather."

"Yeah," the other woman said, "so, I've been observing a lot of angels that I'm going to dub 'Cherubim' heading up north. You know. Four faces, more human shaped than balloon, lots of fire. They're not the only ones heading north, though—shit tons of angels are passing above us every day. I don't know and I don't care what they're doing there, but I think we should move down south and start living on a beach somewhere instead of in this hellhole."

"You know we can't do that. This job is our job."

"I want a raise."

"You know we can't do that either. Please continue your report."

"Oh, whatever. So anyway, bye-bye Cherubim. We've been hearing of an increase in Messenger activity as well, but until someone sends us actual evidence, we're going to politely ignore it."

"I think that concludes the news for today," said Naomi. "This has been Angel Radio."

*"See you next time, dear listeners, and remember: you are always being watched,"* Emil said, and there was a sharp wave of static.

ONE THING was clear: there had to be a colony of humans nearby, fighting the angels, their broadcasts a beacon of hope for other survivors. They were even comfortable enough to joke around.

I was too hyper to sit still. Never before had everything seemed so possible. I paced the floor of the church a couple times before deciding I was just too amped to fall back asleep. I gathered my stuff, double-checking that the radio was completely sealed in its plastic case, and departed.

There were more angels floating around me the longer I walked, their bodies so intricate and layered that they made me think of fleshy castles. I thought of them as Watchers, and they started to appear the moment the rain let up. Surely the angels didn't have a problem with water? That would be ridiculously bad planning on their part if so.

There was another kind of angel in the sky, ones I had dubbed Messengers. They were large and often quite shapeless. Most were like ovals, a sort of reverse pyramid that lacked any features besides wings and eyes. There was a feeling of serenity about them, still, as they hung throughout the sky. Their feathers ruffled in the breeze as they bobbed slightly, huge eyes framed with long eyelashes. I had grown used to them.

The Watchers were similar—in fact, I wouldn't have differentiated between them if I hadn't spent so long watching them as I walked. They had more eyes than the Messengers and were more circular. Often, they'd have one large eye covering one face of their body, with smaller ones spiraling off from that. Unlike Messengers, they rarely closed them.

For one of the last remaining humans on an empty Earth, things were going well for me. It would have been better if there were some way to find the other humans, but I liked to think of myself as an optimist.

The angels, like particularly slow butterflies, seemed farther away now. I mean that very literally, as they were the farthest I'd ever seen them before.

It was one of those sort of comical but really horrifying moments when I noticed a shadow on the ground that wasn't there before.

And with a pained movement that ended in me falling on the ground, I looked behind me.

And then I looked up.

I had never seen an angel like this one before. Its body was massive and constantly writhing with its wings; wings of all sorts, like sparrows and eagles and birds of paradise, were all balled into one form. Each wing had its eyes, and all of its eyes were incredibly human and incredibly terrifying.

Its head was not attached to its body at all, but floating above it and peering down with its incredibly long maw. Its face was that of a bird's skull, the true face below covered by a pair of enormous wings.

Another pair of wings gaped to the sky, feathers to the stars, and yet another pair covered its feet and swept the ground. It had five hands, each ending in a different creature's paw, with the fifth coming straight from the center of its chest and ending in a human hand.

About its head twirled two cosmic rings, their whole being covered in eyes. The rings interlocked under the floating head of the angel in such a way that the head was fully surrounded. Where the neck should have been on the body below was just a hollow tube.

It was an Ophanim, I decided. A throne. And sitting on its shoulders—or perhaps they were part of it?—were several other angels.

It bobbed like it was walking, one foot was moving at a time, but glancing at its body revealed it was floating about two feet off the ground.

I scurried to get to my feet, but as I looked at its eyes I fell straight back down again. I watched it move closer to me, and I pressed my back to the ground and held my breath.

And then it passed over me, and for a moment I was in the eye of the hurricane. Inside the angel was darkness and moving shapes and tiny dots of light, like white dust on black paper. And all the way on the other side, much farther away than it should've been, was the neck hole.

As it moved over me entirely and I sat looking up to the center, it stopped.

It hung above me, and suddenly I was gasping for air and choking on fear, and I could only feel adrenaline and a need to not move at all. I lay transfixed, staring straight through the pinhole of light that felt more and more like a spotlight. There was a delay before I realized I was hyperventilating.

I was trembling in the darkness and staring at the light. Ignoring the lack of danger I seemed to be in. It took too much work to force myself to stand, so I crawled across the asphalt until I came to the edge of the shadows. I didn't feel better until I hit the sunlight and cleared a distance of fifteen feet. I lay back on the road, hands covering my eyes, and slowed my breathing.

Then I got up, the Ophanim already long past me and making its way down the road.

I think I had fainted at some point.

The rain started up again too suddenly, a violent storm that passed in short bursts. Lightning flashed and struck, thunder roared, and I found myself a car to huddle up in.

But I didn't sleep.

I couldn't.

Not right now.

The radio, its power low from lack of charging, could only manage a little more than a whisper, and I leaned my ear against the speakers.

There wasn't static, but there weren't any words either. Just strange, strange sounds that carried into my sleep.

# 3

I DIDN'T wake up feeling any better, but at least the rain had stopped. The scent of wet asphalt calmed my nerves a bit, but the sight of the empty sky brought back my anxiety. I didn't want to encounter another monster like that again.

Still. I had to keep moving on. At this point that was my responsibility. Keeping myself alive—or the betterment of humanity. Or whatever. I just had to keep myself motivated.

Walking is a really monotonous activity, especially if you're all by yourself on a country highway. I kept the radio on. Broadcasts were becoming more and more frequent, though few were Angel Radio.

Sometimes there'd just be a little voice whispering, "Checking, one two three. Checking, two three one. Checking, three one two." For hours at a time. Sometimes music would play, though it was always an electric cathedralesque melody I had maybe heard once before. I enjoyed it all. Anything was good enough for me if it broke up the everything else of the world. Even the strange sounds that floated out of the radio, like moans and groans and screams, even they were appreciated.

I ended up taking a bike one woman had left on the highway, her corpse having fallen a ways from it. However, I found it such a pain to balance my stuff while I rode that I quickly disposed of it.

At one point I did step off the road. But only because the radio told me to. Emil's voice crept quietly, even at full volume, and all I heard was *"Stop stop stop stop stop"* over and over. I did stop. But I probably would have without the radio's orders—I had seen something move in the bushes. It looked too big to be an animal.

I hadn't seen many angels on land. There had been a few earthly ones, but they always seemed to be floating a few inches off the ground. It was either a new sort of angel or a bear.

The woods were old and healthy, with a lot of space between the trees and only little ground vegetation. I followed the movement to a large white oak.

I saw part of the mystery creature peep out occasionally as if it was shy, but I couldn't make out what it was. I rounded the trunk of the oak slowly, feeling my way across the bark. The thing moved with me, always staying a little out of sight.

Then I heard a gunshot and a guttural whimper that made me jump out of my skin. I instinctively flattened up against the tree and held myself calm for a few moments. Then I allowed myself to glance around the edge. Whoever had fired their gun seemed gone, but the creature lay dead at my feet.

It was a deer. A buck. I reached out to examine it closer when a decidedly human voice cried out.

"Don't!"

"What?" I said, unbelievingly. "What?" If anything, I was questioning if the voice was real, not why I couldn't touch the deer corpse.

He did not reveal himself to me, but then I could hear hesitation in his voice. "Don't touch it."

"It's a deer," I said, resorting to the confused tactic of stating the obvious.

"No it's not."

I glanced down again at the body. "It's literally a deer."

"No."

"I'm going to touch this deer if you don't show yourself to me, you know."

"No!" He caught himself and spoke more calmly. "No, you don't want to do that. And I mean no to both those things. You don't want either."

"So you're saying if I touch this deer, I'll die?" I moved my hand steadily toward the deer's head.

"It's not a deer, for the last time. And no."

"I'll get sick?"

"No."

"Is there any adverse effects to touching this deer?"

"Not technically. Just don't do it!" he said, alarm in his voice as I held my hand just an inch from the deer.

"Let me tell you, suspicious forest voice, I don't really feel like valuing your opinions for some reason."

"I'm sorry, but you don't want to see me or touch that not-deer creature."

"You've got that wrong, buddy, because I think I'm going to do it 'in about ten seconds."

"No! Don't!"

"One… two… thre—"

"Come on!" he stressed. "Come on!"

"Four."

"I can't believe this!"

"Five!"

But at that very moment, he shouted, "Erika!" And I went dead still.

"How the hell do you know my name?"

"I've been following you."

"Thanks for that info and all, but it's not like I say my name in my sleep."

"I've been following you for a while."

"Define a while."

"The sixth day."

I paused.

"All right, creep," I said, "just reveal yourself already." But I had a nasty feeling I knew exactly who I was going to see.

As expected the boy with the beautiful eyes emerged from behind a tree, holding a shotgun loosely in his arms.

"You. Now what's this about the dead deer?" I said, gesturing over to it.

"It's an angel," he said with a sigh.

"Looks like a deer to me."

"And it's not dead." Sighing again, the boy used his gun to lift the deer's neck, and I saw it had one giant eye in the center of its head. The eye rolled itself open and looked between the both of us frantically. Then on its body a hundred more eyes opened and the deer-angel got back on its feet, bobbing in the air.

"Stand back," the boy said, and he shot at it again. It fell to the ground again, immediately returning to its deer facade. He shot a couple more times, reloaded, and continued to shoot.

"And why is that angel pretending to be a deer again?"

"To trick you, of course."

"Into touching it?"

"Into coming into the woods in general."

"What would happen if I touched it, then?"

"Some awful things."

I was beginning to feel fed up with his cryptic answers and brash ways, but I wasn't going to let the only other human just walk away from me. I still needed answers.

I asked him, "Are we going to talk about how you somehow snuck into my house, protected me but not my family, and followed me all the way out here or not?"

"We'd be better off not discussing it."

"Am I supposed to just leave you here and forget everything?"

"Yes."

"And you'll continue to watch me sleep?"

"I have to sleep too. But yes."

"I doubt you have a reason for this."

"There are reasons but… I can't risk saying anything. Do not worry about me."

"I'm not letting you go."

"I guess it's a good thing I'm light on my feet," he said. And indeed he was fast, dashing away behind a patch of maples, already gone from my sight.

"What's your name?" I yelled as loud as I could.

From nearby the boy with beautiful eyes called back, "Gav!"

"Like Gavin…?" I said quietly to myself, and from somewhere in the treetops I heard a voice whisper, "Yeah." I had to resist the urge to laugh.

I TRUDGED out of the woods feeling a bit annoyed and generally unnerved. It figures the only other surviving human I'd meet would be a weirdo stalker.

# ANGEL RADIO

The deer-angel had followed me to the forest edge, floating with a sort of ethereal quality. Sometimes I thought I heard laughter from back in the woods, but I figured it was probably in my imagination. Or, I suppose, it may not have been. I was almost expecting something else crazy to happen before I reached my bag again.

In an almost reassuring way, I was correct. At the bridge between the woods and the road, the deer-angel paused. Then it unhinged its jaw, let a great deal of steam out, and ran away. In the still-standing mist, I heard a distinct sound ring in my head—*Orifiel*—before dispersing.

All right. Whatever. Angels were weird as hell, but that was a well-established fact at this point. Time to move on.

The sun was starting to set, and out of the corner of my eye I thought I saw the occasional movement along the border of the forest— the deer-angel, I decided. Following me still. Was there a wild chance it was working with Gav? Yes. Absolutely. At this point, any ridiculous thought might as well be considered fact.

Gav was in general weirding me out, which is a quality I tend to dislike in gorgeous people. And yet I was almost excited to see what excuse he had for breaking into my house on the sixth day of angels and holding me like that. I knew this certainly wasn't the last time we would meet. I was going to make sure it wasn't—there was no way I was letting him go like that.

Sure, he could run about for now, pretending he was guileful—I liked to believe I'd best him by the end. I didn't know what "besting" him meant yet, but I assumed I'd build a fantasy to explain it by the next half hour of walking.

I like to pride myself on my tenacity. I can still remember what bad things people have said about me from years past. And I haven't forgiven them. I guess now is the time for that, though. Now is a time for peace with the dead.

It's a terrible sort of way to be, I guess, assuming most of your personality. I've never been pushed to do much of anything. But I've always run with the assumption that I am worthy to be feared. That I am the sort girl that no one wants to make mad.

But there was no way to know for certain, not anymore.

The broadcast came with the setting sun.

"*HAVE YOU* heard the next big thing?" Naomi was saying. "*Farming!* Everyone's doing it. Good way to get food if you have the time for it. Vegetarian is definitely the way to go in times like these."

"Cowards," Ada mumbled.

"Especially," chimed Emil, "with the state of game! It's getting harder and harder to find wild animals. I, personally, haven't seen a living deer in weeks. But hey, who needs meat? We can all go vegan again, just like the good old days! Or at least until we find some good meat."

"Humans have always been omnivores," said Ada. She sounded like she was chewing something. "Did you know you can eat bugs? People thought that was going to solve global hunger. Bugs."

"No one's eating any bugs! Plus, it's not like we're going to have to worry about hunger ever again," Naomi stated. "I mean, there's so much food just lying around everywhere. I guess we'll probably die if we eat too much of the prepackaged stuff, though."

"I want to eat some bugs. Like ants and shit. And scorpions. They're really good."

"Ladies, I feel like we're getting off track," Emil said. "Why don't we—"

"Whatever, gentleman," interrupted Ada.

"Yeah, okay. Anyway, Lucimi has a special report today. Lay it on us, Naomi!"

"Yeah! So I've been doing some research lately into forest management. Did you know that trees can be harvested like any other crop? Did you know trees are a crop? It's so weird."

"That's not what I asked you to look into."

"I got sidetracked."

"All right, I'll do it instead. Today, dears, we're looking at Messenger angels. Just like Watcher angels, except they specialize in messages. They're real lugs, sort of boring to observe actually. They don't move much. Barely have a brain. Getting any sort of weapon to pierce them is nigh impossible, though I'd suggest something small and precise. Bullets, as always, are suggested. However, you shouldn't even bother shooting a Messenger angel—they are relatively harmless, though capable of killing when provoked. Their role is what it sounds—

*they carry messages. How do they do it? Who knows? But they sure seem to be doing it constantly."*

"Lengthy.... So unlike you, Emil!" said Ada, having found herself a drink to slurp. *"But boring as ever."*

"Let's just get to the weather and finish this thing up. Ada? Your turn."

"Well, here in the city, we're expecting a huge tide of Cherubim, so much so that I don't feel safe leaving the house. Not much new to talk about. Uh, also it looks like the rumors were true. Lots of angels have been swarming the area lately, Messengers and Watchers and warriors alike. It's like raining angels. Clouds of them, welling up. Annoying little tykes."

*"And...?"* said Emil expectantly.

"And keep on the lookout for any bad news Bambis out there, as evidently some angels have been taking the form of adorable little woodland animals. We pretty much said it at the start of the show. Why were we even trying to do it subtly at the beginning if you wanted me to just say it right out at the end? Like yeah, we heard there's this—"

*"Shush, Ada,"* said Lucimi with the air of someone trying to laugh off a threat.

*"And thus ends the Angel Radio! Tune in tomorrow!"* Emil said very hurriedly, and the program closed not a millisecond later.

# 4

FOUR DAYS in and I had a feeling I was getting close. The signal was impeccable now, more and more featuring upbeat electronica or softly familiar piano tunes. However, when there was nothing playing, there was still static instead of silence.

I had seen Gav a couple times now, usually only when I changed roads and he was forced to run across to the forest on the other side. Once or twice, when I'd stopped to eat or rest I would see him leaning against a tree and patiently waiting for me to finish. He had yet to return any questions I had yelled at him. I kept yelling, though, finding the act incredibly therapeutic.

It was only five minutes after I departed one morning that I noticed a rather curious sight off the main highway. A circle of angels, all of them the same crystalline sort, floating a ways off the ground and spinning.

Careful to avoid entering the ring, I paced their perimeter. They ignored me, naturally, but at this point I was far enough off the highway that I thought there wasn't much harm in continuing forward. As I approached a small town named Norwich, I realized it had been a while since I had seen any angels. And off in the distance, I swore I could see smoke.

The radio was off at the moment, but this place was looking a lot like it might contain humans. And even if it didn't, it wouldn't hurt to check. I could use some new supplies anyway, like maybe a compact tent and a warmer coat.

As I walked toward the town, the trees began to thin out, and I could distinctly see Gav walking along next to me. "Am I supposed to be heading here, or is this detour not allowed by your standards?" I called over.

To my surprise, he answered. "You're supposed to head here, yes. But I wouldn't suggest it. Turn back."

"No."

"All right, whatever." Such casual speech didn't translate well when yelled, and Gav sounded pretty bitter.

He followed me into the town, though still doing his best to remain in the shadows. He hid around corners and behind trees, moving only when I wasn't looking and being careful not to make a sound. I had to question the point of it—and did—but of course he didn't respond.

I followed the smoke trail to a traditional sort of campsite conspicuously next to the woodlands. Three tents sat around a fire pit. It seemed to have been left in a hurry.

"Maybe you should investigate those broken branches and footprints in the mud over there?" said Gav, but there was a very resentful edge to his voice.

"Thank you, I would've seen that without your help, you know."

"Just follow the trail."

"Again, thanks for the obvious."

The end of the pathway came to a rocky clearing overlooking a little valley, and down in the valley was a village. It was made entirely of tents and tarps, and a couple people looked up at me.

A man laughed. "We've never seen a drifter before! Come down, we'll take good care of you."

Gav, naturally, had fallen into the shadows, though I thought I heard him hiss something as I made my way down.

I fell into a euphoric state as a crowd of people parted around me. My journey was over, and I didn't even have to track down the radio station. Or maybe the radio station was here somewhere? It might be possible that all the necessary equipment had been moved into one of the tents.

"Hello, I'm Broderick," said the man who had greeted me, shaking my hand. I looked about at the camp. It seemed to consist exclusively of tents scattered in roughly a circle. I could make out a small clearing to one side, but otherwise every tent was pitched directly next to another, leaving very little room to navigate. Broderick smiled warmly at me, but the other humans seemed nervous, watching me with dead eyes. Everyone seemed to be covered in a thin layer of dirt.

"Hi, I'm Erika. Uh, Cantor. I can't believe I've finally found a settlement of people! I've been out traveling on my own for a couple days now, and I was stuck alone for—well, you know. Since the whole angel thing," I said all in one breath.

He smiled. "I think you'll find us very hospitable. We haven't had any outsiders before, so everyone's a bit nervous, but you seem safe."

"Very safe. I don't think I even have the strength to lift most blunt weapons." I chattered on excitedly. I honestly wasn't even paying that much attention to my surroundings. Just knowing they *existed* was enough.

He was leading me toward the center of the camp as we walked. "We'll find you a place here. Everyone has a job they can do for the good of everyone else."

Suddenly a woman came forth from the crowd and roughly grabbed me by my coat and shook me around. "What have been the movements? Where are the Cherubim heading?"

"Jaen, please. Get back," Broderick snapped, and the woman retreated. "Sorry about that, some people are still a little… discouraged by the existence of the angels. Not fully committed to survival yet."

"I get that. I mean, I'm constantly discouraged by their existence. Anything less would be a bit weird. And God forbid growing comfortable."

"Yes, but we have to learn to move on."

"Do you have any problems with angels here? I didn't see any in town, but there must be a reason you're living in the woods like this."

"I suppose it's because we all have bad memories of Norwich."

"Oh, are you all from Norwich, then? How did so many of you survive? I was the only one in my area."

"Luck. Just pure luck."

I was certain Broderick was hiding something, but I didn't feel comfortable pressing him about it. I wanted these people to like me, since I was going to be staying with them for the foreseeable future.

"How many angels were in your area? I had three, but I'm from a bigger town. Just one, then? I wonder what was wrong with it that it missed so many of you."

Broderick spoke abruptly. "I imagine you're very tired from all the wandering you've been doing; why don't you rest up? You can stay in this tent until we find you a more permanent dwelling."

"I'm not that tired. I'd love a tour if you don't mind," I said, dismissing his aversion to my questions.

"A tour? I suppose that makes sense. You," he said, pointing a boy out of the crowd, "show our new member around. Tour her."

After Broderick left the boy came up to me. "Uh, I'm Fex, and I guess I can guide you about? Yeah." He was pretty cute, with slightly curly, dark hair past his ears and face red with a blush. My whole perception of people might've been off, though, after months of isolation. Just scanning the crowd, I could pick out numerous people I thought were pretty cute. Everyone was, at the very least, wholeheartedly appreciated in their existence.

"Fe... cks? Weird name you got there."

"Ah, yes, it's foreign. My parents are foreigners."

"Oh, what country?"

"Eh...." He paused for a few seconds. "America? They were Americans."

"Like native? That doesn't really make you a foreigner, then."

"Oh! Yeah. Yeah. Yeah, that's right," Fex said, nodding.

We were walking through the camp, and Fex stayed silent. "Ah, what's going on over there?" I prompted, pointing to a circle of people. They were too densely packed for me to tell if they were surrounding anything of interest.

"That? They're just relaxing."

"While standing motionless in a circle?"

"Yes."

"That's weird."

"Let me guide you to a tent. You should sleep for a few hours."

"It's the middle of the day."

"Sleep is vital to a fast recovery. I want the best for you."

Somehow, I doubted that. "I'm not sleeping. Show me around more."

"Okay." He walked me to the other side of the camp, to the edge of a river. "You can gather water here if you need to drink something."

"I actually still have some bottled water in my backpack, but thanks."

"Okay, that's all," Fex said, and he walked away. I was too dazed to stop him.

"That was an amazing tour, I have to say. Fex has potential," Gav said after Fex left and I noticed him leaning against a tree on the other bank.

"I know we're living in a crazy world these days, but I'm sort of beginning to fear everyone here has gone completely mad."

Gav raised an eyebrow. "That's an interesting thought, isn't it?"

"Why don't you come here and find out for yourself?"

"Trust me, I know." He tossed a rock into the stream. "Damn! I was hoping that'd skip. Ah, I have another game for you to play. Why don't we see how many differences you spotted?"

"Differences from what?"

"An actual civilization." He looked me dead in the eyes.

"Well." I nearly laughed at his unwavering eye contact. "Uh. I don't know?"

"Isn't this place a bit weird?"

"Sure. But it's, you know, the end of days. Things are supposed to get a bit weird. At *most* these guys are going to be cultists or cannibals. Which would suck, but again, it's sort of a given during the apocalypse."

"Think it over a bit more. Try listing the odd things you've noticed about the place."

"Odd? I guess there's a lot of people here, but no angels. No one has any weapons. No one seemed willing to answer my questions, but it wasn't even like they were rude. They just seemed unaware." My previous joy still haunted my mind, slowly fading as I forced myself to face these obvious discouragements. "And Broderick looked like he had rolled in mud and then tossed a little in his hair, while Fex clearly had no idea who he even was. And that circle of people was clearly unnatural."

"And what could this all mean?" Gav asked, leading me on like a condescending teacher.

"Oh my God, don't tell me that I've just stumbled into some sort of… angels-disguised-as-humans camp. Like, as the world's most elaborately ill-planned trap. Because, if so, I have to get out of here before I die of stupidity. Which angel thought this was a good idea? Why would they even do this?" There were further implications to mull over—so angels could look like humans? But those were for later. Right now I was just struck by how ridiculous this trap was.

"Don't worry, they're not going to kill you," said Gav slowly, rolling his eyes, "but don't say I hadn't told you so. I was like, 'Don't go in there!' and you were like 'Whatever, I do what I want!' It's all your fault. Anyway, don't expect they're ready to let you go. You're probably going to have to play along for a day or two until they're all set to release you into the wild again."

"Why are they doing this? And should I be concerned that you clearly know all about it?"

"Don't worry, I've just run through the paces a few times. I know what's up. Maybe one day you'll know what's up as well," he said as he turned back into the shadows.

"Go to hell!" I called after him. "Useless bastard."

"Why are you yelling? Are you distressed?" asked Fex, who had crept up behind me without a sound. Never before had I taken such a second look at someone. The aesthetics were still there: the dark, curly hair and the bright eyes. But I now noticed how *off* he looked. His hands were so clean, I had trouble believing he had ever lifted anything heavier than a couple pounds, and his face, which had seemed delightfully sculpted, now seemed to lack depth. It certainly was missing laugh lines.

So this was the face of an angel. Pure and unworn. Why weren't these angels killing me? What end would justify these effortful means?

"Why are you doing this?" I asked. I didn't bother thinking what might happen if they realized I knew about their trickery.

"Doing what? Showing concern for someone who is clearly feeling ill?"

"I feel fine," I said curtly, and I headed back into camp.

The circle of motionless angel-people had expanded since I left; even Broderick had joined their ranks.

"I'm taking you to a tent immediately. Don't resist it, or I will have to move you physically."

"Wow, that's no way to treat your newest community member."

He took me to a tent and made me go in. Standing before me, holding on to the zipper to close the door, his expression remained blank. He tilted his head slightly.

"You know what is happening. I will not alert my superiors, as I feel pity for you, but it would be best to do whatever I say. As your new commanding master, we will have a mutually beneficial relationship, as you will not be destroyed for your corruption of foreknowledge and I will have a servant to carry out matters I could not normally delve into. This will be a wonderful few days, I do believe."

After he left I waited patiently. I wasn't a bit scared about Fex and these angels, as everything was beginning to feel all too real and yet overwhelmingly surreal. My life felt fake, like a sitcom I had never seen playing at midnight in an empty bowling alley. I couldn't feel fear if I was occupied with muddled thoughts of dreary acceptance.

Luckily, the amazing trick about tents is that they open from both the outside and the inside, and a few minutes after Fex left, I let myself out. I still had my bag, and I set out to get out of camp as soon as possible.

I made it to the border of the woods when I felt a hand on my shoulder. Lots of people will tell you they have cold skin, but Fex's was cold as a corpse, and it occurred to me with the little I knew of these angel-people, he might very well be one.

"I was watching you. And I will still be watching you. When they are done with their communications, I will ask to be assigned as your official Watcher. I'm not letting you out of my sight."

His hand was just resting on my shoulder, but it was heavy enough to lead me right back to his tent.

"Yes, of course," I told Fex, and I glimpsed him briefly smirk, breaking his previous demeanor.

What I was answering, I did not yet know.

# 5

I FELL asleep very quickly, almost disappointingly so. Evidently I actually had been tired.

It was still day when I woke up, maybe just about midday by now. I ate a breakfast of cold canned corn and stale water, and not long after I had finished eating, Fex came to get me from the tent.

An unfamiliar man was standing behind him, and in the background I could spot many people out and about. The circle of weirdos had ended.

Perhaps that also explained Fex's new demeanor. "I-I've come to wake you up, if you don't mind," he said, blushing heavily. "Isa here is our leader, and he'll be helping you settle in today."

Isa shook my hand. "Did you have a good sleep? We're very concerned about your well-being." Though he looked the most sincere and human of the angel-people I had seen, he spoke clumsily, pausing after each word.

We walked directly out of the campgrounds and onto an old trail through a meadow.

"Thank you, sir. I slept quite well. I'm sorry I was a bit hyper from exhaustion with Broderick yesterday. Please send him my apologies." There was no way I was going to act on how I really felt about all this, and I decided on a polite and charming persona.

Isa smiled reassuringly. "Good. Fex, you're dismissed. Now Erika… would you care to answer a few questions?"

"Absolutely. I wish to—" I paused. I had no idea what purpose this was actually going to serve, so I took a wild guess. "—assimilate here as easily as possible."

"Off to a good start, then. Not everyone has been so graceful about it. First off, then—do you consider yourself brave?"

"What, when dealing with angels? Or like, socially brave? I don't know. Not really, but you know, as of late I've been handling myself pretty well." I wasn't sure what I was supposed to be saying. Would it be bad to tell the truth? Or was I supposed to make myself a threat, and to make him fear me?

"That's fine. So you've been on your own for a long time now—do you think you could have survived much longer like that?"

It was a hard question to really answer. "I'm not sure I would have wanted to. But... probably. I'm not very social. And I guess it wasn't the first time I've had to live on my own either."

"You'd rather live than die, right?"

"Well—yes. But if I had to live in a ghost town for the rest of my life, well, I'm not sure it'd end well for me."

Isa made a sort of twitching movement with his mouth. I guess he didn't like my answer. "You're compliant, yes? And biologically female?"

These questions were starting to tread on a level I was uncomfortable with. Especially with the order in which the questions were asked. "Why do you ask?" I said in what I hoped was still a friendly voice.

"It's not always easy to be certain," he said. "You don't look wholly female."

I absolutely made a face of repulsion at that, and fixed it a moment too late. It was probably the pettiest of things to get upset at these days, but I had endured enough questions about my gender that it had left a mark on me. I do have a fairly masculine face, angled and often frowning, and I had turned to growing my hair out in recent years to combat this. Since I'd been traveling, I'd cut my hair off, and had nearly forgotten it might confuse people.

But I do have a fairly feminine voice, I think. There was a good chance this angel was just lacking in his human knowledge, and I was overreacting for nothing. I paused for a few more seconds. "Yes, I'm a girl."

I would have thought it was exactly what he wanted to hear, but he still had a kind of half frown on his face. "I'm not sure this is going to work. May I touch your hand?"

He really wasn't trying to uphold his human facade, was he? Surely he knew how odd that was? Still, I let him take my hand and examine it thoroughly. After a minute, he let go.

"Have you ever considered dying?"

"Uh, maybe a couple times. No more than average, really."

"Unsatisfactory." He took a few steps forward. "I'm sorry, Erika, but we can't stand for that level of uncertainty. You've come close, but there are better options. Unfortunately, this means I will have to kill you."

"What?" I started, but Isa came at me with a heavy punch, and I swung aside right in time to dodge it. Didn't he have some kind of magical angel power he could tap into? Then again, it was likely for the best that he was sticking to more traditional ways of fighting—I couldn't handle him as it was.

Again he went with a simple punch, and this time he hit me squarely in the shoulder. It wasn't too bad, but I stumbled backward. He moved in for another simple punch, and, hyped up with adrenaline, I dropped my legs and fell down so suddenly that he was caught off guard. I caught myself with my hands before I hit the ground, and sprang up again. I had no idea what I was doing, but luckily, it seemed he didn't either.

I kicked his legs out from the back, and he fell to his knees. I knew I needed to run away, but I was curious. I kept my distance at about three feet away and stared Isa in his newly blank eyes. Already his pupils were just outlines and his irises were merely suggestions. All at once his movements began to stagger mechanically.

He stopped. Straight-out stopped moving and breathing and just stood there.

I backed away slowly at first, but then as fast as I could. I was halfway across the field when I heard Isa call after me.

"Erika! Wait up!"

"No!" I shouted back.

"Erika, it's okay! I'm no longer Isa. My name's Kasos. Isa has been removed for disorderly conduct." I did not want to rule out a bizarre trick by Isa, but it seemed he was telling the truth. Kasos spoke entirely differently from Isa, somehow working the same voice into a distinctly new one.

"I don't want to deal with you either."

"You will have to. As you are no doubt aware, we are all angels here. And we have a purpose for you. We feel Isa's lapse of logic should not affect whether we deem you a proper candidate for the job we require of you, but you must cooperate with me here. It is simple enough. As long as you choose to forget about me speaking to you like this, the judgment can carry on unbiased."

"I have zero interest in being a pawn in whatever you're planning. Leave me alone. I'm going back into the wild to look for other humans."

"There are no more humans, Erika. We have only saved a select few for our judgments. There is nowhere for you to go."

I didn't want to mention the radio. I certainly didn't want to mention Gav, who, while he wasn't quite giving me purely human signals, didn't feel angelic. He sort of felt like an enigma, someone acting outside of it all and made purely of shadows.

"I want no part in whatever all this is."

"You really want to die, then?"

I chewed my words before I spoke, mulling it over for a dangerous amount of time. "No."

"Then stay here, work with us, and we will let you go. We will collect you again when the time is right, of course, if you end up being chosen." He dipped his head to me as he passed. "Once more I offer apologies for any emotional and or physical damage you may have sustained from Isaiel's actions, and I wish you the best. I know this body is not one you will be wishing to associate with, so I will be disposing of it and finding myself a new one in a short time."

"Uh, thanks for that, I guess," I said, feeling a bit awkward and very put off.

I waited in the meadow for a bit, pacing around and watching the woods for any sign of Gav. He wasn't showing up, and I really could've used someone to talk to at that moment.

I wasn't desperate, and you know, I wasn't even that angry that Isa had attacked me. I had won, in the end, and honestly my situation wasn't any different.

Plus, it seemed he was pretty much dead. God knows where he went, but I'm guessing he broke a few rules and was going to pay for it.

It was all too strange to think of the angels as beings with a society, but they must have some sort of hierarchy. And they certainly were collaborating on something here—something nefarious and badly put together, perhaps, but something nevertheless. Something I had to get away from as soon as possible.

The angels, now that I thought of it, had always been angels. There were some mentions of aliens in the beginning, sure, and of demons. But neither had stuck. Even the devout religious types, still holding out for brave winged humanoids, admitted these angels were definitely the real deal.

Come to think of it, I remember doubting that they really were angels the day I heard the news. But by the time I saw them in person, I knew it to be true.

I headed down to the river and waded in. After a moment of meditative breathing, I got out again, feeling quite dumb for bothering to get my legs wet. I looked again to the other side of the bank, and, finding it deserted, went back to camp.

I still had not had a proper tour of the campgrounds, and I took the time to survey it. It was almost entirely tents. The only actual pathway was the one I had entered on, a very wide one that ran straight down the middle. In the center was an open space where all the angel-people had gathered, a corner set aside for the ones who were still standing motionless. There was no area to eat, and in general no room for anything. It was absolutely clear that this had been planned with very little understanding of what a campsite is or how one works.

My tent was, conspicuously enough, one of six that had been placed in the central open area. I grabbed my stuff, eager to experiment with how far I could get without anyone noticing my absence.

Almost immediately Fex came to my side. "I'm sorry, miss, we can't let you leave the grounds alone for your safety. And I'm sorry to hear about what that downright awful Isa tried to do to you."

"Are you guys a hive mind or something?"

"Ha, what a funny joke that is. I think I will accompany you into the woods so you can look at nature for a while," he said, his speech very stilted and monotonous.

"I don't want to look at nature. I'm more interested in leaving into it."

"You sure like to child around. You're a very funny person, in fact. You were just telling me how much you're interested in the local population of white pine and were concerned for their health, thus prompting a request to go look at them. Very funny indeed."

I figured this was Fex's way of trying to talk to me alone, and I went with it. He didn't actually have anything he could hold against me, not since Kasos also was aware I knew this was just a huge setup, but I figured playing along with a slightly rebellious angel could have its benefits. With a bit of luck, I could get him working for me.

He took me up an overgrown trail, which actually did end in a grove of white pine.

"You really need to watch yourself."

"Is this about Isa?" I asked. "Because that was all his fault. He just said I was 'unfit' and tried to kill me."

"Oh, obviously not! The thing with Isa was—look, just don't try to leave like that ever again."

"Why? I wanted to know how long it would take before someone stopped me."

"The trick is that they wouldn't. You're being judged here, you know. And if you leave, you'll be deemed unworthy—"

"Again? You know, I don't exactly want to be worthy to you angels anyway," I interrupted.

"—and hunted down and killed. The lesser angels ignore you now only because they're ordered to. Lose the ego. I thought we were working together here."

"Yeah, because of blackmail."

"If you really hate us all that much and want to leave, do as I say. What I need is to get out of here, and you want the same thing. If we kill the leader, Isa—or wait, Kasos now—then there will be enough chaos that you'll be deemed in need of a retesting. They'll leave you alone until you wander into another of these camps. I will use the chaos to become the hero of the crisis and get promoted. We are both victors."

"Wouldn't they kill me?"

"They wouldn't know who killed Kasos, and they would assume you never knew this was an angelic camp. They'd hope you'd run away in fear and wind up at another camp, where they could comfort you and continue the testing."

"This is sounding, frighteningly enough, like a good plan. Except how am I supposed to kill Kasos?"

"Anything you want. As long as he retains his human form he is as harmless as one. Bash his head in while he sleeps. Shoot him in the heart. It doesn't matter what you do, just kill him."

"I'm afraid to trust you on this one hundred percent, but it looks like I'm in."

"Excellent. And believe me, I'm very trustworthy."

"When you say it like that, it doesn't help."

"Just trust me."

I sighed. "Whatever. Let's kill this bastard."

# 6

I WASN'T sure what I was going to use as a weapon, but I eventually settled on a large rock. I dug one up near my tent and hauled it in. It weighed a good couple of pounds, and I figured it probably was enough to bash a head in.

A passerby-angel had stopped me and asked what I was doing, and I earnestly replied that I had taken an interest in geology from a young age and wanted to work on my rock collection. She nodded sweetly and left me alone.

The only thing left was to find a moment where Kasos was off guard. This proved impossible, as she—having done as promised and switched bodies—didn't even sleep.

It was the second day of me being in the camp, and not once had I seen her in a moment that would have allowed me to kill her. I followed her as much as I could, and I never caught her resting. She seemed to exclusively wander around camp and talk to the others, usually about exceedingly mundane subjects. Catching her asleep, as planned, seemed unlikely.

I was watching her from a safe distance—Fex waiting behind and giving me a look of urgency—when I noticed there was a new girl in camp. Admittedly, I could not recognize everyone yet, but I was very certain this girl was new.

She had a certain look to her, and I imagined her the type who might've run a blog devoted to flowers and blurry photographs of wolves. She had long brunette hair that somehow still had a faded green hue on the tips, and a long dress that was entirely inappropriate for the weather. She had a crown of fake flowers on her head, and was looking around the camp and nodding at everything she saw.

I knew she had to be an angel, but my instinct refused to agree with my mind. She seemed too sincere, too good-looking, and too human for that. I subdued my doubt the best I could. There had to be other humans out there. No reason a pretty girl couldn't be one of them.

"Oh, Erika, come over here!" said Kasos, catching me unaware. "I'd like you to meet Midori."

I went up and shook her hand. Kasos spoke to Midori. "This is Erika, another wanderer who arrived just yesterday. You two should spend some time together."

"It's nice to meet you," said Midori with a small smile.

Kasos left us alone, and I decided that if she was human, then it was my duty to enlighten her about what this camp was as soon as possible.

"Let's go out to the woods and talk there. It's good to breathe in the forest air, isn't it?"

"Um, well, if you don't mind, I'd like to look around here some more first. I really only just arrived a moment ago." She had a singsongy voice, like a bunch of birds talking through a human avatar. It wasn't one of those sarcastic horror movie singsongs either, just one her voice fell into naturally.

"It'll just be a short walk. I'll get my friend, and we'll be off and back in ten minutes."

"Can't this wait?" She yawned as if to emphasize her point.

"All right, but we should go soon. Let me show you around at least."

I tried to subtly clue Midori in to everything off about the place, but she seemed genuinely interested and very sincerely accepting of everything weird.

"This here is a circle of people. They don't really breathe or move much like this. They do this for hours on end, actually," I said.

"Oh, like meditation? That's a good idea, especially with all the terrible stuff that's happened. It's a good way to clear your mind, and I love that it's so popular here! I can't wait to join in when I get the chance."

"You shouldn't. It's weird."

"You should try to be more open to alternative lifestyle choices."

And when I was showing her the layout of the tents, I said, "See, they're all cramped together except for this one clearing. And we're the only ones with tents in the clearing and actually ample room to move around."

"I think it's awfully clever of them to arrange them like this. It helps build a feeling of community to have a center square sort of place, as if this was a real town. It's a bit abnormal, but there's nothing wrong with it."

When I had finished my tour, I took her aside one more time. "Can we make a little time to go into the woods yet?"

"No. I think I'm going to head to my tent now and rest. Maybe later?"

Frustrated, I took Midori to her tent and stomped off to keep watch on Kasos. It was so hard to instill a sense of danger when you couldn't actually name it.

Kasos was doing what she often did, watching the other angels convene in their circle. She never joined in, but sat a few feet away and watched. She was almost in the same sort of trance that the others were in, but occasionally she'd shift or open her eyes and look around.

I guess if I was light on my feet, I could've killed her then and there, but there were always a few other people hanging around in the clearing.

"How'd it go with Midori?" asked Kasos, unmoving.

"Oh, fine enough."

"You were very desperate to walk with her in the woods."

"Uh, I just thought she would want to. She looked the hippie type, and I don't know, I guess we could've bonded through that."

"If you were to go in the woods, who would have overseen your safety?"

"Probably Fex; he is my Watcher after all."

"Perhaps I should switch it up a little, give Fex a break from his strenuous job of keeping an eye on you."

"If you wish." I didn't want to alert her that I actually needed Fex around, especially with her suspicions already raised.

"Also, we are expecting another visitor quite soon. Make sure to rouse Midori when the time comes. You will both need to be present for this."

"You can just drop the guise here, you know. Just tell me what's about to go down."

"You should aim not to be so emotional. We will be having another test for you shortly."

"A test on what?"

"Play along now. It isn't a large problem that you know we are angels. I only ask that you pretend you don't. I am being quite kind to you in saying this, but we are looking for your genuine personality and reactions. These tests will not harm you, so please, try to cooperate."

I decided to head down to the river and spend my time looking for Gav instead of standing around until this visitor arrived. I hadn't seen him at all today, and I was getting sort of concerned about his well-being. He was the one sane person I knew at this point, though I guess that could be up for debate. At least he sort of knew what he was doing.

I took maybe ten minutes to wait before I got tired of it. Gav wasn't coming, and I couldn't stand to stay still that long.

I went back to Midori's tent and knocked stupidly on the fabric of her door.

"Come in?" was her slightly confused-sounding answer.

I let myself in and settled on the floor. I doubted she had had much sleep since I brought her here, as she had evidently unpacked her entire bag and made the tent very homey. Two blankets were laid over the sleeping bag for comfort, and on the other side of the tent she had arranged a collection of various objects.

She had an unlit candle, a parcel of herbs, and a peacock feather carefully put together into a display that she sat in front of.

"What are you doing?" I asked.

She took a deep breath. "Just thinking."

"Can't sleep?"

"Not at all. I'd love to, though."

"Do you want me to leave?"

"Not particularly."

"Oh." I didn't actually have anything interesting to talk about, I realized.

"Where are you from?" Midori asked suddenly.

"New York, though I don't remember much of living there. We moved up here when I was a kid, right when my mom started getting sick. I guess the mountain air was supposed to help."

"Did it?"

"Oh, yeah, I guess it did. She made it right 'til the end, you know? Died in a fire later, of course, but at least it wasn't from the illness. What about you?"

"What, about my family? We never were close, and I moved here from California last year to escape them and city life in general. Reconnect with nature. I sort of wish there was a way to go back there. I mean, we survived. I hate my father, but I still would want him safe."

"He's going to be dead. It's better you don't see the bodies, trust me."

"I'm guessing you did." She looked at me glumly. "I'm so sorry about that. I just mean, I can't help but cling on to the hope that someone I knew survived. Or that I'm somehow stuck in the only patch of land where this happened, and that I can escape back to civilization. Or that it's all one nasty, long, and vivid dream."

"I don't blame you." The topic seemed to have run out, and I struggled for something else to say. "What's all this, then?" I said, gesturing to her display.

"Oh this? Nothing really. Just junk." She sighed heavily. "Alluring and pretty, yet useless possessions that I still lug around for some reason."

"You seem attached to them, though."

"I used to have more," she said, almost too soft for me to hear.

There was a commotion outside. The visitor had arrived.

HE LOOKED like the epitome of a wanderer; a long coat and a long scarf obscuring most of his appearance. His hair had grown out poorly, for it was mangy and thin and not at all suited to being tied in a bun.

His scarf had been covering most of his face like a mask, but he undid it and gazed around impassively.

I regarded him with suspicion, for if he was involved in this upcoming test of the angels, then he surely was one of them.

Midori, meanwhile, greeted him enthusiastically. "Hello!" she said. "I only just arrived here myself. It's nice to see this place is constantly growing. At this rate we'll soon be a village."

After a look from Kasos, I went up and shook his hand. "I'm Erika. Hello."

His voice was heavy and sounded like a mountain. "Call me Haywood. Where will I be staying?"

"One of the tents in this clearing, no doubt."

Kasos smiled at me. "You're correct. Please, why don't you and Midori help him settle in?"

"Of course," answered Midori, picking up Haywood's bag.

I watched Haywood very carefully. He looked strange enough, certainly quite dangerous in that "wasteland wanderer" sort of way. I just wasn't sure how his presence was a test.

He was very tall, a stubbly beard growing in patches across his chin, and bright hazel eyes that were surprisingly full of light. There was a feeling to him that he had done much in his life, his hands callused and rough and his forehead bearing an uneven scar.

I didn't get an angelic vibe from him, honestly, but he was still part of their plans in one way or another.

His backpack looked like it weighed a good amount, and as he unpacked, I began to understand what problem this man was supposed to present.

He had several pistols in his bag, which he placed near his sleeping bag. Now, I'm personally glad he had the sense to carry a gun with him. I wish I had carried one with me, because even if I was a bit scared of firing one, it would have made me feel a million times safer.

Midori, however, said what she was supposed to. "We're aren't allowed to have weapons in camp. For the safety of everyone else."

"Oh? I wouldn't worry about it. I'm not even sure if I want to settle down here or not. Might be gone by tomorrow's sun."

I had a strong guess that he would be gone by tomorrow. Whether he planned to leave or not.

"Have a nice rest, then, Haywood," Midori said with the slightest of bows. Once we had left, she pulled me aside. "We have to tell someone. I don't think Haywood is very trustworthy. What if he's a madman and shoots someone?"

"Please. If I had a gun I would've done the same thing and kept it with me. He just got here, and he wants to be safe."

"I still think someone has to know."

"Why should anyone? It's his business what he keeps in his tent. I didn't report you for having a candle, which is clearly a fire hazard."

"I don't have anything to light it with, though! Come on, it's better safe than sorry. Let's just tell Kasos and explain the situation; I'm sure she'll be reasonable with him. At most she's just going to take away the guns."

"I'm not so sure."

"What do you think is going to happen? Like they're just going to kick him out for a misunderstanding?"

They would probably find a way to kill him. But I couldn't sway Midori in the slightest, and she brought me over to Kasos, who was still sitting on a log in front of the circle.

"What is it, ladies? Is Haywood all set up yet?"

"Yes, but we noticed he has a collection of firearms with him."

"Oh dear."

"Well," I said, "who can blame him? I mean, he only arrived a few minutes ago; why should he be trusting enough to let us know about his guns? He wasn't even aware that you don't allow weapons in camp."

"That's a good point, Erika, but I'm afraid the risk outweighs the logic."

"Yeah," Midori chimed in. "He could totally be unhinged and violent. We can't let him hang around if he poses a threat."

Kasos looked to Midori. "Very correct."

I had the feeling I was failing this test.

Together, we went back to Haywood's tent. Kasos and Midori led the way, and I begrudgingly followed.

When we met him again, standing with his back to us, I could instantly tell something was wrong. One of his hands was pressed to his forehead, and the other one was gripping a gun and shaking wildly.

"Drop your weapon," said Kasos, with the flair of a poorly scripted actor.

"No," he answered, in an equally fake tone.

Midori seemed gripped by the conflict. "Please, Haywood," she pleaded, "we can't let you bring dangerous things into camp."

"No," he said again, in what could have been a tape recording of his previous statement.

"I'll have no choice but to engage you directly if you don't do as I say," said Kasos.

"Don't do it," I said at last. "He's obviously possessed."

"What do you mean?" asked Midori, seeming frightened.

"Like, by an angel. He's acting and sounding entirely different. I bet if he turns around we'll be able to see it in his eyes."

"Angels can *do* that?"

"If he's 'possessed by an angel,' then we have all the more reason to attack him, don't we?" said Kasos, and she ran at him suddenly and punched him in the back.

I might not know much about fighting, but I feel she could have made a better move strategically. The punch met his broad back weakly. Kasos was stuck for a moment, fist still clenched.

Then Haywood reacted, spinning on his feet and drawing his gun directly to Kasos's forehead. As expected, his eyes had been drained completely white, with hundreds of tiny eyes springing up to replace them.

Not only was it painfully obvious how scripted the whole encounter was, it was also obvious the angel that was (possessing or not) Haywood had little idea of how to use a gun. While the muzzle was right to Kasos's head, he held the gun loosely with one hand, fingers not even near the trigger. If he had meant harm, he would have acted by now.

Midori was gripped by the situation, though, sitting down and watching with wide eyes. I joined her on the floor, and she grabbed my hand, squeezing it for security. She really was taken by this show.

"Give me a reason I shouldn't kill you all right now." Haywood was now speaking in a voice completely unlike his own, much more mechanical and wooden.

"Common sense?" I suggested. "Pity?" I eyed the rest of Haywood's firearms just a few inches from my feet.

"Erika, don't," said Kasos, looking at me with wary eyes. "Wait for help to arrive. Or sacrifice me if you will. But don't risk yourself. Wait for someone who can handle this. Your life is your most important asset."

"I'll get help!" offered Midori, scurrying to her feet. A look from Haywood and a quiver of his gun stilled her.

"I don't see the problem here, frankly." I wasn't even sweating.

"Erika!" shouted Kasos and Midori at almost the same time.

I grabbed a pistol from Haywood's bag and fidgeted with it for a few seconds before figuring out a good grip. I aimed it toward Haywood, and, finding it shaking, took a deep breath.

He immediately took his gun off Kasos and aimed it back at me. "Seems like this is a standoff."

"We wouldn't be if my allies would actually do something."

"I don't want to break it to you," he said, "but that's not what you're expected to do."

"Somehow, I don't think I'm missing out," I said.

Haywood's hold on his gun was just as loose as I expected, and it only took a sudden grab at it for him to drop it to the floor in surprise.

When he went to reach for it, I took another deep breath and shot.

And then I shot again.

And one more time for good measure.

"Erika!" Kasos yelled, visibly angry. She seemed to be crying, but I doubted her tears were genuine.

"I'm not done yet," I said.

And I shot her next.

# 7

THE UNFORTUNATE thing about shooting an angel was, it turned out, that they took more than one shot to die.

Haywood seemed dead enough, but Kasos reeled, seeming to no longer try and maintain her human shape. She was still on her feet, but she seemed to have lost gravity, her body held at an impossible angle as she shook off the bullet. In a few moments she settled about an inch in the air, absolutely still.

I didn't want to look away, but glanced to Midori. She seemed to have fainted, and I was nearly relieved. I wasn't sure if I should try to shoot again—the first one clearly hadn't had much of an effect.

Kasos then seemed to surge as her body glowed at the seams, tugging at the skin, and all at once like a million pores, her skin erupted into a sea of eyes.

Always with the eyes, these angels.

Her skin had gone a sickly metallic cerulean, and from her back blossomed a pair of great wings that tugged at the edges of the tent.

Then, like she knew what I was thinking, she tore the tent open in one swift move. All at once we were exposed to the unwelcome night air.

I got up steadily, using the gun like a shield. Kasos rose a few more feet before settling at one elevation. She bobbed in the air slightly, but made no motion to attack.

"Don't bother," she croaked.

"Let me go and I won't shoot," I said, rattling the gun as if that helped emphasize the threat.

"You shouldn't bother with this, Erika."

I shot at Kasos two more times, my hands shaking so much that I doubted either bullet made contact.

"Please," Kasos said.

"I'm sorry for shooting at you, but can't you just let me go? I'm not a threat to you. I have no interest in anything you're doing. I just want to... go."

I think Kasos sighed then. It was rather hard to tell, her body fading in and out of the corporeal realm, but something in her throat shook and breathed. "We like to be precise."

"Ah," I said, stuttering on the sound. I looked about—Midori was still on the ground, and camp appeared to suddenly be deserted.

I was, admittedly, out of ideas, but I was sure I'd think of something. Or maybe Fex would; after all, he had to be somewhere around here. He surely knew he depended on me if he wanted someone to do his dirty work, and I dimly hoped he'd find a way to step in and insure my survival.

Nothing happened for what felt like too long. Finally, I decided enough was enough and made a run for it. Midori's body only crossed my mind when it was too late for me to go back for her.

I had dropped the pistol somewhere in the process of making a mad dash for the forest, but I regretted that the moment I realized Kasos had begun to follow me. The gun had proven useless, but it was still a comforting weight to carry, and I felt frantically naked as I tried not to look behind me.

I ran as fast as I could, which when I think about it, isn't that fast. But I was hyped up and moving fast as my feet could carry me, jumping around and zigzagging, like Kasos was some easily confused animal.

She lunged at me suddenly, her claws grazing my cheek with a long gash. I kept moving and weaving around the tents with little sense of direction. The fact Kasos hadn't stabbed me through the gut by now was likely a decision on her part. What, did she want me alive?

I am notably not athletic, and I only made it to the border of the campsite before I succumbed to exhaustion. Taking huge, shuddering breaths, I ducked behind a tree. It was instinct, if anything, that caused me to hide, as Kasos had obviously seen where I went.

"You don't have to die," Kasos said. Something in her voice made it sound like an offer.

"I don't want to die," I wheezed pathetically.

"We'll find a way to preserve you as we search for someone better. We are not unkind. I only wish you wouldn't run."

And then everything began to burn.

I don't know where the blaze came from, but all at once it was there and terribly everywhere. I was facing the woodlands, but I could feel the heat and hear the crackling embers. It had started in the same way sound rushes you after you take off a pair of earmuffs: very, very quickly.

The heat waves battered my skin, and I got up slowly. The smoke was not doing wonders for my shortness of breath.

Kasos had turned to face the camp, and I stood beside her, cautiously glancing to see if she noticed. The brush around the perimeter of the campsite was aflame and slowly branching between tents along small patches of grass. There was no clear sign of an origin point.

I looked up at Kasos again. Midori was still in the camp. I considered asking Kasos, quite politely, if I could grab her. Then I decided to just make a run for it.

Running was not my strong suit, but it was aided by a sense of desperation only a forest fire can bring to a situation. I took off my coat and one of my jackets, using the latter to cover my mouth and eyes. I was nearly blind, and had to stop to lift the shirt and check my surroundings every few seconds. The fire was growing unnaturally fast, so much so that I met it in the center of camp.

I hurriedly removed my masking shirt and suffered through the smoke in order to search. I found the tent Kasos had destroyed, but Midori wasn't there. Had she woken up and already found her way to safety? My head was hazy enough that I spent another minute in the center of the camp, running in circles and checking each tent.

As the fire approached me, I started to run back. And then, as I came coughing back to where Kasos still stood, I had the sense to follow her line of sight.

Even through the thick smog I could see the angels and their glowing forms. They had returned to their true states, most of them the balls of wings and eyes I had grown accustomed to. While they hung in the air without much movement at all, a great slowly rotating circle of them had formed a perimeter around the campgrounds.

In the very center, slightly lower than the rest, was an odd sort of angel I had never seen before. It took a moment for me to recognize this new addition as Midori, and my heart sank. I suppose I had seen it coming.

She was quite a sight, skin radiating light, hair suspended around her head like she was underwater, and a halo of eyes encompassing her head. She was nearly beautiful, but I wasn't willing to let the whole "creepy eye monster" thing get past me yet. She was an angel, and she was burning everything.

She waved her hand and a pattern of sparks elicited another wave of flames. I watched next to Kasos with an odd sort of kinship, a heavy air of confusion as to what was happening and why.

Then Midori turned her head in a slow circle. When she was facing me, she stopped. And dove.

I stepped back, tripping on my heels and falling to the ground. I got up and faltered for a few more steps until I was securely behind a tree, and forced myself to stay there. No need to turn around and see what was happening. Kasos would defend me. Maybe.

There was a high-pitched screeching and a physical thud. Then a sound precisely like scissors. I edged my way around the tree.

Seeing her up close, I was again struck by how pleasant Midori looked with calmly closed eyes and surrounded by soft light. Unfortunately, this observation was hindered by the scene before me. Midori had Kasos pinned to a tree, struck through with a blade that resembled a sword but was fused with her flesh.

Midori looked like a religious icon, and barely moved her arm to strike again, this time cutting one of Kasos's arms cleanly off. Strange vine-like tendrils struggled to reconnect it, but Midori neatly severed them too.

Kasos withered, letting out a pitiful whine as Midori cut her to shreds. Was this the only way to kill her, or was Midori reveling in her attack?

Midori struck her blade directly into Kasos's head, right between what remained of her human form's eyes. She screeched and retched, throwing her body around. Soon she was struggling to move, and within seconds she was barely twitching.

I peeked out farther from behind the tree. "Uh…," I said, hoping to politely catch her interest. When she caught my eyes, I stepped back.

Midori turned her head and raised her palm to the sky, and the circle of angels stopped moving and scattered like flies. And then she lowered her hand, and the resulting gale put out all the fires and smelled sweet like mint.

She began to drift back into the campground, and I followed her from a few feet behind. She was visibly losing energy, and by the time she reached the center of the ashy camp, she had collapsed. Above her, the night sky seemed to glimmer, the stars barely shining from above the smoke.

I ran to her body and cradled her head in my hands. She was breathing calmly, evidently fast asleep.

I was unable to lift her, so I decided to wait for her to wake in the dying ashes. She was an angel, and she hadn't so much as saved my life as she had suddenly killed another angel. I didn't know why, and I didn't need to, but I wanted to wait for her to wake. I liked her. Or at least, I liked the *idea* of her. A naïve girl, who needs me to survive, hiding a dangerous secret. It felt like an element from a bad bit of drama.

Plus, I hated being alone. I needed to regularly talk to someone who wasn't myself.

A new scent began to well up around me, like a thousand herbs and a drop of dew, and I was joined in waiting by a moth made of crystals and starlight.

I almost didn't notice it; I certainly didn't bother to move away from it. The moth was only sitting there, waiting. There was only one eye located in its transparent body, a sphere whose pupil was always facing me no matter where I looked. I almost wanted to pet it. It wasn't that freaky; actually it was almost sort of pretty.

It looked at me, and like a cicada it began to split open and a familiar creature's head emerged. It was the deer from the forest, and it blinked at me, settling down by my side.

There was little to be surprised by when it came to dealing with angels. They very rarely followed the laws of logic, physics, and God knows what else. So I was actually apathetic about the whole one-eyed, crystal moth-deer-angel thing. Call it overexposure, if you will.

I guess it was... *nice* of the deer thing to show up, though. I wasn't sure what was happening. All I knew was I was waiting, and that I had to wait, and I was going to wait until Midori woke up again.

And then we'd hit the road.

I assumed I'd learn about what happened to Fex at some point. And where Gav had gone. And maybe I'd get an explanation about why and how Midori had killed Kasos.

But for now, waiting.

## 8

THE DEER-ANGEL settled next to me with a hiss of steam. We sat for an hour before Midori stirred, blinking awake slowly.

I leaned in close. "Are you okay?"

"I think so. I'm not sure what happened. Where are we?"

"We haven't really moved."

I helped her stand up, and we surveyed the long dead embers.

"Was there a fire?"

"Don't you remember anything?"

She shook her head. "Not at all. There was some fighting in the tent, with Haywood and Kasos, but I don't remember past that...."

"Uh, well. A lot happened. They're both dead; everyone else fled."

"But how? And why?"

"You don't remember a thing?" I didn't want to mention what had really happened. If she didn't remember being an angel, then maybe.... I didn't have an end to that thought. There was something hopeful about the concept. "Angels came. They killed Kasos, burned the place down, and left. I decided to wait and check you were okay."

"Weren't you scared the angels were going to kill you too?"

I shrugged. "I've made it this long."

"So where do we go from here?" She dusted her clothes off, but the pristine white of her dress wasn't going to come back that easily. "I guess it's time we took that walk in the woods."

"Might as well."

I'm not an idiot; I know how unwise it is to withhold information in times like these. I just didn't want to spoil Midori's bright outlook or have to be the one to inform her about her whole "magical death angel" secret identity. In fact, I wanted to spend as little time possible mulling it over. I'd come clean to her later.

"So why did angels attack the camp?" Midori asked as we set out on our way.

"They attacked because they're dicks," I said. "Oh. And because Kasos was an angel too. Most people in the camp were, in fact. I don't know why, but I do know we're going to avoid camps like that in the future."

"She seemed so nice," Midori said brightly. "And to think, all she ever wanted was to live with other humans."

"All angels are bad, Midori."

"Who are you to judge? It's not like every angel can be cut from the same cloth—they're just as diverse as us, maybe even more so considering all the orders and forms they come in."

"Maybe you're right; maybe they're not all the same. They're all different shades of evil, but trust me, they're seriously up to no good. Kasos was killed probably because of some angelic turf war, not because she was a brave and holy rebel. I think most of the angels are some sort of hive mind anyway."

"I'm not going to trust you. In fact, I'm going to keep believing what I want to believe. You are free to do the same."

"The closest thing to a good angel that I met was one who was dead set on murdering Kasos so he could get a promotion."

"Just because we've yet to see proof of something, doesn't mean it isn't real."

I did sort of know of a good angel. At least one that wasn't immediately malevolent. But the moth-deer angel had left without a sound a while ago.

Suddenly, Midori mumbled miserably, "Damn it!" I realized she had noticed her tent, or rather, the remains of it. She ran over and dug through the cinders. "Nothing!"

"I'm sorry all your... stuff burned up."

She sighed. "It's nothing. I mean, they're nothing. I've been meaning to throw it all away anyway. I just—I guess I'm still reluctant to let it all go."

"What is all of it, though?"

"Oh, nothing at all," she said airily, which was my cue to stop asking.

I decided to check my tent as well, which had miraculously avoided much damage. My possessions hadn't, though, and I found my backpack too severely damaged to continue using, as well as the clothes inside. I wasn't sure if the food was good, but I figured I would find more to eat later.

In the corner, unscratched, was my radio. I picked it up and brought it out for Midori to see.

"Is that yours?" she asked. "Seems pretty bulky to lug around."

"There's a radio show that comes on at night. Real human voices. It's amazing!"

"Please listen to it away from me, then. I don't sleep too well with background noise."

"I guess we're all set to leave, then. Let's find our way back to the highway and continue north."

"I've been meaning to ask you," Midori said as we left the valley, "what happened to your face?"

I touched the mark Kasos had left. It was still throbbing, but the pain had begun to lessen. "I fell down."

"That's a cut, not a bruise."

"Okay, fine, Kasos attacked me."

"Why would you lie about that? And why would she do that?"

"Because she's an angel and angels want to kill us all. Why not? I lied because I—I don't know. It just sort of happened."

"Whatever. Let me see your cut." She lightly brushed the cut, dancing around it with her fingertips.

I averted my eyes as she studied the wound. "Um…. What are you doing?"

"Looking it over. Don't worry," she said, looking up and smiling at me. "I'll take care of it."

"Do you… know first aid?"

"Not at all. But don't worry. I'll wait until we're done moving for the day—or night now, I guess—before doing anything."

We climbed out of the thicket and onto the highway once more. The moon was full and the night had no clouds. I hated walking at night, and I was glad that at least I wasn't alone anymore. The ground was illuminated like the streetlights were still working.

I could only spot two angels in the sky, both of them passive and distant. Still, their presence also gave me peace of mind. The last two times I had noticed a lack of angels, something bad had happened.

I fiddled with the radio as we walked, at last finding the broadcast I was looking for.

*"...In? Oh well, it's been a bit!"* said Emil cheerily.

"It's on!" I nudged Midori softly.

Naomi asked him curiously, *"A bit since what, Emil?"*

*"Since we've had the studio to ourselves! Yes, that is correct listeners, Ada hasn't shown up today at all. So for this broadcast, it's just me and Naomi."*

"What kind of show is this anyway?" asked Midori, and I shushed her.

*"This is Angel Radio, and I'm your host, Emil. How's everyone doing tonight?"*

*"Lovely, lovely,"* chirped Naomi.

*"I was asking our listeners!"* He chuckled wholeheartedly, like some '50s sitcom father. *"We start today with a good look at angel classification by the ever lovely Naomi."*

*"Aw, you're not too bad yourself, Emil! Anyway, the gist of angels is that there's a lot of them, and they're all like little snowflakes of uniqueness. Well, the upper orders are. Lower down you get a lot more lazy cookie-cutter types if anything. I'm looking at Messengers especially. So boring. Next up is the archangels, who are just slightly more pimped out versions of the lower angels. Also lame. The last order of the third sphere dares to be different—applause goes here—and those are the Principalities. Unlike their other first sphere brethren, Principalities have distinctive faces, arms, legs, and bodies. Like their name implies, they used to watch over cities and communities. But watching over sure doesn't imply protection—they don't attack others without orders."*

*"Very informative today. I like it. I guess it's on me to do the weather, then?"*

*"We can do it together,"* Naomi giggled.

*"All right, so...."* There was a rustling of papers, and they both began to talk slowly at the same time. *"Tonight we're looking at a calm and temperate night. Tomorrow, expect changes and rainfall. Cover yourself up."* There was a lot of laughing as the two of them struggled to speak at the same pace. *"Watch out for—watch out for—okay, one, two, three—watch out—"* They continued laughing, unable to talk straight.

*"I'm sorry, listeners. I think we're done for tonight,"* managed Emil. The broadcast abruptly cut off before his last syllable was through.

"So it's some sort of… show you can…?"

"No, it's purely informational. And comforting. It's normally more professional than that, and there's three of them, and—" I realized I was blushing.

"So it's—"

"No, just forget about it."

Midori looked at me oddly, and I looked away. I'm not sure what triggered me to get so defensive.

"If you insist."

"Let's just find somewhere to settle for the night."

"Why not one of these cars? That's where I mostly slept."

"There's dead bodies in them."

"Not always! Rarely. And you can move dead bodies."

"But it's gross!" I protested, but Midori had made up her mind.

"You can sleep outside, then." She found herself a van and pulled the rotting corpse of its previous owner out onto the ground. I moved a ways away and settled on the grass, using my coat as a blanket.

"Guess what?" called Midori. "I found a can of air freshener. You can't even smell the decomposition!"

I rolled over. The grass itched my skin and a bug buzzed near my ears. I was thoroughly uncomfortable, and I eventually gave in.

"All right fine, make room," I said, climbing into the backseat with her.

"You sleep on the floor, since it's your fault for taking so long to see I was right."

I settled on the carpeted floor. The air smelled like chemical flowers, but at least I was comfortable.


I AWOKE to rain falling on the roof of the van, a familiar sound that made me yearn for the days of dozing off during long road trips. Midori had left the van and her clothes behind, and I looked out the window to find her lying on the ground with her eyes closed.

I stripped down to my underwear and joined her outside. The rain was heavy enough for a summer storm, louder than sounds of our breathing. It pelted my skin relentlessly like a bad massage, and I took to keeping a hand over my eyes to be able to see. Rainstorms were one of the things I nearly enjoyed about the empty earth, the incredible smell of foliage and the rejuvenating feeling of cold droplets on my skin.

"I'm sorry I forgot about healing your cut last night. Maybe this rain will help," she said, without opening her eyes.

"Probably just with preventing infection." I sat on the grass next to her.

"No need to be self-conscious," she said, sitting up suddenly and taking in my soaked underwear.

"I'm beginning to regret keeping them on myself."

"Then take them off and toss them in the car to dry."

"I've made it this far," I said, though I knew I was being ridiculous.

"Whatever. Say, I could still try to fix your cut, you know. Let's head into the woods and look around."

"Isn't it dangerous to walk around naked in there? Like branches could scratch you, or you could step on a rock."

"Not if you pay attention. Come on!"

She dragged me up and pulled me into the pine forest.

"What are we looking for exactly?" I asked as she began to search every tree in sight.

"Here!" she said suddenly, and I went over and watched as she began to coil a spider web around her fingers.

"Is the spider still in that? Because I don't want a spider on my face. Or a web for that matter."

"Don't fret so much and sit down. Here, I'll be careful applying it."

I hesitated, but allowed her to trace the gash out, circling its edges three times before applying the web like a glaze over it. Her eyes were closed in concentration, and with her pinky she lightly pressed some of it down the very center of the wound, and when she was done, she covered it with her hands for a few more seconds.

"What was that?"

"Healing, I hope. I don't know if I did it right, though."

"Well it doesn't feel any better."

"Stop being so cynical about it. Do pills work instantly? You've got to give it time to heal."

"Well, thanks, I guess." I seriously doubted the medical efficiency of cobwebs, but I felt it would be rude to mention this to Midori.

"You really need to work on your attitude, you know that, right?" Smiling, she took me back out into the roadway. "Look at how beautiful it is!"

I was smiling, and I turned my head to check if she was as well. She had to be kidding if she found a highway particularly pleasant to the eyes. I didn't say anything to her, though. I just laughed a little bit, and she grinned.

"The sun's shining," I said. The day wasn't cold but crisp, and the sun brought some appreciated heat to my goose-bump-laden skin.

"Exactly." She seemed particularly enthused, clenching her fists above her heart and nodding slightly.

"It's nice," I said, and she continued in her excitement. Something about her was infectious, and as she looked about the roadway with delight, I couldn't help but be reminded of a child. Maybe she wasn't bright, or perhaps she was an angel, but something in me wanted to protect her. No matter what had happened, she was the only person I had left. Human or not.

# 9

A FEW hours later, the rain succumbed to a light drizzle. I had a lunch of soggy crackers while Midori swam in the river. We had decided not to move until the rain had stopped and we could dry off, but the rain showed no signs of stopping.

Instead we had busied ourselves with whatever we could think of. I was mostly walking through nature, as I didn't want to join Midori in the ice-cold brook.

The rain had brought a heavy fog and with it the eerie eyes of angels still lurking in the woods. Midori was quite keen on them, though.

"They're just watching. It's like they're guardians of the forest!"

"They unsettle me." In the mist their eyes reflected light, and with the mist obscuring much of their bodies, it was like the forest was staring at us.

"Stop worrying about them. You know they won't harm us. They're just spirits."

Midori hadn't seen the things I had; that had become abundantly clear. She still refused to talk about her life, but her carefree attitude suggested one without much hardship. I had picked up that she was from a well-off family, and she told me that when the angels had arrived, she had been camping.

"I was out conversing with nature for the week," she told me. "Perfect timing, right? I was out on Bread Loaf Mountain when it happened. I did see an angel pass right over me, and a few smaller ones had found perches on the mountain. But I paid them no mind. It was not my business to intervene. None had interrupted me, and I continued to live for the rest of the week in isolation. Only when I returned back to town did I realize what had happened—but it wasn't really my business. I left town and headed southeast on an urge, and followed my instincts the rest of the way. None of the angels acknowledged me, and I thought it may have been my destiny."

"Weren't you scared, though? Everyone was dead except for you."

"I had few friends. I'm a nomad at heart anyway; I travel around. And most importantly of all, I've always believed I've had a higher purpose."

"Seems a little cocky to think that you alone were chosen to live while everyone else was unworthy."

"Self-confidence isn't a sin, Erika. And it wasn't that I was better than everyone else. I'd never think that. It was more that I had been chosen for my regularity. For whatever reason, I was just average enough to be spared. Don't you feel the same way?"

"Definitely not."

"Surely there's a reason we are alive, and being kept alive?"

"I really don't think so."

"You've got to work on your faith."

As we sat by the brook, we both saw the angel at the same time. It was unwieldy, like a melting wax sculpture, and indeed it appeared to drip pale droplets of strange essence as it walked. It was maybe ten feet tall, weaving carelessly through the trees, leaving bits of itself on the branches.

"It looks scared," Midori said immediately, climbing out of the water and standing next to me on a nearby boulder. "We should offer it assistance."

"It looks like it's going to be in my nightmares tonight." Its face was the closest to human I had seen in an angel, though like everything else on its body, it looked like partly melted wax. It had six arms, each hand ending in a mass of at least ten fingers. Its whole body radiated a pinkish color, and at its core a light like a candle's flame massed.

Midori jumped down and walked toward it, hands in the air to prove she was unarmed. I didn't follow her but observed from a safe distance.

The angel stopped in front of her, swaying quickly from side to side like grass in the wind. It did not look down on her, but rather its face fell from its head and slid down to come with her.

Carefully, Midori put out a shaking hand, slowly touching the angel's skin. I could hear its heavy breaths even from here. As her fingers made contact she shouted with glee, "I told you it's friendly, Erika!"

I noticed something was wrong with it, though. The bubbling on its back seemed very irregular, and stranger still was the angel itself: its only eyes were the two on its face area, and it lacked wings entirely.

It made a jerky movement, and I yelled, "Wait, Midori!"

But it was too late. First it was her hand, suddenly slipping through the soft surface of its face and getting lodged there. As she tried in vain to remove her arm, the angel's body swooped down onto Midori, covering her and consuming her.

It fixed itself up in seconds, standing perhaps a little taller. Floating inside its nearly translucent body, I thought I could make out Midori, murkily obscured.

With a creaking sound, it turned to face me. My heart raced, ready to flee, but I kept still. I wasn't just going to let that thing take Midori like that.

I didn't have a weapon, and I scrambled to grab a heavy rock. Before the angel-thing got too close, I lobbed the rock at it. The rock was simply absorbed, causing nothing more than ripples in its body where the rock had first made contact.

While the angel continued its advance, I tried my next best idea— a full charge. It wasn't even an idea, honestly, just a bad decision.

Its feet were soft spires, perfectly pointed and carefully sidestepping across the brook. I only came a bit above its legs, and I drove my hands wildly into its body.

I lost control of my arms right away, but I still had some control of the rest of my body. I jerked myself backward, tugging repeatedly at it. It was incredibly unbalanced; that was made even the more obvious as it began to topple.

As it tried to right itself, it began to drop some body mass, presumably to act as a base for the rest of its body. In response I quickly jumped backward one more time and pulled the angel with me. For a moment I was suspended an inch above the brook as the angel slowly toppled over. The moment it touched the water, however, it began to dissolve.

Out of its body came several egg-like capsules, which dissolved as they fell into the water. Midori emerged from one of them, as well as several other forest creatures such as deer and foxes.

"Oh," she said, swimming in the goo that now covered the water like a thin membrane.

"I killed it," I said triumphantly. "Now do you see what I meant by 'angels are bad news'?"

"It dissolves in water. Poor thing was just trying to get out of the rain before it melted."

"It also tried to… eat you or whatever."

"I think it just needed some things to help hold its body together. I also think it isn't dead," she said, pointing to some of the other capsules that had yet to open.

She swam over to one and pried it open. There was a rabbit inside the first one, long dead. The trend continued as she opened more of them, next a turkey vulture, and then a honeybee's nest, and finally, a human man. He was in a particularly bad state, veinlike structures from the capsule covering most of his body. His skin had been preserved, but he was very much dead.

"Or not." Midori sighed. "I can't be right about everything. Let's head upstream so I can get this stuff off me. I think the rain is letting up, a real shame since that angel couldn't live to see it."

When we made it back to the car, the rain had long stopped, and a cool breeze had mostly dried us off. I was shivering by the time we fully dried off (using a towel found in a suitcase), and I was very glad to be fully dressed again.

"I'm not even sure that was an angel, to be honest," I said. "It didn't look like one."

"Maybe it was something else."

"Yes, that's what I'm saying."

"I think it was just another kind. When I was inside it—well, I was actually unconscious. But I think I was connected with it for a moment, sort of a link between our minds, and I could tell it was an angel in a lot of pain."

"How do you know you aren't imagining it? Like you're just experiencing what you want to experience, but in truth it was nothing."

"I know what I felt. And I still feel its presence. I believe it to still be alive, and perhaps if we were to head back to the brook it would have reformed itself by now."

"So what kind of angel was it? It didn't even have wings."

"I sensed a very old soul within it, one that was full of fear. It is my belief that it was not just avoiding the rain but also running away from something greater than it. Perhaps its strange appearance and its terrible fear are connected?"

"If you're correct, I'm just glad we're getting away from there. Hate to run into whatever made that thing cower like that."

"It may still be advancing. Nothing's stopping it, and I do say we are a point of interest amidst everything else left on this planet."

"Don't freak me out. You sort of freak me out a lot and make me worry far too often."

"Sorry!"

We were traveling down the highway once more. The supplies we had looted from a particularly cautious man's car included plenty of weather-worthy clothing, a new bag for the both of us, new water rations, and food. There was also a shotgun and plenty of ammo, but Midori refused to let me take it. She did allow me to take a flare gun, although only after a lot of whining.

Neither of us had mentioned a destination, as I had only the vaguest of directions toward the radio station and Midori preferred to trust fate with our path. We were pretty much heading north, though slightly to the west. It wouldn't be that long before we actually did cross into Canada. Mostly we were following the road.

There was no sign of some sort of super-angel or whatever Midori had been expecting, but she remained adamant. "I can feel something coming, I'm telling you."

With her luck, she'd be absolutely right. But I didn't want to deal with another angel, even if this time I was slightly better prepared to take one on. Water melts them, huh? How cliché. And probably not all of them, actually, as I had seen a few angels in the rain before.

It was one in the afternoon, according to Midori's watch, that I spotted Gav again. I don't think she noticed him, but he certainly noticed me and disappeared a second later. But as we continued, he emerged again with a slightly subdued step.

I nudged Midori softly. "Hey. Look over there. That's this kid who's been following me since before the camp. I thought he had stopped."

"Is he human?" she asked curiously. "You'd think a human would want to spend time with us."

"I think he's just weird. He certainly is convinced I can't see him sneaking about."

"Why don't you ask him to join us? The more the merrier, right?"

"I don't think he'll accept. I think he actually prefers slinking around like that. But don't think I'm letting that stop me," I said. Then I called over to him. "Hey, Gav! We can still see you, you know!"

He ran deeper into the woods as soon as he heard my voice. "I still know you're there, you loser."

"You're not suppos—okay, fine, you win. I'll come out." He was wearing the same outfit as when I had last seen him. Not like I changed my outfits much these days, either, but at least I washed them. His clothes were caked in mud and ash.

"Hello there, Gav," said Midori.

"Hi, Midori. Hey look, you guys, I'm not really supposed to be hanging with you right now. I got other things to do."

"And here I thought your only matter of business was stalking me! Do explain."

Midori put a hand on my shoulder. "Don't question him. If he has other things to do, so be it. We may cause more harm than good in the long run if we pursue interaction with him."

"Oh, who says? I'd rather settle things once and for all. So tell me: what are you doing? Who do you work for?"

"I'm a lone wolf by nature, and I'm certainly not working for anyone or even working at all. I just got lots of things to attend to that lie in the border between the woods and this highway, and by a crazy coincidence, it trails you guys exactly."

"Like shape-shifting immortal deer, right?"

He clicked with his tongue. "You got it! Well, not really. But you're almost correct, so I'll give you the point this time. Bye, ladies!" He ducked back into the thicket.

"We should leave him be. I worry for him."

"You're worried about *him*? What about us?"

"He seemed frightened."

"By what? I swear, you see every living thing as a wounded puppy," I said. I handed her my bag. "Don't think I'm letting him go, by the way. Wait here."

I entered through the gap he had trampled in the bracken and began my pursuit, hoping he had taken the logical path of straight forward. At some point he probably realized I was following, as I had never seen him in this deep before. However, perhaps he hadn't been fleeing after all. Just waiting.

At the end of the path he had weaved and I had followed; he was standing still. A field had opened up very suddenly. A beaver pond filled most of the open space, and an unmarked building took up the rest.

Gav watched me carefully with unwavering eyes. "Sorry for the strange setting. Had to get you alone somewhere with a lot of space," he said. "Are you ready?"

## 10

"Could you have phrased that any freakier?"

"Sorry," he apologized. "What I mean is—look, forget it. I do want to talk to you, though."

"Without Midori."

"Not without her, per se, but rather with you alone. I have nothing against her. She seemed nice."

"Well, then, spit it out. What's up?"

"Uh, you had the questions, right? Why don't we work off those?"

"Are you actually going to answer me?"

"Well, let's hear what you're asking first before I make any promises."

"All right, who are you? Why have you been following me? Why do you know so much about the angels? Who do you really work for?"

"That was a lot to take in! This will take a moment to sort through." He sighed. "I guess we have the time. I've told you my name, Gav, which is sort of a real treat since I never intended to. I've been following you for ages now because… well, I feel inclined to." He paused and took a deep breath. "I don't know, to be honest. I found you on the sixth day of the angels, when that angel went into your house and killed your family. I saw you faint, I ran in to check you were okay."

"But you didn't stay to talk with me. You left me alone while I went mad, and I only saw you once I left."

"I actually was gone at that point. Came back just in time for you to leave. And I never talked to you because I—uh—don't like people. I don't like talking. It's not how I do things. So I settled with just watching."

"And about the angels?"

"I have no idea what you mean. I know just as much as you. Perhaps a bit more because I prefer to observe rather than barge in. The camp was the most obvious ploy I've ever seen, and even you realized it after a while."

"There's something far too casual about you and the angels that I really don't want to delve into. But sometimes I worry...."

"That? You think I'm an angel stuffed into a human body? I like to imagine I come off as a bit more realistic than those idiots. It's nice to see someone praise my observation and preparation skills, but I don't like being accused of being a monster for them. And to answer your last one, I seriously don't work for anyone. I'm just a human, similar to you, who is out here doing his own thing."

"Why did you disappear after that one time in the camp? I was looking for you."

"Fex saw me. I had to leave."

"Oh, really? Is that so?"

"Yes. He saw me talking to you, so I had to lie low. It didn't help that you were yelling at me either."

"Really. And lastly, about the super-deer—"

"Is that what we're calling it now?" He smirked. "I told you once and I'll tell you again. Stay away from that hell beast. It's an angel trying to lure you to touch it, and you definitely should never touch it."

"You shouldn't touch any angel, right?"

"Absolutely. I saw you out there fighting that gelatinous one. What a stunning combination of terrible decisions and good moves. You're lucky you didn't die."

"I'm somehow not surprised that you were spying on us bathing this morning, pervert."

"Pervert?" he asked, pausing for a moment. "Oh. Right. It's not my fault you ran around naked for the first half of the day. If it helps, I am quite asexual. Now, is that all you have for me to answer?"

I thought about it, but I couldn't figure anything else to ask. He really hadn't clarified anything, but there was no way for me to form my feelings into questions.

"I guess so."

"Have I proved myself fine and in need of no more investigation by you?"

"That's asking quite a lot of me. I'm not exactly happy with you."

"So what else do you need to know before you feel like you can trust me?"

"Nothing. I just—I barely know you. Why would I trust you at all?"

"I will answer any questions you have until you trust me."

"That's not how trust is formed. How about I just go back?"

"No, I insist. I want you to not feel threatened by my presence."

"I have nothing left to say." I gave an exaggerated shrug to emphasize my point.

"No, really, really, really, I seriously insist," he said, looking around nervously.

"What is going on? Is this some sort of trap? A trick?"

"No, no, no! Of course not. I just mean—I uh… I want to be close friends with you, and I wish for this to go as well as possible. Let's be friends."

"You're not going to just be my friend by… asking me. That's like the most awkward thing I can think of."

"I-I'm sorry."

"I think I'm going to go."

"Wait!"

"No. See you later, I guess."

Suspicious, suspicious, suspicious. That was all Gav was—or rather, continued to be. And by suspicious, I mean: there was no way he should have known Fex's name.

He appeared genuinely human, certainly more real than any of the other "humans" I had met, but there was no doubt that he was working with them somehow. Maybe without his knowledge, if such a thing was possible? I'd be lying if I said I wasn't hoping he was somehow innocent. I wanted to find as many humans as possible, even if it would make traveling very hectic. But I couldn't even pretend he was fully normal, and I was definitely not about to allow him to travel with us. Except from his safe stalking distance, since I couldn't really help that.

Midori was leaning against a truck, appearing to have dozed off, but she sprang awake as I stepped back onto the road.

"How was it?"

"He's untrustworthy. I want nothing to do with him."

"He was just doing his best."

"You seem very keen on him, and you barely had a chance to glance at him."

"I'm very good at first impressions."

"Well, this is one time where you're wrong. Actually, you were wrong about most things so far. Kasos, the camp, the jelly angel."

"I've noticed that," she said, "but I politely disagree."

I couldn't change her mind about it, not to mention it'd be really pointless to even try. We headed out again.

There's only so much walking to do before you tire of it. I really hoped the rest of my life wasn't going to be walking on highways and walking in the woods. But what can you do, right? Just head straight down the path.

Gav didn't reappear. I wanted to secretly hope we were going to leave him behind, but then I remembered we were following a very straight and predictable path, and even then I didn't want to leave him. Not quite yet.

"Look up," said Midori, very quiet suddenly.

It was like—and no matter how much I repeat it, I cannot stress it enough—a hot air balloon show of angels above us. They were clustered right above our heads, hovering and jittering like a swarm.

"They look agitated," she said. We had stopped to look, but I itched to get away from them as soon as possible. Being this close was never good.

"C'mon, let's hurry."

"Why? I want to know what's bothering them."

"They're not animals. But if you really want to stay and observe, maybe together we can observe what happens when I shoot a flare at them."

"Erika! I said no guns. That flare is for signaling only."

"I bet they'd explode. They must be full of hot air, after all they do just sort of float there. We should find out. I bet guts will go *everywhere*."

"No!"

"So you think they don't have any guts? Very interesting theory that we should totally test as soon as possible."

"No way!"

I laughed. "You're like a crazy animal rights activist. These things aren't harmless little bunnies. They are totally able to kill us."

"By comparing them to humans you're finally admitting they're beings who can show emotion and intelligence," she pointed out.

"Yes, but at least I know they can handle themselves and that we should just leave them alone—and get as far away from here as possible."

"You're overreacting. They're all crowded together like this because they've been spooked. I want to see what's spooked them."

"Again with the frankly suicidal desire to see some sort of mega-angel or whatever. Let's just leave them alone and start praying we never see that thing."

"It might be too late for that."

"See? This is what I meant! If we had just left—oh goddammit," I said, realizing what she meant. I looked behind me.

Something was pooling out of the shadows. It wouldn't be a bad guess to say it was some sort of angel, but it didn't seem to have much of a corporeal form. It was like an oil slick or a glass of spilled water that was rapidly advancing on us. While most of its body was a solid black, now and then there were portions of diluted gray and translucency, like watercolor ink.

While it was very much a dripping blob, it weaved in a serpentine fashion toward us, curling infinitely just beyond my line of sight.

Neither of us dared to move, as that seemed like a pointless waste of energy. In horror, I felt my heart pound, and I reached for Midori's hand, finding it and gripping it tight.

It did not attack us, but did acknowledge our presence. It began to circle us, its body ringing itself like a snake. Up close I could see the bubbly texture of its skin and the pockets of air like scales that lined its upper side. It did not appear to have a headlike appendage, as when I spun in circles to look for one I got too dizzy to continue.

Its body formed a pillar around us, and for a moment it seemed like it was going to seal itself off. Instead it stopped some twenty feet tall and paused.

Then I realized this thing wasn't interested in us, it seemed to only have eyes for the flock of angels gathered above like gulls. Carefully, a dripping tendril formed from its body, and then fifty more all at once. These tentacles crept around the panicking angels, before striking faster than a flash of lightning. It had almost been like a whip, wrapping around the angel's entire body and dragging it straight into the giant creature's body.

Not all of the angels were drawn in. A few had somehow eluded attack, or otherwise were too high up. The tentacles began to reform immediately, and curiously tested themselves around the angels, who, for whatever reason, refused to flee.

There was a sudden and very human shout compared to the shrill calls of the angels and the hissing of the oil snake. Gav swung out of nowhere—and I do mean nowhere, considering he was about twenty-five feet in the air—and landed on the creature's body.

"Hi!" he shouted down to us, oddly unharmed by the creature's muck.

"Hi?" I managed, very much confused.

He jumped on top of the creature once, ran its entire length in a circle, jumped again, paused, and finally lit the whole thing on fire. Why did everything end up dying in fire these days?

Where he even got the flames was beyond me, but suddenly I was standing in a literal ring of fire, and while the walls were surprisingly spacious they were still on fire. My eyes began to sting from the smoke, and Midori brought me to the ground.

A strong arm grabbed me around the waist and attempted to lift me up. I clung to Midori in a moment of heat-caused delusion. I stuck to the burning ground blindly, and felt Midori leave my side. Finally I was lifted, but by what I had no idea. By Gav, obviously, for there really couldn't have been anyone else, but there are certain things you have to ask yourself in life. For example: how was Gav going to explain his sudden ability to leap twenty-five feet in the air and carry people with just one arm?

"Rope" was how he explained it. "Or more accurately, steel cables. Accidentally dropped it all when bringing Erika down, though."

The creature's body was still burning, having collapsed into what was essentially a pile of... whatever it was made of. Parts of it seemed to have hardened, and I imagined it would turn into a little mountain when the next rain came.

"That's ridiculous." I said, shaking my head. It really made no sense, but I didn't feel like dwelling. "But what is—was that thing, though? Not an angel, right?"

"Correct. I call them demons. They're a lot heavier than the angels, and more or less made of liquid."

Midori stayed quiet, but I saw her lips tighten.

Gav sat us down to talk and check for injury, but we were all fine. Still, he insisted on sharing fresh bread and clean water with us from his brand new backpack.

"You came back," I said.

"He never left," interjected Midori.

"She is about right, yes. I never said I was going to stop following you, so why do you sound so surprised?"

"Somehow I was expecting—I don't know, not this." I held my tongue, unsure if it was wise to speak my suspicions. Maybe there was some sort of value in not making him aware? There had to be. Instead, I decided to see what information I could shake from him by pretending to be oblivious at the game he was trying to play.

"I changed my mind," he said.

"I'm sorry?"

"I changed my mind, I mean, about following you. I'd like to travel with you, if that's possible. Power in numbers, yes?"

I had to grit my teeth in order not to laugh. More and more he was slipping up. I'd be damned if he wasn't an angel at this point. Maybe one who had done a bit more research on humans, but certainly not to be trusted. "I don't know about that. What do you think, Midori?"

There was some ill-thought logic in trusting Midori, the unaware angel, on her opinion on what was likely another angel. There was probably a mistake in trusting her at all. I knew it was a stupid thing to do, and I had no defense. I wasn't some logical mastermind. I was a seventeen-year-old girl who had spent the last few months in utter isolation. I was going to stick with Midori until it bit me in the ass. Whatever.

"I really like you," said Gav before Midori could respond. She closed her mouth and pouted again, silent.

"That's great. I mean, who knows? We'll see. By the way, I was wondering. The deer thing. You never really explained what that was about, and I mean if you're going to come with us you ought to stop being so mysterious about everything."

"Oh! Of course. One sec, just gotta word it out in my head before I explain." He made a bizarre face of concentration, and I probably made a similar one. Why was he suddenly so awful at being human? "Yes, so that deer-angel—"

"Excuse me," said Midori in a quiet voice. "What deer-angel?"

"I'm getting to it. That angel had possessed a deer, and was highly dangerous because of it. As you've noted, angels really do best in human hosts, though to be honest they really are ill suited to possession in general. Angels that take over animals become highly unstable—something about the wild mind of the creature matched with the energy of the angel has toxic results."

"And touching one?"

"How do you think they possess their hosts? It's bad enough to touch an angel, but at least they don't usually bother possessing bodies. Feral angels will always go for a human body, and that has disastrous results."

"Like what?"

"Terrible stuff. I saw it happen once. Very unclean. The human had no doubt died from the process, and I doubt that even if the angel had been removed, the old body would have functioned properly anymore. Always keep your distance and shoot to kill."

"Then why—when you attacked that demon thing, you left those angels in peace. Why didn't you try anything on them?"

I was a bit nervous that I had cornered him into admitting he was on their side, but he came back strong. "You can't kill every angel, Erika. There's too many of them and too few bullets for that."

"Excuse me?" tested Midori quietly, repeating it to herself several times. Then she finally spoke above the both of us, yelling a little bit. "Excuse me, I'm going for a walk."

"Of course, go right ahead," said Gav.

"Are you all right? Should I come along?" I asked.

"She's fine. Let's stay and talk some more," Gav replied, dragging my attention away from Midori's retreating figure.

"I have nothing left to say."

"Oh, come on! I'm sure you do. Where's your sense of curiosity? Here's an example for you: How did I know how to kill that demon? Well, the truth is I've been doing a lot of that kind of stuff lately. I've been killing off all the monsters I find in the forest, not to mention occasionally I go ahead of you and get rid of some of the ones that would have slowed you down."

"Thanks, but I think I want to talk to Midori right now."

"Please, stay here." I almost felt bad for him. He obviously had some sort of order to keep an eye on me, but there was no way for him to enforce it if I didn't play along.

"Erika, please, sit back down."

"No can do, pretty boy. Wait here, I'll be back in like twenty minutes."

"It's probably too late for her, Erika," he said, stone-cold, and I spun around on my heel.

"Don't you start with the cryptic shit again. If this is another badly phrased sentence, I swear to God I'm going to bash your face in."

"Erika, watch yourself. This is not a joke."

"And you're not Gav."

"Correct. Please, sit down. Let us talk this out."

# 11

"Midori," I said. "I'm not leaving her to whatever you're doing."

"So between learning the truth of what is truly happening and potentially saving someone you barely know, you choose her?"

"Always. The truth can wait, because it's always going to be there. She won't."

"I might be gone by the time you return. Wouldn't you rather speak to me? Even for a few seconds. See what you can learn."

"I've told you all I want to. Leave if you have to. I know I am."

The thing that perhaps was Gav, or maybe used to be him, did not stir. The air was heavy with a wet fog, the sort that only rolled in after a storm, and brought with it the tranquil scent of pine and soil. The sky was darkening rapidly, sun long gone behind the clouds, and the moon was nowhere in sight.

There was no way to tell where Midori had gone, but somehow I just knew. Something in the moss led me down a steep hill into a gorge. A hiking path intersected with my route, and I followed it to the bottom of the gorge and the serene waterfall pool where Midori was kneeling.

She looked like radiance.

"I'm scared," she said, one hand idly turning the water of the pool about.

"And?"

"Uneasy?" She looked to me with wide and trembling eyes.

"Is this about Gav? Because you know, it turns out that that wasn't—"

"No!" she shouted, but her hands clamped over her mouth immediately. "I'm sorry. What I mean to say is, it's not him. I don't care about him. I don't care about any of this, all these monsters and angels and forest guardians—I just want it to end."

"I thought you were all… cocky about it earlier. You're chosen, right? Meant to live on."

"But I hate it. I hate all of this so much. I just want a normal life, and I want normal things, and most of all I want everything to be logical and make sense. I hate these spirits so much."

"Why?"

She closed her eyes, and her face told me she wasn't about to open them anytime soon. "Because I'm just a dumb kid. I'm nineteen years old. I ran away from home when I was sixteen because I thought my family hated me and my online friends were my only real ones. But most of all, I wanted to leave the city. I didn't hate the crowds or the noise, even if I always complained about them. Looking back, it was comforting. All those people, always living right outside my window. But I had it set in my heart that I was a creature of the earth, meant to wander the woods and frolic among deer and wear flowers in my hair all day long and sleep under the stars. I was a witch—or at least, called myself one. I never really did any spellcraft. I barely understand what modern witches are. I just wanted to be one, to be independent and unique and live with plants."

"Doesn't everyone do this kind of thing, though? It's perfectly normal to want to be special."

"No one's actually special or unique. We're all the same. I couch surfed my way through two years of my life, living off friends and night-shift jobs. I read dumb books and made an altar and believed myself to be finally at peace with myself."

"There's nothing wrong with any of that, Midori—"

"I'm not Midori, okay? That's not my name. My real name's Sarah Rosenthal. I renamed myself Midori because it means 'green' in Japanese, and I thought it was nice and earthy, because everything in my goddamn life was nice and earthy. I traveled around New England for those two years in the best state of being I've ever been in, but I was thoroughly miserable. Every night I'd toss and turn to the pace of the wind, and every morning I'd shiver at the birdsongs and the touch of the falling leaves. I hated organic food, I hated gardening, and I hated my new wardrobe of flowing clothes made of flowing fabrics and asymmetrical skirts. I was not at home, but I had to be at home, because this was all I ever wanted."

"That's... really sort of awful. I want to say something, but...."

"Don't bother. The worst part of this story is yet to come. There is no conclusion. I'm still wandering the earth pretending I know anything about psychics and spirits, but for some reason I'm entirely right. Why am I suddenly so right? I am dreaming? No one said this would happen. No one said life would be like this."

"You shouldn't be so caught up like this. Nothing's your fault. And you know, I think you shouldn't be so caught up on your past like this. You should never live as who you used to be, only as who you want to be."

"This is who I want to be. I wanted this, I asked for this, I imagined this. And now this is real and perfect and absolutely awful."

"I don't want to try to make this about me—because it isn't—but I sort of want to say that, well, I get what you're going through. Not to imply you're going through some sort of phase or whatever. Unless you want to think of it that way? Please, disregard that. What I mean to say is, I've dealt with a lot of shit in my life and I know where you're coming from. My whole life, I've never had more than one or two distant friends, and every day I would tell myself I was going to start changing—wear what I wanted, talk to anyone I liked, show more interest in the world. But I never could. I wish I could have done something like you did, to be honest."

"Running away was the worst thing I ever did. My life was hell."

"But at least you tried! I was wallowing around feeling terrible for myself, hating who I was, and at least you were trying to live your dreams. So what if things weren't how you expected? At least you lived them. At least you had a chance to grow."

"Everything that grows has to wither."

"But we aren't plants. We're people."

"Yeah, fuck plants." She wiped a hand across her cheek, but she wasn't crying anymore. She took a deep breath. "Even now I can't admit you're right. But thanks for trying. Thanks for trying."

There was no moon, but the sky had lightened. A couple stars peeked down over us, and again I had the feeling Midori was the one emitting the light—there was just something about her.

"But there's one more thing. I don't want to appear like I just ran off like this for no reason but to sulk. Something else has been bothering me, something that he had said."

"What is it?"

"He said humans should never come in contact with angels, especially ones in the shape of animals. And I know I have. Am I possessed?"

"What? When did this happen?"

"A while ago. A long time ago, I think. Before the angels even arrived. I had been out for a walk around a particularly pleasant field when I saw this great beast appear suddenly. I was afraid to approach it, but it seemed like some sort of sign—like some sort of patron god to me. It was like a gazelle, mixed with a rose bush. Long limbed, covered in thorns, and colored in the deepest green. Absolutely beautiful and very frightening. Ever so real. I walked to it and I kneeled to it and I think it might have possessed me."

"Why would you think that? And how do you know it was an angel?"

"The eyes. So many of them, always watching me. And it had two feathery pairs of wings set upon its back as well. And I think it was possession because I can't remember much else after that moment. Darkness. And then, several days later, I resumed life like nothing had happened. And nothing had, oddly enough, for no one noted my absence. It was like they had all forgotten about me."

"Gav was pretty clear that people who had been possessed by an angel died. Maybe you just had a blackout? Some sort of ill-brought hallucination?"

She shook her head. "It was too real for that. I know it happened. The only problem is, I don't know why. Since that day I haven't gained any new abilities or even lost consciousness. If it's possessing me, it's not doing much."

"So... maybe it didn't? Maybe it just let you be, whatever it was."

"Well.... There's been one thing. I haven't really been hungry. Or thirsty. Or even tired since that day."

"Oh," I said. "*Oh*. That's certainly something. A whole hell of a something."

She shifted uncomfortably. "And ever since I woke up yesterday in that burning field, I've felt empty. I'm missing something. I think it's finally left me."

"So what, you think that elk-angel had just been chilling out in your body for however long, stopping your major bodily functions, and then just got up and left suddenly last night?"

"As weird as it sounds, yes. But it isn't like I've recovered at all—I still can't sleep. I just want to know why."

"Nothing's weird anymore, Midori. Or should I start calling you Sarah?"

"Please don't," she said weakly. "I'm not yet ready to be true to myself like that."

"Just let me know when you're ready." I took her hand in mine and gripped it tightly, helping her to her feet. It was entirely dark now, but we found our way back without trouble.

I was almost disappointed to see the-thing-that-was-Gav was still there waiting. He had started a fire, in fact, and was waiting beside it.

"I can't feel heat," he said.

"That's a lovely fact that I don't care about," I said. "What happened to 'I'll be gone if you decide to chase down Midori'?"

"I am gone. Or I will be shortly. I just wanted to check up on you two."

"What's going on?" asked Midori, looking to me.

I shook my head. "Who are you?"

"I am, say—" He looked up as he paused, evidently thinking it over. "—pretty much the game master. The show runner. Nearly the one in charge." There was a long, quiet moment where I watched his cold face and pondered the implications of him holding power. Then, very quickly, he made a sound like a snort of laughter. "Uh, you know what? I'm mostly joking. I have to go."

"Seriously?" I said.

"Yes." And he delivered that promise quickly, slipping away from our campsite and into the shadows with great agility.

We halfheartedly grabbed our bags, but the still-burning fire was very inviting.

"Do you want to listen to the radio with me?" I asked.

"Not really. Today's been pretty loud. Too much talking. But I know you like it for some reason, so go ahead."

"I don't know why you don't. Isn't it nice to just hear something regular for once? Isn't it hopeful to hear something from a civilization that exists, even if it's somewhere far away?"

"What kind of radio is that anyway? Shortwave?"

"Huh? I don't know, actually. Some sort of ultimate radio I found in a wilderness shop. Why?"

"Don't mind me. I'm just curious."

I flicked the radio on and settled on the ground, curling up on a blanket I had laid on the ground and watching the fire's flicker. Midori remained sitting, but she too was gazing into the flames.

Emil's voice came out of the static after three minutes. *"Hello listeners. Miss me?"*

*"I'm the one who was missing, dickweed,"* Ada said.

*"But I'm the favorite!"* he protested. *"All right, Naomi is the actual diamond among us, but let's not get too caught up on that. We have a lot of news to cover tonight.*

*"Since the last broadcast was cut off rudely, a lot was missed. We're sorry that any vital information may have not been delivered, but hopefully things have worked in your favor regardless.*

*"I guess we should head right in. What's tonight's theme again? Care to take us away, Ada?"*

*"Today we're reporting on an outbreak of environmental disasters that seem to be sweeping the nation—or rather, our little corner of it. Rivers are flooding, trees are uprooting, and lots of fires are burning tonight. Could the angels be to blame? If so, why? Like seriously, why? They already killed the humans, so do they also have some sort of grudge against wildlife? Not to mention the confusing idea behind them even causing floods and windstorms. Are they that strong?"*

*"That's all very intriguing. Have any answers for us, Naomi?"*

*"I do believe so! I have noticed some interesting activity of the Ophanim recently, perhaps they are the arsonists we've been seeking? As for the winds, well, many of the larger angels have wings large enough to summon such a gale. I've yet to see an angel go anywhere near the water, though. Not even a stream! So I suppose that's one mystery left standing."*

*"Very interesting indeed,"* Emil said, *"and now, the weather. Clear days ahead full of sunshine. Expect some chilly winds, though. It'd be best to bundle up early in preparation for the coming frost. About now would be a good time to plant bulbs, if there was anyone left to plant them. Such a weird thought, isn't it, that so many bulbs are left to die in flower shops around the world. I wish them the best."*

*"I have one more thing to say today. Watch yourselves out there, listeners. Bad things are coming. Not like they had ever stopped coming, but it'd be good to start being more aware of their existence."*

*"Thank you, Ada. I suppose this concludes Angel Radio. A bit shorter than I was expecting, honestly! Ah well, I suppose that's for the best,"* said Emil.

*"When isn't it?"* said Naomi from a ways off, and I heard the slamming of a door before the station let out to static once more.

"It's done," I said, sort of dumbly.

"Can you turn it off now?"

"Oh yes, sorry. I guess I'm heading to bed."

"I'll be up watching the sky, I guess."

"Aren't you...?" I started. "Oh wait, sorry. Right. Good night."

"Good night and good morning," she said, watching the clouds idly.

I had gotten up already before I realized I had no intention of cleaning out a car of its previous owner to find somewhere to sleep. I was quite tired, but the grass wasn't feeling very appealing right now either. Instead I made my way back to Midori and sat next to her.

The fire was beginning to die from lack of timber, and I watched it suffer in silence. I didn't have anything more to say to Midori, but I didn't quite want to leave her yet either. And it was in this way that I drifted off: silent, drowsy, and by her side.

## 12

I AWOKE on the ground alone, and as I got up and rubbed my eyes idly, I spotted Midori a ways off standing on the roof of a car. I stretched out and joined her.

"What do you think that is?" she asked, pointing to something off in the distance from where we had come from. It didn't quite look like anything at all, resembling a black dust cloud. But a dust cloud was something that probably shouldn't be cloaking a forest, so it was definitely of some interest.

"I have no idea. Likely something we don't want to get tangled with, though."

"I have little doubt we're going to go into it at some point. I would like to get its existence cleared up before that happens, though."

"Eh." I shrugged. "Not much we can do besides commit its appearance to memory and get a head start. We should be hitting Lake Champlain any day now, huh?" I said, looking back in the direction we were heading. We were situated on a hill, and from the crest, the landscape stretched a great deal forward. However, all that could be seen was the trees, which were now beginning to don their fall colors, and the mountains. A river also ran beside the highway as it had since the last city.

"Once we get to the lake, what will we do?"

"I suppose we're either crossing it or walking around it. I bet there's some boats docked up somewhere with their keys nearby that we could steal, but I'm not taking a rowboat."

"Do you have some sort of ultimate goal in mind, though?"

"I guess I'm hoping we'll eventually find civilization? I mean, the first cities grew around rivers. A lake is a good place to start."

"Plus, you want to find those radio people, right?"

"Yeah, I mean the signal has yet to fade, so we must be getting close."

I hopped off the roof and got ready to go. After the events of last night, we were both restless to leave this place.

"Do you think we're going to see Gav again?" asked Midori, but her expression made it clear she was asking more for my sake than her own.

"I hope so. Whatever is going on inside him, I have a feeling he'll be back. Or at least, his body will be."

"The sky looks healthy today, at least," Midori pointed out, referring to the many clusters of peaceful angels that were floating about this morning. I was unnerved by their seemingly inflated numbers, but Midori was right: bad things only seemed to happen when their numbers were low or agitated. Hopefully this meant today would be smooth sailing.

We had gone another hour down the road when we decided to stop and take a snack break. It was mostly for my sake, but Midori kept her eye out for any valuable nonconsumables.

A traffic jam on the exit ramp was where we dispersed to begin searching for food. I came out with some canned bread and a package of gummy candies. Midori had found a few cans of fruits as well. We continued to quickly scavenge through the cars, though, to see if anything interesting caught our eye.

I noticed a pile of wrappers and bottles on the ground, and I cautiously peeked into the back of the pickup truck that they led to.

"Holy shit!" I swore, falling backward in surprise. "You!"

Looking tired and ill-kept, Fex sat up and ran his hands through his dark hair in a poor effort to fix it. "Yes, me. I've been waiting for you for a day now, but you definitely took your time. And then I discovered alcohol."

He yawned and got up, dusting himself off and jumping out of the truck with a slight wobble. "I'm not intoxicated now, though. By many technicalities, I can't be. I wish I was, though. What was keeping you? Wait, I already know, scratch that."

"Aren't you supposed to be 'promoted'? Or maybe dead?"

"Erika!" Midori called from the other end of the car pileup. "Is someone there?"

"I got off unscratched, very luckily. No one suspected my involvement with the fight thing. Good move by the way, with that fire. I wasn't expecting you to utilize our weaknesses so efficiently like that."

"Who is this?" Midori inquired as she approached us.

"This is Fex, an angel from that camp, and who has evidently been following us."

"If you want to get technical, my name is really Nu-faxielimuth. Fex was a very quickly thought-out humanlike name. You may use it if it makes you more comfortable, however. You're Midori, right? I'm very unpleasantly surprised you survived."

"What's that supposed to mean?" she asked.

"Well, I'm sorry to say, you weren't supposed to," he said with great disdain. "Hasn't Erika filled you in on everything? We were testing you too, but only one was going to pass and make it to the next round. You were actually the favorite, but there will still be problems if certain people see you both alive and together."

"You guys are like a hive mind, right? Shouldn't all of you know by now?" I said.

He cringed. "For serious, we are not a hive mind in the slightest. Stop saying that."

"That is pretty rude," Midori chimed in.

"Some of us are linked, but even they are not unanimous. Many of us are watching you, as per orders, but most of them are simply 'Watchers.' They watch. They do not form thoughts based on what they see; they just watch. And *even then*, what they see is not brought to the rest of us for some time."

"How deep does this go?" asked Midori, shaking her head lightly. "This whole watching thing? What are your people planning?"

"Thank you for calling us people," Fex said with a look of wonder. "See, now you're even becoming my favorite! But alas, I really cannot go into details. I know I might be coming out of nowhere here to fill you in on all these wondrous facts, but I'm still on my own side. I can't go about spoiling everything and thus getting killed."

"So if you're not here to help us, what are you doing?"

"I was just leading right into that, Erika. Last time's attempt to boost me up to power failed, but just barely. There's a little encampment just a little bit away from here where I'm expected to be in a few minutes. From there on out, the plan is the same. Kill the leader, I rise up and become more powerful. We all win."

"That sounds risky for us, and we don't get anything out of it," Midori pointed out.

"You get the sweet feeling of having rid the world of another high-ranked angel. I believe currently running this camp is an angel by the name of Rohandral, pretending to be a man named Han. He should be even easier, if such a thing exists, to kill than Kasos, who was a Cherub. And Cherubs are a bitch to kill. Are you in?"

"No," said Midori.

At the same time, I answered, "Yes."

"What?" she said. "You can't be serious? I don't know how we even lived last time. Last time Kasos was killed by another angel, right? There's no way you can do it on your own."

"I fled the scene early, but I was under the impression you killed Kasos, Erika. Is this not true?"

"It's... complicated. I'll explain it to you later," I promised Midori. "But I think I can handle this. You don't have to come along—though it might be for the best if you do."

"Excellent. I am going to say I have your word now that you'll do this for me. See you at the camp. Bring your own weapons this time." Fex waved without looking back as he starting trekking down the hill.

Midori shook her head again. "This is just awful. I guess it's nice that you seem to be over your prejudice against angels enough to work with one, but trying to team up just to kill someone you know you can't kill seems very dangerous. Why would you trust him?"

"I don't trust him. I just want to try it out. I mean, I trust him to the point that I believe he's telling the truth and that he doesn't want anything more from me. So I don't see many negatives about this."

"I don't know." She sighed. "I don't want to split up, though. That's always an awful idea. But I do think we should be cautious."

"Don't worry. We'll be fine," I said, heading down the road. Fex was long out of sight, and I had to wonder if he had dropped his human form and flown off. "If you want, I can tell you all the details when we get there, but here's the short of what really happened at camp: Everyone was an angel, they were testing us for some reason, I shot Haywood and Kasos, Kasos attacked me, and then she died. The end."

"How did she die?"

"That was the doing of another angel, like I told you."

She was quiet for a while, and I was afraid she was going to ask why I hadn't told her any of this. But she said nothing.

Until, finally, "How will we know where the camp is?"

"It will be obvious. Really obvious. They want us to find it, after all."

The lead off was the same as the last one: brush cleared in the same obvious way by what appeared to be clippers, and to the right there was a large pile about a foot tall of lanterns, wires, and knives. It was like they weren't even trying.

There was a shorter trail this time, leading up to a grassy knoll, which was once again densely packed with very large tents. Once more a crowd of people encircled us, looking curious and yet very distracted. A man came out from the chaos, and I was suddenly very certain we wouldn't have much trouble killing him. He was what I would call a wimp, very frail looking, tall, and thin. Last time Kasos had lived when I shot her in the head. I decided this was because she had been expecting it, having seen me raise the gun, and thus had time to switch to her angelic form. I guessed we could kill this man in less than an hour.

My own commitment to Fex's sudden scheme nearly took me by surprise. Violence had never really been my game before, and God knows I had never dallied in manslaughter. However, I liked the idea of killing angels. I liked that I could take a stand, leave an impact in the only way possible postsociety.

Maybe this would change something. Maybe this would do nothing. I wanted to find out either way.

"Greetings," the man said. "My name's Han. It's always pleasant to find more survivors." His glasses, I noticed, had had their lenses punched out.

"Hi," I said, wanting to move this along as fast as possible. "I'm Erika, this is Midori. We'd like to take some time to look around right now, if that's okay with you?"

"Sure it is!" he said, tilting his head with a broad grin. "Why don't I assign someone to show you around? How about you, Fex?"

Fex stepped out of the crowd. "Hi!" he said enthusiastically. "It's very nice to meet you!" In between fake smiles, his cold eyes reminded me how much he wanted this to end already.

He rushed through showing us around, before leaving us unceremoniously at a set of tents identical to the ones at the other camp.

"That sure was something." Midori bit her lip. "Do I have enough time to rest in my tent or do you think you'll... be done before that?"

"I'm pretty determined to make this a speed run. I mean, we spent way too long at that other camp. Stay here if you want, but stay alert. I'm going to try to isolate Han."

"Good luck," said Midori, before she went into her tent. I guess I probably should have explained to her earlier about how she actually had been the one to kill Kasos—but how was I supposed to do that? She was probably stressed enough because she thought she was a vessel for an angel for the last couple months of her life—how was I supposed to tell her that I had evidently seen the angel that had been possessing her and that it had saved my life?

Okay, maybe it wouldn't go that badly. She was smart; it wasn't likely she'd overreact. It wasn't even that scandalous of a secret. I just didn't want to upset her. She deserved some rest, and I didn't want to make her worry any more than she already was.

Han, like Kasos, did not seem to have a moment of solitude. I had yet to spy a creepy circle of angels for him to observe, but that did not stop him from constantly surrounding himself with others. No matter what Fex said, there was something ever so hive mind about the way the angel-people looked at me, like they only had one pair of eyes between them.

"Hey, Han," I said, stepping in front of the group that had amassed around him and trying to ignore their singular looks. "I was wondering if I could talk to you for a moment. Maybe we could walk together in the woods?"

"Absolutely. I know just the trail we could take too," he said, getting up and waving good-bye to everyone.

"Could I also join you?" said Fex, coming out of nowhere with a smile. "I have been meaning to do some walking."

What was he doing here? "This is private business, I'd rather you didn't," I told him, giving him a confused look.

He stared back with what seemed to be irritation. "No, I insist."

"It's fine, Erika." Han placed a hand on my shoulder. "Let him join us."

The forest path was suspiciously cleared out, laid with new wooden railings, and the upper brush of the trees had been trimmed. I could see through the gaps of the canopy the sky was still full of angels.

"So what is it you wanted to talk to me about?" Han asked.

A strong look from Fex told me now wasn't the time to whip out my flare gun and shoot him in the face. I wasn't even sure if that'd work. I mean, it would catch him off guard, but would that split second be enough for him to drop his human body?

Instead, I thought fast. "The angels. I guess. I mean, my family all died because of them, and I was hoping that as the leader, you might be able to help me with them."

"What do you mean?"

"You know. Angels. What are they all about? Everyone I know is dead and I want to know why the angels did that."

"Why are you asking me?" he asked with a forced laugh. "What would I know about angels?"

"I'm not expecting you to answer; I guess I'm just looking for condolences? Some sort of spiritual speech about God's plan for us all? It was a bad idea to drag you out like this. Sorry."

His smile grew, and he poorly tried to disguise its relieved nature. "That is true. Perhaps we should head back, then?"

Fex, who had yet to even make a sound, stood still. "I'd like to continue walking. If she's up to it, she may join me. I'll make sure she gets home safely."

"I'd like that," I said, trying not to sound too happy.

"Hm, I suppose it can't hurt. I will leave you two alone, then," Han said, turning around.

"What's this all—" I started as soon as Han was gone, but Fex shushed me.

"Let's walk in silence. Allows more time to think, I'd say," he said cheerfully.

Just a short way down the trail Fex pointed dramatically to the left. "What's that? I think I just saw something run into the woods. Let's check it out!"

I saw nothing, but I followed him as he wove deeper and deeper into the tangled brush. At last he pulled me under a low-growing bush. "There are some things I hoped I would never have to explain to you," he whispered harshly. "Because they are so obvious. Number one: don't fall into a simple trap. And no matter what you do, take time to think. If you killed him on that trail, even ignoring how clear it was you were being watched from above, all of the camp-bound angels saw you leave with him. You'd be marked as his killer in two seconds and eliminated."

"All right, all right, I'm sorry. I was just trying to end this as soon as possible."

"Your sloppy job would have cost you your life, and if you continue being sloppy, mine. You have to kill him in camp so I can pin the blame on someone else, kill his supposed killer, and reap the rewards. And I hope this is very clear to you, because I can't spend much time with you without people talking. It's odd enough for some we both ended up in the same camp after the last one burned up; the last thing we need is people getting suspicious of our involvement with each other."

"How'd you even get chosen as my tour guide again?"

"I'm one of few angels equipped for the job, I suppose you could say. The others are Watchers. But again, that's sort of the point—*they watch*."

"Seriously, I got it. I'll be more careful next time. I've just got to take some time to strategize."

"Let's hurry back, then. Remember to think things through. And also, Han is going to be a bit more on alert because of you; you know that, right? Way to ask him about the one topic you should have known to avoid."

"No need to rub it in." I sighed.

We made our way back to the main trail without a word, and continued the trend all the way back to camp. We split as soon as we arrived, leaving me free to pace the camp.

It looked like this might take a while after all.

## 13

By nightfall, I was no better off. I paced the surprisingly roomy interior of Midori's tent trying to think of ideas, but I came up with nothing.

"I mean, it shouldn't be too hard. Han doesn't suspect us yet, and he looks to be quite weak. But still, he is never alone. And there isn't one easy way to kill him in isolation in this camp without someone knowing it was me."

"Can't you do this in your own tent?"

"I was hoping you'd be able to help."

"Right now I'd rather meditate. And even then, I never agreed to help you here. I suggest we just bail on him and get back on the road."

"Don't you have a single idea?"

She sighed and ran her hands through her hair. "Create a distraction? Look, why are you so bent on risking your life like this? Fex's never done anything for us."

"It's not about him. It's about me. I want to use this opportunity to practice killing angels. I think it's best I learn now instead of dying later because I have no idea what I'm doing."

"The angels don't even want us dead. You said it yourself. They want to test us, and no matter how creepy that is, we don't need to worry about combat with them."

"They want to test only one of us. And I don't want you to die."

"All right. Fine. But keep yourself safe out there, okay? They're always watching."

"That's exactly it, though. They are always watching. I don't care what Fex claims, there's something all too similar about most of the angel-people here. It's like they're just here to fill empty space."

"I think you just have a biased view of the angels. It's like… speciesism or something. They're not all the same."

I was starting to feel like I was onto something however. "It's night. Han doesn't sleep but stays awake in the center of camp with a group of those weirdo angels. But think about the last camp we were at: by the end, every angel was in the sky watching my fight with Kasos. So why am I allowed here; why haven't they heard I'm not to be trusted?"

"I think—" Midori started, but I stopped her with a hand raised in front of her face.

"It was rhetorical, I know why. It's as Fex said: many angels are simply Watchers. They watch but do not think. They see, but do not tell."

"Then what's the point of them? Why do they watch? Why would the more advanced angels even bother keeping them around?"

"You may have me there. But I'm not even sure there is a reason. All I know is, Han may keep himself surrounded at night, but I doubt any of those angels are smart enough to remember who killed him. I could do it tonight, and it wouldn't even matter if they saw."

"What if you're wrong and they are the smart sort who could quite easily tear you to shreds? Or what if they *can* communicate with other angels and alert them that you're not to be trusted?"

"I'm fairly confident. But you probably ought to kiss me for luck before I go."

Midori rolled her eyes. "You're such a reckless idiot! I'd better not even wish for luck and head right to straight-up praying," she said with great exasperation.

"Don't sweat it. I'll be back before you know it," I promised, and I went out the door.

The air was heavy with the sweet mist of autumn, and the crackling of the fire appealed so much to me that I almost wished to sit down for a moment before I dealt with Han. He and his companions sat perfectly side by side a few feet from the fire.

"Erika," said Han. He still had a friendly air to him that I would miss when he was dead. "What are you still doing up?"

"Enjoying the fire. Are you cold?"

"Cold? Why, the fire is right there. I'm searing with heat."

"Are you sure?" I walked over in front of him, barely feeling the heat dance on my back. A breeze kicked up. I began to walk around behind him.

"What are you doing, Erika?" he asked.

I came around again behind his head. I had brought my bag, and despite my desire to just go all out on the drama, I reached in and took a step back before firing.

It's a good thing I winced when the flare ignited, for the light it provided was as bright as the sun. At such a close range, the flare's shell really just bounced off Han's head, but it was enough. The force knocked his head down a bit, but the fire caught on with unnatural enthusiasm, like oil on water.

The still-burning shell also set the ground aflame. As much as I wanted to put it out and prevent another incident like the first camp, I knew I had to run. I dropped the flare gun and dashed as fast as I could back to the tents.

"Everything is going to be on fire. We have to move."

Midori looked up from her book. "Again? What is it with you and fire?"

"You do know I had a flare gun, right? Now come on, grab your stuff."

This time we hadn't even bothered unpacking, so cleanup was short. Back outside the flames had spread. While I had no way to tell if Han was indeed dead, nothing seemed to indicate otherwise.

"Should we sneak out somewhere?" asked Midori.

"I don't know, maybe it'd be more convincing if we ran?"

"I don't feel like running right now," Midori complained.

We watched the center of the camp burn for a minute. "Let's just go with a fast walk, okay?" As we started for the perimeter of camp, I looked back one last time.

Obviously something had to go wrong. God forbid anything work out the way I planned.

It may have been a simple detail that might not matter at all, but it seemed to me there should be more angels in the sky. When the last camp had burned, they had all flocked together, free of their human forms. But where were they now?

"Something's up," I said to Midori, before running back to the site of the campfire. Fex stood a way off, kneeling in front of someone's body. Han's body was entirely missing. But most importantly of all, the Watcher angels were waiting for me.

They had dropped most of their human forms, just enough to show off their array of eyes and their long misshaped heads. They had moved themselves to a number of places to avoid the slowly creeping graze of flames, but they all turned to me at once.

"Are you sure?" they said as one. From across the site, I saw Fex look up and give me a panicked look. He obviously hadn't been expecting this either.

"What?" I said. Maybe it was more for myself than anyone.

"Are you cold? Are you enjoying the fire?"

"What?" I said again. The flames were causing me to sweat. I watched Fex bail on me and began to step backward slowly.

"Are you sure?" they said once more in unison. "Are you cold?"

"Wait." I stopped. As hard as my heart was pounding, it was clear I had been right. They could watch, but they could not think. They could repeat, but they could not form their own words.

"Are you enjoying the fire?" they repeated. Still, I didn't want them around. They were stuck on speaking just my words, but if they lived to say anything from Han's side of the conversation to someone capable of thought, I would be doomed.

As if in response, the Watchers said, "Erika. What are you doing, Erika?"

I pursed my lips. This was going to be tricky. The flare gun was amidst the flames, and even if the fire was growing slowly this time, it was still a fire. I couldn't get too close.

I had an idea then, very luckily I might add. Things are only tricky if you allow them to be, or if you think only in elaborate schemes. Sometimes the simplest ideas can be all you need.

These Watchers were a group of seven, all scattered by flame into little pockets where they'd be safe. Atop rocks and old still-wet logs mostly. Cautiously I picked up a solid tree branch that had not begun to catch fire. Wielding it with two hands, I held it carefully as I made my way to the closest Watcher.

As I thought, the Watcher did not move at my approach.

"Are you cold?" they said.

I brought the end of the branch to the Watcher's chest, and pushed at it lightly to test its reaction. Nothing but a wobble.

"Cold?" they said. "Why, the fire is right here." I pushed the Watcher strongly, forcing it to lose its balance. At last the Watcher stumbled backward and into the fire. "I'm searing with heat." The other six echoed the cries of their seventh member.

They did not seem to mind the death of their own. They did not move, except to shuffle whenever the flames got too close. It was downright easy to push the rest of them to their deaths; once they fell on their backs, they simply sat there and burned.

The fire stung my eyes as I got to work poking the Watchers into the fire, trying not to breathe in the smoke or the scent of burning flesh. This was downright disgusting, and God knows how many problems with breathing I was going to have in a number of years if this habit of everything I visited burning to the ground continued.

Still, in a couple minutes the Watchers were all gone. The last one had looked at me with what seemed to be a painful twinge of awareness, and feebly whimpered, "What are you doing, Erika?" before finally succumbing to the flames.

As the last Watcher burned to death behind me, a nasty wave of emotions came over me that I fought to suppress. I had wanted to do this. The smell of death and smoke came along with my success, and I had to look past the grotesque nature of my actions to enjoy it. I had come here to do something, and I had done it.

These were Watchers, these were *expendables*, really nothing more than background clutter. Getting caught up in a moral dilemma would do no good. The angels had killed everyone on Earth. Knocking a few of them off should be fair game. There weren't any laws left to the land—if I wanted to kill angels, I could. If I wanted to spare some of them, say Fex, I could.

Midori was still waiting where I left her, and she took a moment before talking.

"Don't run off like that ever again."

"It's okay, I took care of the problem. I had to get rid of the Watchers."

"I could have helped, you know. Don't feel like you need to protect me here."

"There's no way I would have let you come with me. It was dangerous, disturbing, and smelled of burning flesh."

"I know I usually don't want to do anything violent, but in this case, I would have liked to come along. Even if I can't fight, I'm capable of keeping out of danger... and I'd prefer a slight burn over sitting alone and wondering if you're going to come back."

"It's not like I doubt you." Far from it actually. If it had come to a full-out fight against an angel like it had with Kasos, I would have been relying on her to hopefully do the angel thing again and save me. If she even could do it. If the angel possessing her had stayed with her so long before that one fight, was there a chance it was still nearby?

"Then act like it," Midori scolded.

"So have you seen Fex? He ran off when he noticed the Watchers were still alive."

"I may have seen him flee into the forest, but that could have been anyone. Speaking of anyone, have you seen anyone? You just killed Han and his Watchers, but what about all the other angels in the camp?"

"It's night. Maybe they got trapped in their tents?"

"Wouldn't they just turn back to their true forms in this type of situation?"

"Maybe they burned before they had the chance."

Midori looked down. "That's... dreadful."

"And yet, frighteningly necessary."

## 14

"Don't you want to turn the radio on?" asked Midori. The night was too dark and cold to bother walking very far from the camp. We had settled down for the night off to the side of the road on a grassy slope.

"We should have just stolen a tent," I said.

"The radio, Erika. Do you want to listen to it tonight?"

"I thought you hated it?"

"It does seem... unnerving. But if you draw some sort of comfort from it, there's no reason to not listen in. It does fill up the silence of the night at least, which is something I normally detest. But you know, since I stopped sleeping, anything distracting is welcome."

"I don't get what you have against hearing it. It's just people talking about useful things. There's literally no downside."

"Well...," Midori said, trailing off without resolution.

I took the radio out of my bag and started fiddling with the tuner. The channel always seemed to be in a different place, though perhaps the dial had just been moved by accident while still in my bag. I nudged the dial along, going point by point and taking care not to skip a single frequency. All I received was static.

I frowned. "Maybe they're not airing tonight? It's a first, but it's possible."

"Perhaps you flipped a switch or pressed a button by accident? Accidentally changed the settings?" suggested Midori. "Here, let me see it."

She took the radio into her lap and fiddled about with it, taking a closer look. "I don't actually know anything about radios," she said. "Maybe we should just press some buttons and see if anything works?" She did so, trying every button and receiving only static.

And then in what was a frightful occurrence, she tried a button and a light turned on. It was a streetlamp, just a few feet from where we were staying. The static of the radio, now ignored, fizzled out. Another light came on down the road. And then another, and another. Soon the whole length of the highway was lit.

"There's no electricity for them to be running from," said Midori, frozen.

"Obviously." I got up, eager to investigate. It had to be the work of some sort of angel.

I went into the street, marveling at the first artificial light I had seen in ages. I surveyed the surrounding woods, looking for a reflecting eye or a shimmering movement but found nothing.

Midori had not moved, and in fact it appeared she was doing her best to stay very still. "I don't see anything that could have caused this," I said.

From behind my back, a cold voice spoke. "I prefer talking to people in good lighting. Makes it easier to read their faces."

I nearly jumped out of my skin. "Fex!"

"Yes!" He grinned, dropping his creepy facade. Well, almost. "Things went about as smoothly as I was expecting. Good job." He raised a hand. "High five?"

"How do you even know what a high five is?" I asked, but I high-fived him regardless. "I thought things went pretty bad. Way to bail on me, though. I could have used some help knocking those Watchers off."

"You know why I had to go. No way I was going to get caught killing my own. I wasn't even sure you were going to make it."

"Wow, you'd just leave me to die so you would have a slightly better chance of not getting caught killing your superior?"

"I play a rough game, I know." He clicked his tongue.

"So are you two done hanging out yet, or should I wait a couple more minutes?" Midori asked. "Why are you back here now, Fex?"

"Uh, isn't it obvious? The magical lights, the extra skip in my step, my heightened posture—I've been promoted."

"I was hoping you'd look different," I said. "I'm very unimpressed."

"Hey, I do look different. Just not my human shape. Why would my human form even change? It would just confuse you."

"So what are you now?" asked Midori. "Or, what were you before?"

"Well, all technicalities aside, I'm a Seraph. All technicalities counted, I'm like just one-tenth of a Seraph. I've been slightly…

disgraced. Had all my power taken away. But I'm back now! To one-tenth of my actual power, that is."

"That's still pretty pathetic," I said.

"It is," he agreed. "I'm only at the level of a regular angel right now. But it's better than before, where I was quite literally powerless. If you hadn't realized it by now, working those camps is punishment. The only people they cram there are rejects and exiles like myself. But now it shouldn't be long before I've climbed all the way back to full strength."

"Does this mean you're done with us?" Midori asked.

"I hate to break it to you, but none of us will ever be done with you. You, along with a couple others, are why we're even here. It's not like we're here to watch the trees sway. Speaking of which, you two better start watching your backs. You've been noticed, and while my superiors have chosen to keep you alive as an experiment, you might soon be on your last legs. Play nicely."

"You'd think we'd be in much more trouble than that," Midori pointed out. "After all, twice now we have all been together at a camp, and twice now that camp has burned to the ground and had its leader killed. That's a definitive pattern."

"It is fairly obvious, but luckily my boss isn't one for noticing delicate patterns like that."

"Who is your boss?" I asked.

"My boss? My boss?" Fex did a fake and airy laugh. Then he dropped his tone back to business. "I can't talk about such matters with you. We may be illegal conspirators here, but I still have to protect myself. I should be going now, before my absence is noticed."

"Will we meet again?" I asked as he walked away, each streetlight flickering off as he passed.

He turned back to look at me briefly, before continuing forward. "Yes, I think so," he said. "I do like you. You're possibly my favorite right now." He disappeared into the night.

"Hm, he's getting much more friendly now, isn't he?" Midori had her hands on her hips. "Like, what does he think he's doing?"

"Well, at least he'll stay off our backs for a while. I'm going to sleep now. Tomorrow we'll be making a lot of headway to the lake."

"I'll be—" She sighed. "—here." She settled into her sleeping bag every night, but I would never understand how she kept herself busy without sleep. She closed her eyes, and it was almost like she was dozing off. But her breath was too short for that.

The moon still had yet to emerge. It had been a cloudy series of nights. In the pitch dark, it was hard to see my hand in front of me. I decided to fall asleep instead of try.

THE NEXT morning went smoothly enough. We were on the road after I ate a quick breakfast, and the weather was warm and bright. As the fall drew on, the days and nights were starting to get far too chilly. We still had sleeping bags, as well as the ability to find blankets and other supplies in empty cars. It was just that we could only do that for so long. As warm as we could get with piles of blankets and clothes, it wouldn't be enough when the first snow came.

Of course, I wasn't expecting snow until mid-November, which was long enough away that we hopefully would have found shelter, if not civilization.

"The herd looks good today," Midori said.

"'The herd'? What are they, cattle?" I shielded my eyes from the sun to glance at the ever-increasing amount of angels above us.

"They might as well be. They're calm, peaceful, and gigantic. And beautiful. I bet we'll hit lakefront by nightfall. We've been on the road long enough now."

"Yeah, I agree."

The air was that of autumn, the scent of decaying leaves and freezing soil. The wind was harsh on our backs, but the sun gave just enough heat to even it out. The chill of early fall kept my eyes open and my cheeks tingling.

I had a good feeling about today.

It was a feeling that was quickly spoiled when I spotted Gav's familiar face on the sidelines. Frankly, I didn't care if he was possessed by an angel or just himself at this point. I did not want to deal with his inconsistency.

"Don't look now," I said, nudging Midori, "but Gav is back. Maybe if we ignore him he won't bother us."

"I doubt that's going to work on him, no matter who he is at the moment."

I groaned. "I wish it did, though."

Midori was correct, and it was after only five minutes that he came out of the brush and stopped us in our tracks.

"Go away, Gav."

"No, it's me. I mean, one hundred percent me. Not the angel. I wanted to talk to you."

"When I said 'Go away, Gav,' I meant it. You always bring trouble."

"Please? I know I've been really weird the entire time you've known me, and I want to change that. My life is—well, it's complicated. I wanted to apologize, and I hope that if I tell you what's happened, you'll have the heart to forgive me."

"Let's listen to him," offered Midori, and I gave her a dirty look. She was far too keen about Gav and far too mean about Fex, when the opposite should have been true.

"Thank you!" said Gav, delighted. "Okay, so the deal with me is—"

"Wait, who said I wanted to hear this? All Midori said was that *maybe* we should listen to you. My final vote is still no."

"Erika, who said you had the final word around here?" Midori reminded me.

"I don't. We have a democracy going on, and we're at a tie, and thus, a no. Go away, Gav."

"We're listening to his story." Midori crossed her arms.

"Okay, fine," I grumbled.

"All right," started Gav. "Basically, I'm very regular. I lived in your town, Erika. I guess we never bumped into each other, but we went to the same school. But a couple months before the angels arrived, I met one."

"Did you touch it?" Midori asked attentively.

"No. She was unlike these angels. She came in a veil of light and had these great wings like—like stardust. And her head was that of a lion. She spoke to me and told me she had a mission for me. She sounded very feminine, but it's hard to tell with angels. I think she truly was genderless. Anyway, she didn't tell me the mission. She just asked if I accepted the responsibility."

"And you were enough of an idiot to say yes?" I asked.

He smiled weakly. "Unfortunately, yes. What can I say? I was—maybe still am, though honestly it's hard to say—a Christian. And when a beautiful angel tells you she has a mission for you, from God himself, presumably, you accept it. And when I did, she just dissolved into shimmers of light. I didn't notice anything different about me, and I became convinced it was a dream."

"Until the angels came for real," Midori said.

"Yes. Their presence only reminded me more how the kindly angel I had seen was nothing more than a dream, for how could these monsters and that divinity be one and the same? But on the sixth day, the day of killing, I knew it to be true. Because I started feeling a voice in my head—"

"Wait. 'Feeling'? How can you feel a sound?" I asked.

"It wasn't a sound. It really was a feeling, a sort of gnawing at my head that was telling me what to do. But it didn't feel like someone telling me anything. It was like I was acting out of my own free will, but looking back I obviously wasn't. I had no reason to do any of the things I did. I just felt like I had to do them. So when everyone was dying in their homes, I walked right out of my house and walked among the angels without a second thought as to why they were keeping me alive. I walked straight to your house, Erika, and found myself watching your every move."

"So has all your following me around just been some angel whispering in your head?"

"Not quite. It's not some direct order. For example, when I saw you faint, spared in a bath of your family's blood, I ran in and held your head. I was made to leave right after, forced to live in the woods for several weeks as what must have been punishment. Not long after you set out on this journey, the voice left me entirely. I've been following you out of my own will, and out of some sort of obligation to keep you safe."

"An obligation set by the angels, no doubt."

"That is true." Gav shrugged. "But I am sincere about it. Even if it's some sort of software that got installed in my brain, I do feel strongly about keeping you safe from harm."

"But then, what about the other angel? The weird one?" asked Midori.

"It's very recent."

"Don't you know anything about it?"

"It arrived suddenly, and just shoved me aside and took over my body. I don't know how it did it. It happened midway during my conversation in the woods with you, Erika. The second one, without the deer. I had intended to come clean with you and ask to travel with you, but even as I first saw you, I could feel the angel seeping into me. I was awake but powerless. And it obviously could read my mind, knowing what I had intended to say. And it stayed inside me like that for a long time. I fought that monster and… it's been feeding you information too. I didn't know any of that stuff about angels and animals. I don't know what it's been planning."

"How did you get it to leave?"

"I can't get it to do anything. It just left a few hours ago, so I ran up the road and tracked you down."

"So," I said, "now that you've told us this, what are you going to do? Hoping to join us?"

"I-I want to. I want to be with you and travel and all that. But I'm scared the angel will come back. And if not that angel, then maybe a new one. I seem to attract them wherever I go. I'm too dangerous to have along. What I want from you is something else: There's another angel camp just a ways from here, and I want you to destroy them all."

Midori looked at me nervously. "I'd rather not."

"Can you do it?" Gav asked intensely. "Do you know how?"

"I mean, we were at a camp yesterday, and we just destroyed it."

"You did that?"

"Yes. I lit it on fire and it burned to the ground."

"Hm," said Gav, thinking about something I couldn't be sure of. "Isn't that just another reason this is the job for you? It's a very large place, but it should burn fairly easily. You don't even have to go in. It'll be quick, not even a detour—it's right on Lake Champlain."

"I think we should do it," I told Midori.

"You and your angel killing. What are you hoping to achieve? There's no way you can kill enough of them to make an impact. All you're doing is making them annoyed."

"They don't know I'm doing it."

"You can only visit so many places and have them subsequently catch fire before you get labeled an arsonist. Is this some revenge thing?"

"It's *not* about revenge. The first two were to help Fex, right? This time would just be the icing on the cake. You know. Luck in threes. Maybe if we burn enough of these camps down, the angels will give up on building them."

"Are you sure this isn't about revenge?"

"It's not!" I snapped, frustrated.

"I'd almost say all this killing *should* be about revenge." Midori frowned with concern. "It'd be healthier than bloodlust. If I were to suddenly be overcome with feelings worthy of manslaughter, I'd want my actions to be because my parents are dead or something. Not just unspecific rage."

"It's not about revenge for me. I don't know. I'm a bit... *over* being pissed about my friends and family. It's been months! I've been completely alone for *months*. I've grieved. I've cried. There's a chance I lost something about myself during that time. I don't know my own motivation anymore. I only know things. I know I want to live. And I know I want to track down some encampments of angels and just fucking burn them all."

Midori was silent for a moment. "Fine. One more, as long as you're careful. Perhaps we can find another flare gun and burn it from afar," Midori said.

"See? It'll be easy," Gav said. "Anyway, if you could do that it would help immensely. And also, I'm very sorry for the confusion I've caused you. I mean nothing by it, and I hope that as long as angels keep out of my brain, we can be friends."

"I'm still not feeling good about you. But I'll leave your friend request pending. Thanks for the tip on the angel camp, though. We'll finish it off in just a few minutes."

I extended a hand, and Gav shook it firmly. I laughed at how professional it felt, like we were sealing a deal of some sort. Gav again ran off into the woods. Would he continue following us until the next camp, or was he satisfied for a few days? I wonder what he even ate and drank out there.

"You make friends with the strangest boys." Midori sighed.

## 15

FINDING ANOTHER flare gun was proving impossible, as most cars seemed to be filled with just essentials. We did find a number of potentially useful objects, such as flashlights and clocks and even a sword. We didn't bother taking anything, though, afraid we'd get weighed down if we just took whatever we wanted. In the end, all we kept was a good hiking backpack and some more water.

The whole "setting things on fire from far away" was still my favorite plan, but it was looking harder and harder to make happen. I took a couple cases of matches, but I was fairly sure I couldn't toss a match and expect it to burn the camp down. I was going to need something bigger.

"We could try lighting an arrow on fire and shooting it," suggested Midori.

"Do either of us even know how to use a bow?"

"No, but how hard can it be?"

"I think we're better off looking for another solution."

"What about a flamethrower?"

"That would work, if only we could find one. Which I highly doubt we're going to do, since I'm pretty sure they're illegal."

"The odds are still out there. Maybe we should start with finding the camp before we get all caught up in figuring a way to destroy it."

"Wait, I got it—we could like, light a tree branch and drop it off a cliff. That would work."

"We don't even know if there's a cliff or hill above the camp. All we know is that it's along Champlain, which probably means it's on flat land."

"All right, I guess it's time we got to that lake anyway."

The interstate had been weaving about farmlands, country homes and private houses for a while now, but it was only now starting to run nearby actual neighborhoods. At one time we ran parallel to a town, one I almost mistook for Burlington. There wasn't an exit ramp, though, and as we passed, I realized it had been far too small anyway.

"Do you think the road will take us right to Lake Champlain?" I asked.

"I doubt it. Probably it will drop off somewhere near the city center, and we'll have to find our way from there. I wonder why the angels don't camp out in actual buildings instead of a series of identical tents."

Not once had we ventured off the road and gone into a town. We never slept in a wayside motel. Even Midori, who usually would sleep in cars scented like rotting flesh, refused to enter buildings. Somehow going near them felt wrong. The emptiness was just terrible, and no matter how silly it felt to be superstitious in times like these, they felt almost haunted.

Walking through even a few city blocks was going to be harrowing.

Time went fast, probably a bit faster than either of us had been hoping. We came to the outskirts of Burlington much earlier in the day than anticipated, and followed the highway with eyes straight ahead until the last exit before the road looped around out of sight.

"This is it, huh," I said. We stood together, looking ahead and placing perhaps too much drama on simply taking a certain road.

"Are you hungry?" Midori asked suddenly.

"Not really."

"Let's have lunch."

Midori couldn't eat anything, and I didn't care to, but we still had lunch. We spread a sleeping bag on the asphalt, took a meal of nutrition bars and crackers out of the bag, and sat in silence.

It was Midori who dragged out the radio.

"The show's never on during the day."

"Doesn't hurt," she said. I understood what she was trying to do: find another way to delay, an alternative to moving forward.

She tuned the dial without paying much attention to it, spinning it back and forth without having any ear for the frequencies of static she brought forth. In one of her perhaps slower rotations, a break in the static caught our attention. She ticked the dial like the seconds on a clock until a voice rang out, loud and clear.

*"Attention. The time is now twelve o'clock. This is a broadcast from the Colony of New Haven. Hello. If anyone is out there, please*

*respond. Hello. This is a broadcast from the Colony of New Haven. If anyone is out there, please respond. We are locate—"* The radio quit unexpectedly, with a sound like a TV turning off. Then not even static came from the speakers.

"What did you do?" I asked, shaking the radio to see if that would fix it. When I messed with the dial, I found all other stations were static as usual. Only this one was broadcasting dead silence.

"Nothing," said Midori.

A few minutes of silence later, the static returned.

"So there's another human colony around here, huh?"

"Looks so."

"I wonder if it's the same one as where Angel Radio broadcasts from? Maybe Angel Radio is the night program, and in the day they just send out help signals."

"That does sound likely. I doubt two human colonies could live that close to each other, both with radio equipment, without finding each other eventually." She looked at me in that mellow way she had been doing a lot lately.

"We should get going. Probably should have done so a long time ago."

"You're right."

We left the picnic behind in the dust.


THE CAMP was lakeside, and indeed, on a flatland. It was situated on a public beach, and though there were a couple trees nearby, they were not close enough to be used as significant cover. Watching it from far off and behind a car, I could see a few people milling about.

"Sand doesn't burn," Midori said.

"I know that. Looks like we're going to need a plan B."

"Got anything?"

"Nope, nothing at all."

"Great."

"But I do know it's going to have to be at night. We have to do it while they're sleeping, or at least doing whatever they do when they're pretending to sleep."

"So what do we do until then?"

"Kill some time, I guess."

We looked nervously at each other. But what else was there to do? We had a number of hours to spend before sundown, and there was no legitimate reason we shouldn't venture downtown and loot what we could.

"Want to split up?" Midori suggested it, but I had been thinking so as well. As nice as she was, there are only so many days you can spend together without needing a bit of a break.

We parted ways, agreeing to meet up at sundown on the outskirts of the camp. I took a turn and headed down a street that ran parallel to the main one. The city of Burlington itself, while technically a city, was too small to have any real skyscrapers. Or perhaps it was too old? Most of the buildings had a certain architectural sense to them of red brick, red clay, and slate roofs on pointed spires. It was all very archetypical for a New England town.

The residential area flowed almost seamlessly into the downtown, often overlapping, the nuclear urban homes standing out amongst the bricks of the commercial venues. I wasn't sure which side of the city to stay clear of: the homes, where people once lived, or the downtown, where people once thrived. Both brought me equal parts melancholy.

I had originally thought of my venture as an opportunity to stock up on supplies, though I realized now there were far too many things out there. I could carry a thermos, a water purifier, a generator and a pistol with me, but did I want to? Probably not. Back pain is not pleasant. And Midori would never let me keep the gun.

Instead, remembering my thought earlier, I found a small lightweight tent that could be rolled up for easier storage. It was only about four pounds, and felt like less when carried with my hiking backpack. I also replenished my water supplies and praised the heavens for artificial brownies, cream-filled cakes, and other foods that had the gall to pretend they weren't candy. Okay, they would wreck my health eventually, but for now they were all I had and tasted delicious.

The wind coursed through the streets, running against the bricks and around the dead buildings. Even if there wasn't traffic or music or people to drown out the sounds of nature, I still had a habit of ignoring them. But now, as I looked over the despair of the empty city, I heard everything. Birds singing, trees creaking, a windblown melody, and a strange, otherworldly rumbling.

Actually, that last one was probably not natural. I thought I might be able to track it by sound alone, but I was unable to locate the source. It was definitely something, for its volume slowly increased and with it the lesser angels in the sky began to become agitated.

I wondered if Midori was close enough to hear it. Right now I was betting the source of the sound was another one of those oil-slicked demons Gav had told us about. Or rather, the angel that was Gav had told us about. It was hard to keep those separate when I barely knew how to tell them apart. I just wish I had a separate name to call it.

I ended up in a small park bordered by rows of aging flowers. For the first time, I saw one of the sky-bound angels rest on the ground. A large one, body like a spire, had curled itself around a statue of a man on a horse. A couple smaller and rounder ones about my height had settled around it.

They looked like they could have been ill. It was the only reason I could think of they would have landed like this. No creature, supernatural or extraterrestrial or whatever else, could resist disease, I supposed. I didn't want to get too close, even if I was unlikely to catch anything.

Their wings had splotches of transparency, even bands of it near the tips of their primary feathers. It looked like it was just another feature of their body, but the glassy look of the markings seemed unnatural for them.

Still, I wasn't about to get into the business of caring. I left them behind and started sorting through another street of shops. Having found everything I needed, it felt halfhearted and pointless to try to window-shop.

I had to kill time, and I felt I had some sort of obligation to kill it in just one way: walking and looking at everything I saw. Even if those things began to feel like they were meshing into the same thing over and over again.

What was Midori doing now? Had she found anything more interesting to occupy herself with? Knowing her, she had found the library or had ventured out and spent time with the angels. Actually, I couldn't really say "knowing her." I didn't know her. We had only been together for a few days, and even if there was an unspoken agreement that we would stay together, we hadn't really become friends. We were caught somewhere in between, and even if we had grown close remarkably fast, we had yet to really know each other.

Chances were she was doing the same thing I was. Walking and looking. Though I bet if she ran into those sickly looking angels, she would have stopped and investigated.

The rumbling hadn't gone away. It was growing, if anything. The sound of it shook me and reverberated through my chest. Sometimes there were other sounds mixed in, like screeches and growls.

Then everything erupted. Like a geyser it sprang out of nothingness so quickly it was like I had blinked it into creation. It started as a quick stream of liquid, but it reformed itself into a great ball-like mass. Its color was almost clear at first, but it shook itself steady and other colors started spreading like ink in water.

The body was about done forming. It had taken a sort of frozen form, gravity-defying droplets suspended in the air next to it, and odd icicle-like protrusions on the bottom of its body. There wasn't a traditional head, or anything that even suggested a head. Mostly, it was just a ball. A giant eye on the center of its body opened.

It had perched itself in the park where the sick angels had been resting. The largest of them was missing, but the others remained. The demon-creature drifted from one to the other, each time enveloping their bodies with a glob of goo and each time sucking the goo back to reveal no remains at all. Considering the demon's mass never increased, I had to wonder what it did with the bodies it took. Did angels even have bones? No matter what they were made of, I'd expect it impossible to just absorb them like that.

I let the demon be. Unfortunately, it did not let me be. At first I thought I was home free, as I had slipped back around the corner and walked fast down the street, taking as many odd turns as I could. But then I saw it—following my path like a hunting dog. It was gigantic, its top slipping over the roof of some of the buildings and its body nearly running against the walls of the street. It was slow, however, and I probably could get away just by running and winding a confusing path.

This thing following me was a threat to my life, but I wasn't feeling particularly frightened. There had been worse. This great ball could kill me, yes, but in the same sort of way a cabinet might: with very little chance.

If anything, this seemed to be a boon. It was early, but surely this demon would be the solution to the death of the camp. All I had to do was lead it in and make my escape. The angels were probably too dull to know what had hit them.

But then again, I wanted this to be clean. At least a few would escape from this lumbering beast on my heels, and surely at least one would report my presence to the higher-ups or whatever. At the very least, there would be survivors. And I couldn't have that.

Which still left me with my original problem: how to kill this thing. It didn't look like it could bleed. It certainly wasn't about to get tired and rest. And it didn't even have skin to speak of, the eye being the only obvious weak spot.

My weapon of choice was always going to be something flashy and dynamic. I detoured into a gun shop, skimming the back counter until I found the owner's still-loaded shotgun. I turned off the safety and aimed, waiting for the demon to approach.

How long was the range of these things, anyway? I waited until it was close, perhaps far too close, before firing. The shot knocked me back, and I staggered, struggling to stay upright.

There was no effect. Was I missing? I fired a few more times, slowly getting used to the pace of the gun's mechanisms, when I ran out of ammo. Unwilling to reload a so-far useless weapon, I dropped it on the ground and ran.

My firing had let the demon gain great ground, advancing at what seemed to be a quickening pace. Its body of suspended animation started to rumble and gurgle, foaming with bubbles that burst from its center like a stop-motion film.

I ran, starting to feel a little bit scared. I got back into zigzagging like it was a pursuing crocodile, but the demon had gained new drive. It was set on me now, and it followed with dead-set precision.

Outrunning it was easy, but not for long. Even if I hadn't run out of steam in a couple minutes, it was definitely accelerating. It was only when it got dangerously close—close enough I could feel the chill its body radiated—that I dove to the ground and grasped for the first thing lying around to swing.

It was a shovel. There are a number of questions as to why a shovel was lying in the middle of the street, but I know this: the demon did not like being hit with the shovel. I struck it just as high as I could swing, but still felt the satisfying shatter of the eye that adorned its body.

Like glass, the cracks grew and splintered at an ever-faster rate, and when they reached the very top the whole eye came crashing down in a flurry of crystal.

The impact didn't appear to cause any grievous harm. In fact, there wasn't even a sign the eye had ever been there, other than an empty spot on its body. But the demon acted as if it had, and stopped for a few moments.

I used this to my advantage, and picked up my lead again. I took the shovel with me, though I doubted I'd catch another lucky break. The rest of its body seemed unlikely to shatter.

Now I just needed to finish the job. Had the demon even sustained injury? It was back on its metaphorical feet once again and continuing at the same rapid pace. Seeing as physical weapons were the ones that seemed to work best against these things, I tried throwing a piece of pavement at it, this time ducking to grab and throw it, and continuing to run forward in one fluid movement. When I looked back, nothing had happened. The rock had probably just bounced off, or else been absorbed.

My next idea was based on what Fex had said earlier, that fire was their weakness. This was a demon, not an angel, but they appeared to be very similar nevertheless. Plus Gav had used fire against that last demon.

The trick about fire was that I couldn't just pick it off the ground; I needed to make it. And though I did have some lighters in my bag, I was doubtful I could light them and throw them while running, and especially doubtful that a single lighter would be enough to light such a giant creature aflame.

Still, I made a tricky series of moves that allowed me to hold my bag on my chest so I could fish a lighter out. I slipped it into my pocket.

The best place to go had to be a park. Grass was generally flammable, and hopefully it would spread enough that the whole demon would get roasted.

Before I could really start searching for a suitable place, I felt the ice of the demon's presence down my spine, and looked back once more to find it hovering just a few feet away. How had it snuck up on me like that?

My hands shook and my teeth clattered. Was it going to eat me? It was straight above me now, and while there was no obvious aperture it could use to consume me, I suspected it would find a way. I struggled with the lighter, nearly dropping it at first, then failing to light it three times.

At last when I had a flame, the cool breeze knocked it right out. This demon was sure taking its time—at least it felt like it was. The next flame I created I cupped with my hand, and raised it slowly until the fire met the watery flesh. With a sudden jerk, the lighter was sucked out of my hand and floated, still aflame, through its body.

I watched with befuddlement as the flame rose with a murky light through the body. Then, reaching what seemed to be high above me, it exploded. Everything burned, and I dashed out from under it as the demon came crashing to the ground. I had to keep moving, as the floating liquid finally became just that: liquid. It flooded behind me, and no matter how regular it looked now, I wanted nothing to do with it.

At the center, cocooned together with sticky crystalline threads, were the bodies of the sickly angels from the park. They were dead and slowly burning to ash.

# 16

As night fell upon the lakeside town, I decided how I was going to burn everything down. To be honest, with the way things were going it seemed like I could do anything and it would somehow burst into flames.

But for now, I was using oil. I was going to sneak into camp, creep around with a can and spread the oil around the perimeter several times. I'd just have to drop a single match for the whole place to burn, and the wall of fire would assure no escape.

I regrouped with Midori at our designated spot, already having gathered all needed supplies. I had been early, actually, having prepared and started waiting almost immediately after killing that demon. Since then I had sat idle, listening on and off to the radio in hopes of a new broadcast. So far, nothing.

I explained everything to Midori, and she gave a much more subdued reaction than I had hoped for. "Okay," she said.

"What happened? Where did you go?"

"Nowhere much. Just enough walking to last a lifetime, and even more nostalgia."

"You've been here before?"

"No, it's more of a nostalgia for everything else. Humans and human life," she said. "Think of it. Our life now is what, wandering on highways, eating canned foods, and burning angels up? What kind of existence is that?" She looked almost confused.

"Well, at least there isn't any more war. Or famine. Or homework," I said, trying to cheer her up. It seemed to have the opposite effect.

"I'm not in the mood to kill anything right now. I never have been, and you can't convince me there's anything good about killing angels. They're the only other lives out there, and even if they're strange, I... just want someone to talk to," she said. "You do the burning; I'll wait here."

I wanted to remind her that she could always talk to me, but I guess that didn't really matter to her.

The sun was setting, but in these fall months it wouldn't take long for it to disappear behind the horizon. Her last sentence had been a farewell, an instruction for me to leave, but it wasn't time yet. Instead it was more of a metaphorical good-bye, in that she sat next to me but stared straight ahead to the moribund angel camp.

"Do you hear that?" asked Midori suddenly, not turning to look me in the eye.

"Hear what?" I clicked the radio off and focused, but I heard nothing. "No. What is it?"

She didn't answer the question. "Isn't it time to burn everything?"

"I think it's still early." Midori's behavior lately had been bothering me, but I couldn't think of a polite way to ask why she was acting so strangely. I didn't want to be too pushy, but I didn't like feeling ignored either.

So I opted to do nothing.

"I guess it's fine. It's dark enough." The sun was still blazing a twilight orange, creating a wonderful filter of honey glow that illuminated everything. I highly doubted anyone was asleep yet. If the angels had even the slightest clue that a fire was threatening them, they'd get up and leave. I had to hope the fire would be faster than they were.

The large can of oil was a tad unwieldy, but perhaps that was due more to my own nerves than the liquid sloshing about inside it. I made a long trail from where Midori and I had been hiding to the camp. Once I got close enough, I walked slow and careful. I could hear voices from all over the camp, even more from near the center where I glimpsed a fire pit.

This camp was laid out a lot different from the others, in general being more spread out and lively. It took me a long time to finish creating the circle of gas, which was obviously helped by my caution. I did see a couple angels on the border of the camp, and a couple times I had to stop and hide while one entered. No one seemed to be leaving, luckily. I'd hate for there to be any stragglers.

It was finally dark by the time I finished. That was good in a sort of sick way, since I was about to light up the night with a bonfire of the dead. When I closed off the circle I just made a run for it, figuring anyone who saw me would be too late to think anything of it.

"We're all set," I said, jumping back next to her. "Should I just go ahead with it?" Midori didn't answer, so I took action. It seemed like something that should have had more fanfare, but all it amounted to was me lighting a match.

And dropping said match.

Fire travels very quickly, unbound by many of the limits that exist for solid matter. It erupted so suddenly I was quite unprepared for the burst of heat it gave off, but the fire didn't last long. It followed the trail at lightning speed, scarcely catching nearby grass on fire.

It almost looked like it wasn't going to work. The ring lasted for just a short time before the oil had all been burned. But luckily, enough fire seemed to have caught on the surroundings to last. Everything began to burn.

Most of the tents were made of plastic, and couldn't really burn. But maybe they were melting in the heat, for I could see them collapse. The ground below the tents was all sand, another thing that doesn't burn. But something was definitely burning, because the fire was raging on.

The smell started to reach me before the sounds. Plastic fumes and the scent of burning flesh engulfed me and stung my eyes. We probably should have been farther away from the fire.

"Let's get going," I said to Midori, but she didn't look up from the radio.

The blaze was too large and lasting too long. What was it subsisting on? Could bodies really sustain a flame for that long? Or was something else at work? I watched carefully as a couple Watcher angels flew in and started circling the camp. They weren't any threat, coming in so late, but I had to wonder their exact purpose. Recording it for later examination, perhaps, but for who?

Far away in the smoke of the fire, the shapes of the angels had become obscured, turning them into nothing more than shadows through the fog. But there were more of them. I saw a lot of movement in the smoke, on the ground, and in the shadow of the flames. The angels were swarming now. I guess I hadn't really killed that many of them.

The sky was much darker now. The only light was the fire, but that light stretched straight into the sky, and was light enough. Midori stared pensively. I had to wonder if we'd ever get anywhere.

"You're right. We should go," said Midori suddenly. She placed both her hands on my shoulders and faced me, eyes on the ground. "But I need to show you something first."

"I WENT downtown," she told me, leading the way in the dark by pulling me along by my hand. The empty storefronts distressed me even more now, and I needed that support. "I think it's best if I show you before I explain anything else."

"Can you at least give me a hint?" We were moving fast enough that the growing breeze hurt my skin. It was a wonder Midori could even find her way in this darkness.

She stopped at a white and flattish building just a single parking lot away from the lakefront. There was a sign on the door, but Midori opened it too fast for me to read. She took me inside, past a little reception area and down a hallway. There she slammed open a glass-windowed door and brought me inside.

It was a studio. A recording one.

"Why are we here?" I asked. The place was derelict, and a small window from the technical booth brought in a very small amount of moonlight.

"This radio of yours. What is up with it?"

"What do you mean?"

"The radio! The voices!"

"You mean like Angel Radio? With Emil and Naomi and Ada?"

"Precisely," she said.

"What of them?"

"'*What of them*?' Stop pretending you have no clue!" She paused suddenly. "Oh God. Don't you have the slightest clue?"

Her tone began to worry me greatly. "What do you mean…?"

"The radio, Erika. There is no radio broadcast. You've been turning on pure static every night now. I thought at first that was the point of it; that you *liked* hearing white noise to sleep. But it's bigger than that, isn't it? You're hearing voices. You're imagining people. You're legitimately crazy."

"What?" I said. It was all I was able to say. "*What?*"

"I took you here because I wanted to prove to you that there is no Angel Radio. This place has been used, however." She flicked the light switch, and the lights slowly dimmed on. "I've found scripts and notes and even coffee mugs around this place. That broadcast we heard, the one from New Haven? It's real. I was thinking we could camp out here and wait until they arrive for tomorrow's broadcast, but I'm starting to feel uncomfortable with the idea of being in the same room as you."

"Look, that sounds like a plan," I said, trying to keep calm. "But while I don't know what's up with Angel Radio, I know it's real. The announcers are too alive to be fake. The information they give is too true to be made up by my mind. Even if they're not this station, who cares? There's more than one station in the state, you know."

"Yes, but that's not even a shortwave radio. It's an emergency one, and can only pick up nearby signals. And you've been hearing that broadcast for far too long now."

"It's real." I gritted my teeth. It defied all logic to deny it, yet here I was. "I know it is. I'm not 'hearing voices.' I know that they're real! Maybe you're the crazy one here, yeah? Maybe you're the only freak who *can't* hear them, ever thought of that?"

"Erika...," she said, trailing my name for far too long.

"I don't want to be near you either. In fact, I think I'll sleep outside tonight, so I don't have to worry about your creepy insomniac angelic ass watching me, *Sarah!*" I shouted as I stormed out the door.

## 17

I IMMEDIATELY regretted the decision, but it felt too soon to apologize. I still refused to believe I was hearing voices or whatever. After all, I did live in a world of eye-covered angels who had some sort of obsession with camping.

So what if the radio wasn't supposed to be working at this range? I'll bet I was somehow picking up on a radio signal far away, with the angels acting as amplifiers. It sounded vaguely possible. And Midori couldn't hear this definitely real show because she just wasn't tuned to it. Hell, maybe it was her lack of belief that prevented her from hearing it. That sounded vaguely possible too in these dark times.

It was cold now, really cold, and though I pulled out a blanket to huddle under, my face began to feel numb. I considered sneaking into just the studio itself, hiding under a counter so Midori wouldn't be able to see me, but I couldn't risk it. I didn't want to lose my pride and admit defeat so soon.

But it sure was chilly. I looked out into the darkness of the night—the empty streets, features lost without lamps or storefronts. The world looked flat and lifeless. The stillness was like a painting—a feeling only prompted by my mind's insistence that the only way the world could be this dark and hollow was if it was nothing more than paint on canvas.

Even the angels seemed far off tonight. Some of them did emit light, but it was such a ghostly glow that they soon looked like nothing more than starlight.

Those angels, those angels, whatever were they thinking?

There was a plan, a plot, an experiment around us, but those angels did nothing for it. They were watching and waiting and floating.

My life would have been better if I was dead, if I had simply died all that time ago with my family. And not even on the sixth day, with my foster family. My life would have carried much more meaning if I had just died in the fire with my parents all those years ago.

If someone else had lived, I'm sure whatever journey and whatever mystery I was being thrown into would have been long solved by now. If I was someone else, everything would have gone smoother. And in most cases, better.

Weren't angels supposed to put only the bravest through their divine tests? The most holy? The ones pure of heart? I was none of those things. So why had I passed their judgments. Why had I lived?

Gav and Midori both made sense as the so-called chosen. Gav had had an angel in his head; of course he would be kept around. Same with Midori—had she not been hosting an angel for however long? But I had never lived at a level any bit more than regular.

Midori more than fit the bill as some sort of divine. She deserved to have lived. She was magic and beautiful and lovely, someone right out of a fairy tale or a legend. But she didn't need me. She needed someone better than me, someone who could heal her and fix her and make her happy, which was clearly not a job I was capable of. If I was someone else, Midori would be my friend, and surely this other me would never have heard voices in her head.

If I was someone else, I would not be freezing outside, and I wouldn't be crazy. We probably wouldn't even be here. We wouldn't have been following a nonexistent radio station. We'd have long ago found humans. And we'd have long ago stopped fighting.

But I am not someone else—I am, however unfortunately, me. I wrapped myself up tighter and waited for daybreak, hoping not to be alone when it came.

Day wasn't going to come for a number of hours. I had perhaps dozed off from the cold, but either way I found myself at full alertness when I heard footsteps on stone. At first I thought it was Midori, being the responsible one and apologizing, but then I realized the sounds were coming from down the street.

And that meant it could only be one of two people. Gav or Fex, both with the ability to sense the perfect moment to arrive. Well, one was an angel and the other was occasionally an angel, so I suppose they did have a way of always observing the ideal time to pester me.

Just as I suspected, Fex turned around the corner. And then Gav. Their feet moved as one, but they broke step and walked a little faster when they saw me. However, neither of them looked concerned as they walked toward me. In truth, they looked identical.

"I wasn't aware you two kept the same company."

They looked at each other. "He is my superior," Fex said as they exchanged nods. Gav went inside without looking again toward me. "How often have you known him?"

"What?"

He clutched his head and then smiled at me. "Sorry, I get a bit too formal when I'm with him. I meant to ask, how many times has he visited you? I know he's been around a couple times, but how often has he actually spoken with you?"

"A couple. Like at least three, I'd wager. Why?"

"As you may have noticed, we've been assigned to bother you two. I've been following you off and on, but this is the first time I've been *really* ordered on you. I have taken it as a sign to be on edge. My boss has always been following you, but the fact that he has spoken to you personally is frankly... worrying. He plays a number of people."

"So why are you here, then? What are your orders?"

"I don't quite know. I'm not worried for you, though. I believe Midori may have been deemed unfit and is about to be exterminated."

"What? And you're just standing here—wait, *I'm* just standing here?" I shouted, and I attempted to shove him out of the way of the door and run inside.

He held me back. "You can't. You're not supposed to know. And I may be wrong about that. My boss can be remarkably unpredictable. All I know is you two are curiosities in our file system, and as I've warned, highly experimental. Your fate hangs on the edge, purely up to the whims of someone else to determine if you're any use."

"So why do you think Midori is at risk any more than I am?"

"Because you've been marked up. She hasn't. You have, I'm hoping accidentally, proven yourself a worthwhile investment for us. So while you're still technically an experiment to us, we are keeping you alive until something changes."

"What did I do?" My thoughts raced to the past couple of days. Since when had I done anything to *help* the angels?

"I can't say. Not even my opinion."

"But Midori...."

"Midori may still have her uses, so I wouldn't worry much. I don't think she'll be dying as long as she keeps being *potentially* useful to us. Again, I can't say anything. As much as I want to help you, I am bound by loyalty to my own."

"Not even the slightest hint about the long-term plan?"

"Well," he said, suddenly caught up in thought, "it's what you'd expect. Maybe. If you've been paying attention."

"Not very helpful. How long is Gav going to be in there anyway?"

"As long as he wants." Fex shrugged. "Like I said, even I don't know what my boss is up to."

"You call him your boss. But is he just like, your district manager, or would he be a bit higher on the corporate ladder than that?"

"Your metaphors do confuse me sometimes. I only have a simple and vague well of human knowledge to work from here. But no, he is only a little bit higher than me. We'd be about equals if I wasn't still a bit disgraced. And keep in mind the both of us are right at the top either way."

"What about his name? I'm tired of calling him Gav."

"What? I was under the impression you knew. Gav is his name. Are you asking about his other names? Because he does have a thing for theatrics. He enjoys playing around with those he meets, much to my disgust."

"Has he always had that form?"

"What, the human shape? Of course that's not his true form. You should know this."

Good. For a moment there I thought that maybe Gav was—well, an angel. Which he was. But now he was at risk of not even being Gav, the strange boy, but Gavreel, the strange angel. A coincidence of name, and nothing more. Bound to happen at some point—

"Wait, has he ever told you otherwise? This is why I was worried that you had spoken to him before. He's a natural trickster. It's dangerous to be alone with him."

"He... has." *Shit. Shit. Shit.*

"What has he told you?" Fex demanded, eyes wide.

"Is it possible... his vessel is still alive? Like if the host was strong willed, and kept fighting, maybe he could occasionally overpower the angel."

"No. This is why I really need to know what he's been lying to you about. Because we don't use hosts. We're shape-shifters."

"Shit!"

Fex gripped my arms tightly and forced me to look him in the eye. "What has he—"

But then the door opened. Gav, who was really the angel Gavreel, emerged with Midori.

"Something the matter?" Gavreel asked.

"Oh, I wouldn't even bother," Midori said, fixing her posture slightly up when she saw me, as if to allow her better access to looking down on me.

"What's happened?" I asked, looking away from the both of them.

"I have somewhere I have to be," Midori said.

"Really, you're going to go with Gav? As in, the angel possessing Gav?" I at least still had the sense to pretend I was still living in ten minutes ago, before I knew anything.

"I've long told you, Erika. The angels are not bad. We should trust them and work with them. And now, I have been told by this angel what my destiny is and I have humbly accepted it."

"Don't do anything he says. We both know the angels are scum."

"You say that, yet never have I seen proof of this. Maybe you're the bad one in this story? All you do is wander and kill. It's hopeless to resist this anymore. And besides, I always knew I was meant for something greater."

"But you're not meant for anything! Okay, shit, that came out wrong. But you told me yourself that you're ordinary, that you just want to be normal."

"Maybe this is the new normal, Erika. And maybe, I just want something organized for once. I hate nature and I hate camping. I want to be with civilization, and let's face it, we're never going to find any more humans."

"What about your plan to wait here for them to arrive? You were almost certain they'd be here tomorrow."

"I know better now. We're the last ones left. It's a good thing I was never as caught up in humanity as you were, or I'd be more distressed."

"The world goes on forever. We aren't the last ones. We can't be. It's like saying there's no such thing as aliens just because we've never met any—conceited and ignoring the statistics."

"I know now," she said again. "And somehow, I don't believe I trust the words of someone who hears voices."

"But you'd trust Gav? As in the one who is periodically human and periodically an angel? The one who has been stalking us? The guy whose emotions change every few seconds, the one who *obviously* has bad intentions and isn't afraid to hide them?"

"Again, your judgments. Never mine. I've always thought of him as nothing more than a tad frightened and a slight bit curious," she said. "Besides, you're not one to talk about distrusting angels when you buddy up to Fex every chance you get."

"Fex doesn't frequently freak me out. At least he acts about the same every time I see him."

"This arguing is tiring me out. You do realize, I hope, that you're not going to change my mind?"

"But surely you can't—"

"Surely I can't… what? Make my own choices? Decide things for myself? Leave me alone, Erika. Just let me be. This will probably be the last time I see you, and you know, I think I'm okay with that."

Fex and Gavreel had just been watching, faces once again matching with a slight smile.

"Don't," I begged.

"Too late. It's already been arranged," she said. As she walked past, Gav and Fex fell in step on either side of her.

As Fex passed, he patted me once on the shoulder. The closest he could get to sympathy, I suppose.

And indeed, once day broke, I was alone.

# PART TWO
## FIRELIGHT

## 18

AT ONE point in life, everyone will either take part in or overhear a conversation that features the line: "But what if none of this is real?"

I had been in algebra, and we had been left alone to do work. A group of kids—Darcy Hallows, Leon Fitz, Kaylee Sparrow, and Caleb Lee, if I remember correctly—were sitting behind me, and suddenly one of them brought it up.

I didn't join in at all, but I listened halfheartedly, the way most people do when they're bored in math class.

"Like *The Matrix*?"

"Or like, a coma. They say people in comas live years in a dream before waking up."

"But if I'm asleep, how would I be able to think I was in a dream? Shouldn't that cancel itself out somehow?"

"Nah, that's the genius of it. You question it, and that only supports the idea."

"How can my dream have science in it? And calculus? What about you? How can you have an entire life that I don't know about right now? How can I even learn new things if none of this is real?"

"Maybe you make it up as you go along?"

"I must be a damn genius, then! Too good to be wasting away like this, that's for sure."

Conversations like this get sidetracked very easily, and soon enough it dissolved into something else entirely.

But often when you keep quiet and keep to yourself, you have the most time to think about what's being said. And I remembered, sitting in class that day, and saving the idea for later. Just as a reminder to myself: if life ever seems odd, maybe it's not even real.

And lately, I was wishing it were true. Maybe not for me, since I'd evidently spend the rest of my days in an eternal sleep or computer simulation, but for everyone else.

At least they still had a world to live in.

IT WAS a cold morning, and now that I was alone for the first time in a while, I was feeling reluctant to follow the expectations of the past. That is, I had given up on trying to wear clothes I thought were nice and just threw a comforter around my shoulders and huddled it around me like a cape while I walked downtown.

To say I was alone was not an exaggeration either. The angels, perhaps following with the exit of their lords, had left Burlington while I slept. Though somewhere in my mind, the part still hoping I was just having a long and disoriented nightmare, thought it a sign. First the radio had been all in my mind, and next, perhaps the angels themselves.

Maybe this city was actually full of people right now, still whole and breathing, and I was nothing more than a cold girl in a comforter stumbling about the parting crowds.

But either way, I had to accept the reality of the situation, even when it rarely made sense. I had one last terrible, terrible suspicion infecting my mind with worry, and I had to follow up on it before I left this lake for good.

There wasn't any noise this morning, besides the waterfowl's cries, and again I found myself retreating to the abstract fantasy that I was just going for a pleasant walk on the beach—not surveying the ashes of my arson with a grudging sense that I knew exactly what I was going to find.

And there, in the impossible ashes of the plastic tents and fiber sleeping bags, were the indisputable signs of a growing community, of a past life and of a lost hope.

But mostly, there were ashes. And no bodies.

It was bizarre, downright, somehow the first happening in so long to truly give me pause: Was this real? Could this actually have been a camp of humans? There was no way to tell, that's what really got me. I had no idea.

There were no bodies, but the tents had been arranged organically, I could remember. The angels had shown up late, the sand seemed to have caught fire—all things that made me think the impossible. Could I have just killed hundreds of humans?

It seemed impossible. The angels didn't need me. They would have done it themselves, the moment they realized the settlement was out there. This was all a trick by Gavreel, a game for him. But I would never know. I never *wanted* to know.

Perhaps it was the mood I had woken up in, or perhaps it was the mood still left from last night. But it took me a long while to cry. And then it was over very, very fast.

Somewhere in my mind, a slow and mocking piano began to play a couple lines of an unknown melody, then ceased with a fading tone.

Unfortunately, this wasn't the first time I had heard music in my head.

But today I didn't have the radio—I had left it, finally, back in the studio. And as the last note died, I looked up and found my reflection in the eye of an angel.

It was a familiar face, I suppose, though I found no comfort in this fact. It was that same deer-angel creature that I had spotted before spying on me. I suppose, as another thing that had been harassed by Gavreel, we were on the same side. But then again, it was a giant one-eyed deer. And I wanted nothing to do with it.

*"And that song, folks, was 'Naval' by Yann Tierson. Lovely piece right there, truly. Next, we'll be featuring a particular composer I've always had a fond ear for—"*

The voice came and went with a flicker of static and a particularly nostalgic noise that tended to accompany electronics shutting off, and I fell again on the sand, lying on my blanket and curling up in a ball.

*"Today's forecast looks sunny. Not a chance of rain! This summer's looking to be a record breaker in good weather for sure, if such a thing exists."*

I rolled over on my back, staring at the cloud-cloaked sun until my vision went green, and was once again greeted by the round face of the deer-angel peering over my body. An old classic song started playing quietly.

"Shut up," I told it, and I threw a fistful of ashy sand at its eye. It simply closed its eye and backed off, blinking rapidly.

Everything went quiet.

The deer-thing had once breathed a name, Orifiel, and left me behind. And I supposed that was its name; it didn't really make sense for it to be anything else. But I wasn't sure if I was ready to acknowledge it yet.

The possibility of working with this figment of my imagination frightened me more than space, and I hadn't been able to so much as read about space since I was a young child and accidentally stumbled into a 3-D IMAX movie on the subject and got scarred for life. It wasn't even a horror film. It had been a documentary. But it had been very loud and very, very big.

It sort of sniffed at me, and I rolled farther away. "I thought I told you to go away," I said, but even then I could feel its breath on my neck. I considered hitting it to emphasize my point, but I realized how gross it would be if I accidentally hit its eye and decided against it.

Orifiel, or at least, the creature that knew the word Orifiel, sat next to me and leaned on my back. I shivered at its touch, but it wasn't cold—in fact, it felt like a furnace.

"Aren't ghosts supposed to go away when you ask them politely?" I said, aware I might or might not be talking to myself. "If a ghost can manage that sort of honest behavior, why can't you?"

It nuzzled against me, a feeling painfully strange and uncomfortable. Its horns bumped my head and shoulders repeatedly and dully, like being hit lightly with a rolled up newspaper.

"That's it," I said, and I rolled over and kicked it in the side.

Naturally, this neither killed nor harmed the creature, and its body split open again and took a long and tall, almost human-shaped form that mostly resembled a silk blanket thrown over a lamppost.

It looked at me a couple times—this I could tell, as the top of the body where I presumed its head to be turned back and forth. I could never know when it was facing me and when it wasn't, but certainly it had to at some point in its rotation.

Finally it made up its mind on whatever had been ailing it, and the once-deer-always-angel dashed (if that was the right word for it) away along the lakefront and toward a park.

I had no desire to follow it, and I felt it would probably start following me again soon regardless. I decided to head back into the city again, thinking I might as well follow the road out of town again and onward.

Because, you know, I had made it here to Burlington. And now it was time to go back—because if I was going to waste away in solitude for the rest of my days, perhaps it was for the best that it was in my own town. The place was full of old memories made painful in just their ancient existence, but at least some of them were good.

And many, if not all of them, were better than the ones I had been making as of late.

When the angel left my presence, another song picked up again in my mind, one that rolled about from ear to ear and had never quite gone silent—one that had risen from the depths of static for air, but never once had truly left me.

And ahead of me, if it even was possible, the clouds were dark and ever reaching—and carried with them a sort of unearthly and unnatural quality, like oil on water, shifting.

## 19

It was day, and the sky was dark and grainy. The clouds weren't advancing, not really, but they seemed to be stirring, and it was only as I moved that they did.

By the entrance ramp to the interstate, it might as well have been night. Obviously there was some sort of external force at work here, something supernatural and related to the angels, no doubt, but it was impossible to pinpoint exactly what that could be. Far away, almost like stars, I could spy holes in the clouds where the sky shone unnaturally blue.

I had time to spare. It was nothing more than a short leap over a concrete fence to enter the wilderness, and from there all I had to do was look up.

But the forest was very odd. Dark and empty. Nothing moved, from insect to angel.

However, I soon found out that the angels were not quite missing. They had simply moved. And it turned out they had fantastic camouflage as well, for I had to step on one to even know it was there.

With its eyes closed and wings folded and body unidentifiably spread out, it looked like nothing more than something slightly out of place. And yet it blended right in, circling the base of a tree, very, very black.

I took a careful step back and crouched cautiously. There were more of them, all over the floor of the forest. They melded together impossibly perfectly, so that I was unable to discern where one started and another ended.

They all looked ill, though, and only a couple eyes out of thousands watched me step through their forms. Somehow I doubted it mattered, the caution I took: angels had never attacked me before, and I had no doubt walked on several others when I had first entered the woods. Still, they made me uneasy.

I could see the spot of light long before I could make out its details. It was blinding even from a distance, but my eyes slowly adjusted as I got closer. And in the center of the clearing of light, there stood a human.

Well, not quite, of course. An almost human. Its features were quite good but had a sort of hazy unfinished quality to them. It had a nosebleed of black blood that ran continuously down its face and merged perfectly with the black spots and bulges that had appeared all over its body. It did not move, but stood slackly, head slightly downturned.

I turned back to walk into the woods but instead walked into a very solid object that looked very much like darkness but was instead completely palpable.

I backed up fast enough that I ended up pushing the human-shaped angel to the ground. Around me, the darkness grew larger and tighter.

In my fit of emotions over the last day, I hadn't bothered packing anything weapon-like with me. I had a couple things of food, water, and a sleeping bag.

I caught a sudden movement from the corner of my eye, and the human-shaped angel was dragged away. I breathed heavily as the darkness got tighter and tighter around me, tapping into my minor claustrophobia, when the creature that was the darkness reared its head and stared me down.

Its head emerged from up high like a fast-growing tree, but as it moved into the fading light, I saw its face to be dragonesque. Its neck, spiked and scaled, circled me several times. It breathed heavily through its nostrils, though its mouth hung slightly open.

I was frozen in place, but as it snapped at me I came suddenly back to my senses. I fell to the ground and desperately crawled to the other side of the clearing and got up, leaning against the solid blackness for support.

The dragon did not give up, and again lunged at me. Its neck almost seemed out of bounds with reality in the way it moved—it circled and seemed to come from anywhere at all, like there wasn't a body below it.

I moved to the side, and the dragon's head rammed into itself and kept going, reforming again a second later on top of the high wall of dark.

I ran to the other side of the clearing—a feat that only took a few steps—and pressed myself against the darkness again, moving carefully so I remained under its neck.

At first this seemed to work, and the dragon was unable to reach me. But then, slowly, I noticed my movement was being restricted. It wasn't that I couldn't move from side to side, but rather that I couldn't move forward.

My arms were stuck to the wall, and suddenly my left one was pulled right in. With a bit of force I managed to free my other arm and my feet, but my left arm seemed thoroughly stuck in the darkness. I tugged, but all I was doing was causing myself pain. My wrist especially hurt, and it felt on the verge of dislocating.

Finally I did make progress, but it was all at once, and not at all on my own terms. The dragon let go and moved to the other side of the clearing, waiting.

However, the force I had been using to free my arm was stronger than it perhaps had expected. I went flying and landed on its snout. One of my shoes caught on one of its teeth, and I quickly slipped it off before the dragon closed its jaws.

I scrambled to find handholds as the dragon's head started to thrash about. I clung at first to one of its large pointed horns but found my grip slipping. I worked my way up the neck instead, finding it significantly more stable.

The head gave up on its thrashing and started to rise. I clung helplessly as its body began to form from the shadows, but even then it still was incomplete. Though there were shapes like legs and claws, they never quite left the mass of darkness; this was even more apparent with the wings, which billowed up like tents, tips still stuck to the ground.

It could only leap so high, but then there was the sudden sound of something tearing, and the rest of its body ripped itself out of the murk. Still, it remained tethered to the ground by its absurdly long tail.

Its wings were giant, almost looking too big, and it seemed to take ages for them to properly flap. But evidently the lift gained was enough to match the slow speed of the flapping, and soon it was airborne and very high up. Its tail extended with it like a loose thread being pulled out of a sweater, and as it grew, it would get larger as well, essentially acting as an extension to the body.

I was almost too busy clinging to its back to stop and appreciate the view, but I found a moment. Everything around was darkness, though the darkness only rose about ten feet. It almost looked like the ground from up high, if not for the sudden drop-off I could see in the distance where the city was. That too would be consumed soon, I realized, because there was no way I was going to kill this thing.

It seemed like it had given up on killing me too, but then I realized we were flying up, not away. And as it flew higher and higher, until I was very much cold and finding it a bit harder to breathe, it suddenly stopped.

Its body melted and dissolved into something like wet sand, and I held a fistful of it before it crumbled.

The once-dragon fell just like anything else, perfectly filling the dragon-shaped hole it had left in itself. It had finished reforming long before I hit the ground. Which wasn't going to be for a while, it seemed—I was impossibly high. While this did mean I had more time to think, it definitely lowered my chances of surviving the fall. I was left in the air, falling and freezing.

I struggled to keep myself steady, but soon started tumbling about in the air dizzyingly. I felt sick, and it was this feeling that accompanied my fall to the ground, and it was this that I felt as I hit the darkness.

I survived, and I was most likely alive. But it was very, very dark. I hadn't really hit the ground so much as decelerated over a long distance, even more so when I hit the fog—it had been like fabric, and I barely even felt the moment of impact.

At least I had survived, even though I was now stuck in the darkness. There was some minimal light, enough for me to see nothing much had changed. I was still in the forest, though there seemed to be a murky fog about the place. Movement seemed harder as well, though perhaps it was the result of the fall.

I had landed on a bed of moss, one that had been coated in a light layer of ice. It helped keep me alert at least. Above me I thought I saw the stars, but I realized instead they were eyes, far off and blinking.

I rolled over and pushed myself up. I couldn't quite get my bearings anymore, but as long as it seemed safe, there was no harm in wandering.

The forest became something like a hallway in the fog and murk, and wherever I stepped, something seemed to be soggy. I had removed my socks and remaining shoe at first to keep them clean, but now I was starting to lose all feeling in my toes. Even when I walked on roots or stones it felt like wading through water.

There were no real sounds out in the woods, just the dripping of moisture and the sound of my feet, walking.

Something was following me, though, and I was only aware of it through whatever extra-sense it is that sends shivers down our spines when we're being watched.

I had been watched for a very long time now, wherever I went, and knew this was different. Something was out there—or really, something was inside this demonic darkness with me.

The something in the darkness wasn't walking, and it wasn't making any sound. But it was there. I was too scared to look around, afraid of whatever I might see. When I did stand still and strain to listen, I felt my feet start to sink into the soil, and I sped up.

The only solution to my problems was to get out of them.

A sudden rain of dust on my face and one painfully slow turn of the head brought me to finally look up. One of the starlike eyes from above had extended toward me, and it bore two mouths, with its great eye above.

For once I didn't trip to the ground. I just ran. Others came down from the sky and joined the pursuit, diving and twirling almost gleefully about. And there was a noise then, but it was gnashing and snapping and something like saliva.

I was spurred far by adrenaline alone, but as I went forward more and more of the tendrils followed. Even if I had a chance to outwit one of them before somehow, maybe by stabbing its eye with a stick, I couldn't do so with this many of them.

Considering I was already inside the dragon's body, it was hard to guess why it was trying to eat me again. I suppose it just wanted me dead.

Far off I could still see some patches of daylight, and I was willing to put myself at risk of another fight with a dragon's head if it meant escaping these things. I willed myself on, and when that started to wear off, just threw myself forward with everything I had.

I dove painfully into the light. The tendrils followed, but only their heads entered the light briefly to snap at me, and then they backed off.

The clearing was empty, and bigger than the one before. I fell face-first into the grass to regain my breath. I felt almost like I could throw up from exhaustion. This was not a safe spot to sleep. But I really needed to.

It was with great pain that I forced myself up, but even then I could only manage to sit.

My head spun, and I fell back again on the grass, still struggling to catch my breath.

"Wow, you look just awful."

"You're no keeper yourself," I replied automatically, before having the sense to turn over and glare at Fex. "Way to show up now."

"Way to show up at all, I think you mean." He was sitting just a few feet from me, looking quite peaceful and relaxed. "This is not a place I'm supposed to be right now, in case you weren't aware. For a very high number of reasons."

"Are you going to magically teleport me out of here or something?"

"Nah, can't risk getting caught carrying you. I'm pretty sure they've marked you down for dead at this point."

"Death?" I said in alarm.

"Dead," he emphasized. "You ran off into this place, so naturally they think you died. Of course, it didn't take much work to find you over here, but most of us don't have the spare time to even bother."

"Aw, were you worried about me?" I asked sarcastically. "Were you searching in misery to check if I really was dead? That's so sweet of you."

"It's great to know you think so highly of my job and its requirements to 'know where you are at any given time.' That really means a lot to me."

"So if you're not teleporting me out, how are you going to save me?"

"I never said I was going to save you."

"Don't tell me you're just going to hang out here until I die."

"I'm going to offer you a tiny bit of help, just because I still owe you for helping me get my power back." He got up and pointed to my left. "The exit is that way."

I grabbed him by his shirt, just in case he tried to leave. "Oh no. That is not enough. I almost got eaten twice today, and I'm not looking for a third time. I think you owe me a bit more than that. You got some crazy power now, right? So use it."

"Uh look, it's not like I'm opposed to helping you. I've told you before, you're probably my favorite over the other girl. But the thing with all my abilities is that I honestly can't use them without everyone else knowing I did. And I can't risk doing something suspicious and getting caught."

"What, you have some sort of beacon in you that connects you to everyone else? So you are confirming my hive mind theory."

"We are not a hive mind. Please stop insisting that." He rolled his eyes, but then his face fell to a grimace. "The truth is complicated and strange. Perhaps not hard to understand, but do realize I still shouldn't tell you."

"Give me some actual help."

He looked lost in thought for a few seconds but then sighed. "All right. I will say I was attacked by a stray outlier or something, and use that as an excuse for this." He then walked to the edge of the darkness and urged me to follow.

The wall had begun to resolidify, and he placed his hand on its surface. He then dug his fingertips into the shadows and a sudden flash of light spread through it.

It was fire, and for a moment the whole wall was covered in small flames like firecrackers. The smoke released blended right with the wall, and soon I could see into the forest.

"That takes care of that," Fex said, looking worried. He took a few very cautious steps into the woods, and I realized he looked terrified.

"You'd think an angel would be able to easily handle some demons. That's how it is in the Bible, I think."

"Demons...," he said, but he was clearly too busy carefully examining everything he saw.

He kept a ball of flame alight in his hand, and he tossed it nervously up and down while he took a couple steps in.

"I really can't go any farther than this," he said. "Walk fast, keep your head down, and breathe quietly."

"Don't you have something you can give me? How long of a walk is this going to be?"

"A while, I'm afraid, and you're just going to have to hope for good luck. If you get out, remember not to go near here again."

"Is there really nothing?"

"Well... I could probably get away with creating a distraction. Here," he said, and he tossed the little ball of flames he had amassed off to the side and straight through the trees.

Above, a couple of the eyed demons suddenly jerked awake and followed it.

"Seems like that actually worked," said Fex, looking very impressed with himself. He turned around, but found the wall had resealed itself.

He started the process of burning the curtain of darkness again, and I started on my way. I looked up, however, and saw that while a couple of the tendrils had been distracted, there were far too many for that to have been effective. One was slowly lowering itself to my level, and I ran back to Fex.

He had yet to finish clearing the wall, and at the sight of the demons he froze up completely. He placed his other hand against the wall in an attempt to speed up the process, and as the demon got closer and closer, resorted to flat-out punching the wall. He was shaking.

"Can't you just burn the thing?" I asked, hiding behind him.

"You do remember what I said about not overusing my power, right?"

I shook him. "Do you want to die?"

"I can't kill them!" he finally confessed. He cracked his knuckles. Other demons were joining the approach, and though they were moving slowly, they were getting very close.

He sighed. "I do not believe this," he said. "Remind me to never offer you any sort of help ever again."

Fex was sort of everything then, almost. It was hard to tell, and indeed, painful to even look at. His body had become fire, and his face had been long distorted into something that indeed reminded me of a dragon, though that could be argued down into a coincidence, for instead of horns he had great folds like wings, and instead of scales he had eyes.

Along the back of his head ran something like a halo, a large ring that looked transparent, and acted as a vessel for the firelight. But it had another purpose as well, and like sails he had wings on his halo, arching out and broad and in every color at once.

He was still almost human in shape, though this was very hard to properly guess, as he had become very much larger than a human. He towered over me, in fact, and I could only really see his torso. He had about six arms, each one coated in feathers and, while looking human, had nails like claws.

He had a mouth on his stomach as well, and none on his face.

And he was entirely silent, and very, very bright.

He raised one of his wings very slowly, like he was still acting with caution, and then at once unfurled another and another, until his three largest pairs were open. Wherever his primary feathers touched was caught by flame, and though the leaves burned, they were not destroyed.

But the demons were. At first they fled, and then they died, falling to the ground like seedlings, tails wrapped around themselves like snakes.

Fex moved forward slowly, almost dragging himself by his hands. I didn't feel safe enough to emerge from under his protection, so I couldn't be sure he even had feet.

It was only a little bit into the woods, with hundreds of demons still falling from the sky, that Fex let out one more great sigh of unearthly flame and bundled himself again to a human-shape.

"It's a straight on walk from here on out," he promised in between pants.

"You okay?" I asked.

"Yeah, yeah," he said, waving off my concern and getting to his feet. "Out of practice, obviously. But you make it sound like going to my natural state is somehow harder than cramming myself up into a tiny little mobile plant like this."

"Humans aren't plants."

"Very similar," he said, showing the supposed distance with his fingers. "Tiny difference."

"Let's get going already," I said, and I almost had to drag him to make him walk fast enough.

## 20

FEX SEEMED to get weaker as we walked, and by the time the exit was in sight he was leaning on my shoulder and breathing very fast. I tried to help him stumble along best I could, though. As it turned out he had in no way killed all the demons. They watched us very carefully as we made our way through the woods.

When we crossed the threshold into the now dampening daylight outside, he looked instantly rejuvenated. Though he continued relying on my support for a couple yards, eventually he began to walk on his own. He only took a few steps before sitting down on the road, however.

"Shouldn't we find somewhere farther away from the giant wall of darkness?" I asked. Even from here I could see it move, advancing slowly.

"It'll take ages to reach us. As long as I'm this close to it, none of my brethren will come and look for me. I need this time to think of an actual excuse for my actions today."

"So what, they already know what you did?"

"No, not yet. But they will when I return." He sighed heavily. "It really figures that I use you to get my rank back, and it's due to you I'll lose it again."

"If you don't want to lose your power, why don't you just not return?"

"They'll know if I don't. Then my punishment will be worse. We're good at watching, if you haven't yet noticed. No one is watching now since we're so close to this void—they may think me for dead. But the moment I leave this area, I will be expected to return. To report."

"Where is it you return to anyway? Is it some sort of extradimensional space you can only access via magical teleportation?"

"It's in Canada."

"Oh."

"It has to be physically real, since, you know, your friend Midori has to be able to go there. Otherwise we totally would have a pocket dimension as a secret headquarters," he said.

"You guys are ridiculous, you know that? Power that humans can only dream of, and you're running around making fake campsites. You've mastered dimensional travel and still feel the need to—" I stopped talking to study Fex's face, which he was twisting oddly.

"I kid!" He broke into a laugh like he was especially unused to it, showing too many teeth and taking large breaths. "Such a thing is very impossible."

I gave him a look as I waited for him to stop. Unfortunately, he seemed especially amused by his own joke, and it took a long time before I could speak. "What are they going to do to Midori?"

"Honestly?" His face fell back into a perfectly rehearsed blank state. "Not much. We put a lot more fanfare into it than it deserves. I'm still surprised they chose her."

"You know, when I ask these sorts of questions, I usually expect concise replies that actually answer them. And what, you thought I'd get chosen for your stupid angel ritual?"

"Obviously not. You're almost entirely unfit. It'd be disastrous. Neither of you is really ideal actually. There was supposed to be a lot more conditioning, but I'm afraid we've gotten desperate. We had other top choices before you two, but... I'm forced to assume Gavreel knew what he was doing when he ordered for Midori instead."

"How many humans really survived?"

"Thousands. I'm afraid we're not that thorough."

"But now how many are left?"

"A lot less. A good 50 percent were set apart for death at the start, and from there we still had to purify the population from un-ideals. And well, eventually it got to the point where we only had a couple with orders to let live. I'm not saying there's no more humans. But I am saying they all have a death sentence hanging over them."

"Amazing. And fantastic, just fantastic really. How many have you killed, anyway? I know you've been hanging around me, but tell me, how many humans have you killed?"

"That's a tricky and loaded question to answer. I honestly can't say for certain."

"What, you can't remember? Is life that meaningless to you?"

"It's... odder than that, I'm afraid. Simple to explain, once again, but I am not allowed to do so."

"Look, aren't you on the equivalent of death row right now? You might as well spill all the secrets you know."

"I'm not going to die," he said quietly, with a mocking edge. "Besides, I'll get off easier if I don't betray my superiors' trust."

"Ugh. How will they know what you tell me? There has got to be some way to weasel the truth out of you. There's just way too much I don't know about what's going on right now."

"Come to Eden, then."

"In Canada?"

"Yes, Canada. We're not that much farther up from here. If you want truth, it's probably going to be your best bet."

"Not to dismiss your suggestion here, but how do you even know what Canada is?"

"What, like we wouldn't do research before putting our plan into action? We know all about various human inventions and actions. I was part of the early research. For example, watch this." He leaned over and widened his eyes and stared unblinkingly at me.

"Why are you staring so intensely into my eyes? Somehow I worry this isn't a regular human interaction in the slightest."

"Think of it as my way of say... holding hands."

"Why don't you just do that, then? Because trust me, this isn't normal."

He looked genuinely offended. "I have no need for your body heat. I produce plenty on my own."

"Oh wow," I said without thinking. Behind Fex I could barely make out what appeared to be a demon just outside the sounds of the wall of darkness. It seemed to be mostly snakelike and lay curled with its eye half open.

"What?" he asked.

"Look out behind you. Another demon. It doesn't seem aggressive, though. We're probably safe."

"Demon, eh?" he asked, looking back at it. "We have a number of names for them. Carapace is probably the closest to accurate." He got up. "It's about time I fess up. See you in Eden or Canada, whichever comes first."

"What are you going to tell them?"

"Tell? I wish. I'm going with 'I was attacked suddenly and accidentally forced to resort to my true form, and likewise accidentally killed hundreds of carapaces.'" He grimaced. "Wish me luck."

He walked away, and this time I saw him leave: it was with a swish of fire and a flash of light, and there was a chance he wasn't really teleporting at all.

THERE WASN'T a point to staying around once Fex had left, and I made my way back to Burlington. I was still feeling sore, but not quite tired enough to sleep. I could maybe go for a quick nap, but the ever impending wall of darkness made me feel much more rushed than I needed to be.

I found another gun shop and chose a small handgun and packed some spare ammo for it in my bag. I also found a map, and once I sat down to plan out my route, I realized I had no idea where I was going.

There was a good chance Fex had not realized Canada was a large country, and had sincerely thought it was a small area I could easily navigate toward. Intention, however, did not make it any easier to guess where I had to go. It was nearby, evidently, but that still left a lot of land. And what exactly was "nearby" to someone who could move at impossible speeds anyway?

First thing I had to do was cross the border, no matter where my endpoint was. There was a road that crossed several islands on the way over the lake. From there I guess I'd head to Montreal? Fex had a habit of showing up every so often, and I was just hoping he'd show up again before I wandered too far off route.

It was looking to be a long walk. There weren't any angels at first, but they soon started to appear in swarms in the sky. Not just the regular angels and the Watchers, but all sorts of varieties. I started to see Ophanim again, twirling in the sky like ballroom dancers, as well as angels I hadn't seen before—some human shaped, others animalistic, and many with multiple faces.

They were not just in the air eventually, but everywhere: hiding in the underbrush and perching on street lamps.

For a moment I almost thought the Eden Fex had spoken of was *all* of Canada, but brushed it off. Midori had to be in a specific spot, and finding Midori was what I was here for.

I think, at least, that was why I was here. I probably had to save her.

I just wasn't feeling too motivated by the idea. I almost felt guilty to realize it, but I was much more excited about learning what was going to happen to her than stopping it. Of course, if it was something awful, I was going to step in and save her. It was, I realized, a matter of a power fantasy.

Midori had left me helpless and alone. She was the valuable one, the one the angels had sought out and taken. And it was she who had the most problems with her life, and the fullest one. All that stuff about a new name and running away from home? It was awful, and no one would want to live it.

Except me.

Because this was also a matter of jealousy.

And I had long lived and thought of the day of disaster, the day when I would earn the pity and attention I had often sought from everyone I met. And now, with two people left, I was the one who had to give pity. I was the one who had to be strong. When I was a child, my therapy after the fire had been normalcy. A forced moving-on meant to make my life feel normal again. But that was not what I needed. I didn't want to be strong.

And I wanted that to fall to someone else.

But strength became my life. Leadership didn't come naturally to me, but independence was what kept the therapists away and my new parents happy. So I began taking it upon myself to be strong. And that's not supposed to be a bad thing—but it was for me. An error I knew about, and felt obliged to continue with.

I used to dream of becoming ill. Not too ill, but almost ill. Cancer perhaps, but never terminal. I wanted to be sick enough to be sick, but never with the real risk of dying.

I would have my head shaved, but hide it under a hat as I took the subway to the hospital. A stranger would make a comment—insulting me for my bald head, or perhaps just in shock of it. And I would smile weakly and explain I was sick, and the whole train car would feel for me.

No one could be mean to me again. No one would make fun of me. They would all have to act better than that, because no one picks on an almost dying girl.

And when I recovered, I would always keep it as a safe card, always as an excuse. Perhaps just a photo in my wallet, to let fall to the floor whenever I needed a little boost of sympathy.

Days were like that. But nights were different. I would stare at my calendar in the light of my nightlight and look at the little boxes and Xs, and dream of days like these. Days of disasters and days of tragedy, and of days where I was a valuable person, a young survivor in a dark time, a ray of hope for all.

And usually I'd try to sleep, but more often, I'd wait. I was disgusted with my thoughts, and I kept thinking over and over again: if the world ended tomorrow, I wouldn't have to act like this. I would grow and I would age years each day, and every day would be an adventure. And I'd change into a better person every day.

It's odd how these things work.

And when I saw Midori again, as helpless as she was, I wasn't going to save her.

Not right away, at least.

Timing is 90 percent of heroics.

## 21

IT WAS two days later, in the morning, that I arrived in a city with a long French name—Saint-Jean-sur-Richelieu. The route hadn't seemed so long from the map, but it had ended up being a lot more than twelve hours of walking. I was probably slowed down by boredom in addition to my terrible sleep schedule.

I had not been, however, delayed by angels or demons in the slightest. The angels around me were becoming more and more ubiquitous as I headed north, but even the land-based ones paid me no mind. If I ever got too close, they would simply move away.

And as for demons, well, I didn't see any. They always had been reclusive.

Now all I needed to do was wait for Fex to show up. It really would have been convenient if he had left some sort of way to contact him. It wasn't like I could seek him myself, unless I somehow stumbled my way into Eden.

I took to the city streets and decided to just keep going. My best bet was to keep moving and waiting for something to happen.

Nothing really did, and on an impulse, I ended up taking matters into my own hands. I had passed an electronics shop, and again found myself going in and picking up a battery-powered radio.

I sat on the hard tile of the shop, held the radio on my lap, and tuned.

I found a lot of signals. I knew there was the very real chance, no matter how I felt about it, that I was hearing things again. But I also knew that the radio was on, and the voices coming out of it felt very real.

But no one could live in a city of angels like this one. Outside they sat and floated and did whatever it was that they did, just *existing*. There were more than I had ever seen, all just waiting for something to happen.

There's no way this city could actually hold life. Besides, that would mean Fex was lying to me, and even if it was a foolish thing to do, I had more trust in him than that.

But there were voices all right, and it seemed almost sensible to me that even if Angel Radio really had been in my mind, there was no way all these different channels were also my own invention. I couldn't be that creative.

I moved through frequencies slowly, catching bits of various sounds and words. Finally, I heard a familiar voice.

"*Well, well, well,*" Emil was saying. "*Well, well, well.*"

"*Again, huh?*" said Naomi.

Were they mocking me? Or wait, was I mocking myself? This was dreadfully confusing.

The signal had somehow locked itself down, and though I tried changing it, nothing happened.

"*I warned her about this a couple times now, and yet here we are. Again. Another denouncement.*"

"*I swear, what is her problem? Ada wasn't always like this.*" Naomi sighed. "*And now look at her. Sneaking around all the time. What a rat!*"

"*I'd think you'd show her more concern. It's been a lot longer than usual.*"

"*Oh, don't worry. She'll show up again at our door one of these days, all beat up, crawling. You know, we have to work twice as hard without her.*"

"*If you can call it that,*" Emil said simply.

"*You know what I mean.*"

It was nice to know even my subconscious didn't care about my problems. I left the radio still running on the shop floor, and as expected, their voices followed me without a falter.

"*Do you intend to even broadcast today?*"

"*Is there even a point to it anymore? Like come on, it almost seems mean.*"

"*We are heard, you know. For someone so willing to dismiss Ada, you're about as downbeat as she was last time we did this.*"

"*Don't lie, you know exactly how I'm feeling right now. Something about the weather lately... I don't know. But it isn't good. You can see it in everyone, everywhere you look.*"

Everyone? There were no people here, only angels. And I suppose in that way what Naomi was saying was right: they were restless and tightly packed. And the weather had been terribly dull as of late.

*"I know of it, but I do not feel it. You shouldn't let yourself become so overwhelmed. Soon we won't have to worry about this sort of feeling again. It's just a matter of patience."*

*"We should really speed the process up a bit. I don't know why it's taking us so long."*

*"Patience, please. We're doing our best. When everything's done and cleaned out, we'll finally be able to live in peace and comfort, and the community will be whole again."*

My subconscious was really working up a storm of confusing dialogue today, that was for sure. But, especially since I still thought of myself as sane, something was sounding very real about the radio's words today. Obviously it was still playing in my head, but that was something I was willing to excuse for now. There was no way I could confuse myself with words I was making up in my own mind, right?

Actually, thinking it over, I was very capable of confusing myself. I was doing it right now. But still—I hung on to the conclusion that Angel Radio was somehow real.

*"Should we go look for her? Ada, I mean,"* Naomi said after a moment of silence. *"It's dangerous out there."*

*"It's dangerous out there for us too. Do you want to get in trouble? The Cherubim will get us."*

*"I can keep safe."*

*"You'll be spotted instantly. There's nowhere to hide up there."*

*"I'll be fine. I just want to check on her—I know exactly where she'll be too. She has a very predictable pattern of interest."*

*"You were calling her a rat just a couple minutes ago."*

*"It's not like I hate her. Or even like her. I have every right to worry about her well-being either way."*

*"Ho hum,"* Emil said. *"You best be on your way, then. Be fast."*

*"No one says 'ho hum,' you idiot,"* Naomi said, and then there was the noise of several things moving about and something like footsteps.

The microphone, it sounded like, was moved across a wooden desk. *"Well, there you have it. How about that?"* Emil said. Then there were a couple electronic noises, before he started to speak again. *"The weather today is looking to be dark, and it might get a bit stormy. We haven't had a thunderstorm in a long time folks, and with any luck, we won't for a long time to come. But keep yourself preened and your eyes forward."*

I was suddenly aware I could tune Emil's voice out, and I did so. I continued to pace the city streets, idly exploring with little mind for what I saw. This waiting game was boring me already.

Still, I felt like something had to happen soon. It was something about what Naomi had said, about going out and hiding from the Cherubim. And Emil had said to be wary up there, about the danger and the few places to hide.

Could it be possible, somehow, that they were underground? Maybe all the humans had fled there. There could be a whole city under the earth!

The logistics behind that thought seemed highly unlikely. How would they get food or water? It'd have to have been set up years ago, and while I could imagine such a bunker existing below Washington, DC, there was no way there was a secret city under a place like this.

I was, however, on edge. I heard something fall to the ground, and I spun around to meet the gaze of a many-footed angel perching on an old apartment roof. It folded its wings at my glare and shifted its weight about.

I kept walking and watched my shoes. New boots, nice and shiny but not at all worn in. They didn't match the rest of me at all—my hair had grown a couple inches, to a length I was quite unused to. It sat poorly on my head, something not helped by the oil and dirt that had accumulated. My clothes were a mess too. I hadn't bothered to replace them, and after all this time they had become quite terrible.

The river, the same one from the lake, ran right through the city. I had passed a bridge a while back that connected the two halves of the city, and I went back to it. It was low-lying, just a couple feet above the river, and long. From the very center, the river stretched wide and relatively still.

It was all quite serene, especially without the angels—they clung to the edge, but none dared to follow me onto the bridge.

I stripped slowly, not even in the sensual, dramatic way but instead like a frightened rabbit. I took off my jacket one sleeve at a time. Taking many pauses to look around and listen hard. I first dropped it, but then I stalled for time by folding it.

By the time I was naked, it was far later than it needed to be, and the night had become chilly. I shivered, and struggled to climb over the fence. It wasn't that high up, but it was a bit higher than I had thought, and I was suddenly reexamining if it was worth the effort to walk back to the shore and get in slowly instead.

I gripped the steel bars of the fence and leaned over the water again. I probably should just get it over with, I knew, but the water was going to be ever so unpleasant.

"Hello," a voice said, and in my surprise I fell right into the water.

For a moment everything was dark and cold.

But I have yet to master swimming underwater without plugging my nose, and the icy water filled my nostrils. I flailed to the surface, gasping and coughing heavily. I couldn't properly swim with so much water still stuck inside me, and I struggled to reach one of the concrete support pillars.

The water wasn't too deep, and once I found a place to hold myself against the pillar, I coughed until my lungs ached. The tiny bit of adrenaline I had gained from falling wore off very quickly, and I started shivering soon after.

I desperately wanted to get out, dry off, and investigate. But I also couldn't let this go to waste, and I quickly ducked under the surface of the water again and ran my hands through my hair. I probably should have brought some sort of soap or shampoo with me, actually. And certainly I should have brought a towel.

Climbing out of the water slowly did nothing to prevent me from getting goose bumps as I cautiously peered around on top of the bridge to see who had spoken. Gavreel was recognizable at a distance. He stood very still in the center of the bridge, likely having not moved since speaking to me. I wanted to move slowly, but I had been shivering ever since I had stripped, and was in a great hurry to pile on my layers of clothes.

"Hello," he said as I walked closer to him.

I ignored him and got dressed, using one of my coats to poorly dry myself off first. I was still uncomfortable as I slipped, slightly damp, into my clothes.

"Why are you back here?"

"There's a couple complications I'm concerned about." He wasn't even trying to address me, instead keeping a solid stance and watching the river. I had to stand in front of him before he bothered to briefly meet my gaze. "And a few loose ends as well, I'm afraid."

"What is it?" I said, catching my head in my hands and sighing with exhaustion. The last thing I needed was a request from him of all things.

"Was Midori... harmed in some sort of way, when you were with her? We did not always have vision on her, and there have been... problems. Solutions are best found when you understand the sort of problem you are facing."

Of course this was about Midori. "Harmed? Definitely not. I was the only one out there who actually did any fighting."

"There is something wrong with her, that is certain. Surely you are aware of this in some way? An observation? A secret?"

Well, if there's one thing I'd learned about Midori, it was that she did have a number of secrets—and one of them was probably the same sort of precise knowledge that Gavreel was missing, the sort of thing he couldn't know. It was before his time.

But I wasn't about to tell him about the angelic creature that had used to haunt her. He had, after all, told me to burn down what might've been a human camp. And we hadn't quite parted on good terms.

"No. We barely knew each other, you know."

"That is most... terrible. We need her. If it fails, I suppose we'll be forced to turn to you. But you're less than ideal. Ah. Well. We will keep our efforts ongoing." He kept steady, but started to rock ever so slightly on his heels while he talked.

"Is that it?" I said, but then he was gone, faster than I could really see but with a short afterglow of heat.

I wrung my hair out for a couple of pointless minutes, brushing it neatly before putting my hat back on. It was really much too cold for any of this.

I had to question, though, where was Midori now? Did they have her in some sort of a cell? They needed her, of course; she was the chosen one. So was she living in luxury right now?

Did she have heat? Was she cozy?

It did not matter what state she was in, because either way I was going to have to burn a house down to get warm again.

And that, I decided, was not an exaggeration. I wanted to burn something. There were plenty of houses around, and if I didn't torch them, they'd probably become dirt in a couple hundred years anyway.

I had matches, and it turned out that was really all I needed. I found a suburban home for myself, a nice little two-story place with white walls and lots of curtains.

The rugs were a good place to start. I placed a match on two corners and pulled up a rocking chair, watching as the fire slowly spread.

I was all set to get out. I just took my time. The fire took a bit to get on anyway.

I took new clothes while I was there: a long, heavy coat, some tall boots, an exaggeratedly large scarf, and one of those thick fur-lined hats with earflaps. I looked ridiculous, but at least I was warm.

My movement was a bit constricted, though, and I contented myself with the idea that in any time of great danger I would be dexterous enough to unbutton my coat in time.

The angels scattered from the flames, hypocritical beasts that they were, and pretty soon the neighborhood was clear of all but one, a particularly lanky angel. Its arms were about twice the length of its body, and they folded above its head as it sat.

It had hair too, or at least something a lot like hair, which fell over its face entirely, like a lampshade. What must have been its neck emerged from below the hair, long and skinny and perfectly straight.

The body below that was like a dead tree mixed with a human. It had a sort of vague dark purplish tint to it that almost came off as real, though the sudden spots of black and white it had laid over its rib cage gave it the semblance of a corpse.

Standing by the street corner, it turned around to face me.

I turned around and went the other way.

## 22

THE ANGEL followed me. It took its steps slowly, one hand at a time before letting its feet follow, but the sheer length of its body made it hard to outmaneuver.

I wasn't feeling up to any sort of fight, and I was just hoping the angel would leave me alone if I ignored it for long enough.

I was getting pretty bored in this long-named French town, so I figured it was about time I left for Montreal. This angel wouldn't follow me the whole way anyway—from what I'd seen, most of them were like pack animals, unwilling to stray.

However, as I took my last customary look back at the city, once I found the highway out, the angel was still there. And it had shifted shape into something slightly more human.

It was never going to be perfect. I had always assumed the only reason Gavreel and Fex came off as real was because they were high-ranking Seraphim, so it made sense that this lower angel couldn't get it right.

But it had come close. Its body kept the same odd color, and though it was squashed down to a human size, its arms were slightly longer than they had to be. It was skinny, but not like the human skinny at all—instead its stomach was like a crevice, and its ribs almost looked bare. Otherwise its body looked female—it was naked—but it was so distorted I could not think of it as so.

Its head was still covered by long strands of hairlike substance that blossomed perfectly from the top of its head. And there was something very weird about its feet—and I realized as it walked closer that they were hard and shiny, like hooves in a foot shape.

It was moving faster now, and I let it approach with a heavy feeling in my stomach. But it wouldn't harm me, right? They never did.

It paced left and right as it moved forward, a sort of meandering walk that gave the impression of a halfhearted awakeness. It stopped about ten feet from me.

I waited, thinking it might speak. But it kept standing. I cautiously moved a few feet closer.

"Hello?" I tried.

It was moving with a sort of twisting motion but little more. It didn't even appear to be breathing.

I took a couple more steps closer. It stilled.

"Hello?" I tried again.

I knew what was going to happen before it did. Its hands dove forward, large enough to envelop my head, and it pulled me right against its body.

I closed my eyes in anticipation but found nothing else happening. Its nails dug into my back and cut into my face—I imagined it left a scar—and they held me firmly in place, but otherwise the creature had stopped all movement. I opened my eyes and found it had thrust my head through its layer of hair and into the cavity behind it.

And yes, indeed, it was a cavity. There was no head or even neck in that space. Its legs and hands emerged from the hair itself, and its center was a simple and rancid space.

I tried struggling out of its grasp, but its hold was too strong. I twisted my head around, and met the gaze of the closest thing to a face the angel had—a masklike feature that held up the hair. It was also pale gray, though chunks of its flesh had been dug out, leaving black marks in their stead.

There was a sudden noise, high-pitched and whiney, and after it ended, I found myself deaf. I tried talking, and found all I could hear was the blood rushing in my ears.

My hearing started returning after thirty stressful seconds, and then the noise happened again—this time it lasted a bit longer.

"Stop it," I said weakly.

The noise stopped again, though it may have been a coincidence.

"What are you trying to do?" I said, maybe too loud or maybe too soft as I started to flail about. The angel dug its nails deeper into me.

I still couldn't hear when the noise happened again. I only knew it was there from the rumble of the base. And then there was a voice.

"This is rather inconvenient." It was a small and even voice, and it sounded like it was whispering in my ear.

"Isn't there an easier way to talk to me?" I realized my hearing was still gone—I could hear the angel's voice but not my own.

"I don't have the ability in this form to speak in the frequencies that you can hear, I'm sorry to say. Please excuse me."

My hearing started working again, and its voice started to fade out. Immediately there was the same high-pitched sound.

"I'm going to suffer from serious hearing loss at this rate."

"Not my problem. Have you seen my friend?"

"What?"

"She has long been interested in you. She has been missing, and I think she must be around you somewhere."

"You're talking about the deer-angel?" I said after another burst of white noise left my ears burning.

"I do not know of this deer thing. Have you seen her? Her name is Adauzial."

I sighed. It was always going to be this, wasn't it? It was always going to be some bullshit angel seeking my help and messing with my life. And talking in my head, with a semblance of humanity.

"You're Naomi."

"That is the short of my name, yes. She may be harmed. I am worried for her. The world isn't safe for us right now."

"Your kind is everywhere. I just saw Gavreel a little bit ago. You know him, right? I can't see Ada getting harmed with him around. He's always watching."

"I am familiar with him."

"Please let me go before I end up deaf," I asked Naomi as my hearing started to surface again. It was still dulled, and I became afraid that my ears were bleeding.

She did let me go, eventually, but she didn't leave me alone.

"I can actually hear you without being constantly in pain when you just broadcast into my mind or whatever, you know."

She didn't stop and go back, or whatever I had been expecting. And it wasn't like she could answer either.

"I would love an answer about all that, by the way. Way to make me feel insane. Why me? I mean, I feel pretty stupid right now, actually, just whining to you like this. You can't answer, and I don't want you to, because I happen to value my hearing. But you know, if you're psychic, maybe you should just talk to me like that."

There was nothing. I tried to see if I could tune into Angel Radio, somehow expecting Emil to offer me answers, but found myself unable to.

"Please leave me alone. I haven't seen Ada, if she is the deer-angel, for days. Your presence is not really welcome. I don't mean anything by it, I swear, but you really weird me out."

She finally turned around, falling back to her proper shape as she did so. I realized then as I watched her run away that she didn't have any wings—or even eyes.

I was really hoping she wasn't anything other than an angel or a demon, though, because my life was already complicated enough.

As soon as she left, I turned around, intending to continue walking.

Fex, naturally, was there.

I jumped a little. "Jesus Christ!"

"Are you really that surprised to see me again? I told you I would come back."

"I swear, it's always one thing after another. You should work on your pacing a bit—I mean I have two days of nothing, and suddenly Gavreel, Naomi, and you all come to bother me right in a row. Have you ever stopped and considered I could use an occasional break after dealing with one of you guys?"

"I suppose our encounters can get a bit intense. But wait—Gavreel was here? What did he say to you?"

"No. Come on, tell me what happened to you first." Half his face was bandaged, and parts of his shoulders and upper arms were likewise wrapped up.

"Some self-inflicted surgery, I'm afraid." He grimaced.

"What did you do to yourself?"

"Oh, let me assure you it wasn't my will. It had to be done, though, so...." He shrugged. "What could I do?"

"I like how artfully you avoid telling me what I'm actually interested in."

"No, I'm not removing my bandages. Now tell me about Gavreel. What kind of lies is he somehow getting you to believe this time?"

"Nothing really. He's told me whatever vague thing you guys are doing to Midori isn't going well, and wanted to know if she was previously 'damaged.'"

"Oh. That was the truth. Is she damaged?"

"Yes. Don't tell anyone, though."

"Would you really rather take her place?"

"No need to make it sound so dramatic. And no, I'm just bored."

"I'm starting to feel concern for you. Ah. Anyway, why I'm here: I need to guide you to Eden, right? It's right down the road."

"Doesn't that seem too convenient?"

"Well, it's down the road, and then off to the side a great deal. It's a mountain."

"A mountain, or *on* a mountain?"

"A little bit of both."

"Sounds exciting. So you're walking the whole way there? Too rude to just fly me over?"

"I can't do anything without everyone else knowing about it. If I use any power, everyone will know and likely seek me out." He reminded me in a rather singsongy voice. Then in his normal tone he said, "And yes, I'll be with you the whole time. Luckily it shouldn't be too many hours."

"How did you get away with it last time? Wait, are your injuries related to last time? Were you beaten?" I asked.

"No, no, don't fret." I couldn't tell if he was lying or not. Had I caused him harm without knowing it? Was he lying to protect me? "I simply haven't returned and submitted my report. I decided it would be a lot easier than just lying about it."

"Won't you be in a lot of trouble when we arrive, then?"

"Maybe it'll take away from the trouble you'll be in."

"I'll be fine. And you'll be fine too, right?" I looked nervously up at him.

He didn't meet my eyes, and my heart dropped. "We'll see. Let's change the subject. Ask me something else."

"Something else? No bounds?" I said. When he nodded, I found myself asking something I hadn't intended. "What did you do that made them take away your power?"

He bit his lip before answering. "Before we all appeared to attack your kind, we scoped the place out a number of times over a number of years. How else do you think I can have rudimentary knowledge of your world? I was one of the scouts once, and I took a long look at your lives. I looked at many things I should not have, and I was cut out because of it. I still haven't returned to proper form since then."

"What was it? Obsession? Friendship? Hatred maybe? Lov—"

"Don't try to humanize me!" Fex snarled, accenting his temporarily sharp teeth. The superfluous change to having only canines was likely a conscious choice to try and scare me. I didn't flinch. "I did nothing more than disobey my calling. I don't have to qualify for your emotional guidelines to fail to do my job—I'm doing that right now."

"You're the one who said no boundaries."

"Then ask something else."

"Who is your leader? And how should I kill him?"

Fex frowned and twitched his nose. "You're *not* going to kill them."

"Them?"

"The Metatron. Ask something else."

"What is 'The Metatron'? Is your leader an organization?"

"No. They are my leader, and they are someone I am *not* going to answer any questions on."

"Are you going to get angry at whatever I ask about?"

"Maybe it's your fault I'm getting angry about these subjects. Maybe you should work on your question-asking ability instead."

"I think you're just oversensitive," I said. "Okay, how about this: are there any other creatures besides you angels and the demons?"

"What do you mean? No. There is no other."

"I just saw something like an angel, but she didn't really look like one. No wings or eyes. And she could talk, which was kind of weird, so she wasn't a demon—a carapace or whatever—and I was in general pretty confused by her. Also she talked by screaming into my ears."

"She must have been some sort of regressed carapace, then. Point her out if you see her again. That is quite odd."

"She was here just a couple seconds before you arrived. Didn't you see her?"

"Not at all." He looked behind us, perhaps expecting to see her there.

"She came to me asking for help. Actually, this reminds me of something else Gav said to me—is it true that angels can possess animals, and that it's terrible if they do?"

"I've told you before, we can't possess living things. So it'd be terrible yes, but only because it's impossible. We're primarily shape-shifters."

"But wait, okay. Midori was telling me a while back that she had been possessed by an angel. I saw it leave her body, actually."

"*What?*" said Fex, seemingly confused. "You know we're shape-shifters."

"I know."

I hadn't forgotten, but that little inconsistency in Midori's story—I had forgotten about it somehow. Angels didn't possess the living. What did that make Midori?

He shook his head. "When did this happen?"

"She killed Kasos, not me."

"I could have really used this information earlier. I'm not really sure what happened to her, then—but I have a couple odd and disorienting guesses, and they're making my skin itch. But my guess for now? Clever thinking, improper conduct, and confusion."

"What do you mean?"

"Look, I'm not saying I'm right. But I am saying that Midori might be an angel. In fact, she might have been one this whole time."

"Wouldn't you know that, though? You'd know just by looking at her if that was true. She can't be an angel. She's told me all about her human life, and she has too many emotions."

"She wouldn't be a regular one, though. She would have to be one like me—someone mostly cut off from the others. And she obviously hasn't been using her power at all, right? Completely unrecognizable. A couple months back, when we were scouting you out for the last time, she must have decided to stay put. We may have sought her out, but she would be impossible to find in her new form." Fex sounded almost excited at his theory, but I just felt sick.

"Is her human form really that convincing? I can tell you're an angel just by how you're holding yourself."

"That body may not be her true one, but it is a body."

"A corpse."

"We'll see."

"Why would she do that, though? Pretend to be someone else entirely?"

"Oh, Erika, it's hard for you to understand. But it gets ever so lonely when you're cut off. And ever so quiet too. You could hear a pin drop onto a patch of moss after an eighth of an inch fall."

"You're telling me."

Because the way things were going, I might be the last human left. Angel or not, Midori was gone, and friendly or not, Fex was still something unknowable.

## 23

IT WAS a long day of walking before we arrived in the Eden Fex had promised, but I was able to see it for a good ten minutes before arrival.

It was like he had said: a mountain. Not quite *on* a mountain but almost; it was great, white, and spun like spiderwebs, and it left no impression that there ever had been a mountain there previously.

I knew that under all that gleam had to be some sort of hill, because along the way were many signs for a ski resort and adventure park by the name of Bromont.

"Why here, of all places?" I asked Fex. He hadn't been talking much since telling me his theory about Midori, and his face had clouded in deep thought. It took him a moment to respond.

"Why here? Why not, I guess. It had to be somewhere. We first began to appear on the other side of the globe, and thusly Eden had to be placed on its opposite."

"Is there something significant about the locations having to be opposite, then?"

"There is something of a… time limit to what we're doing here. So yes, it is important."

"You know, your habit of dodging my questions doesn't really make sense when you consider you're the only one around who actually has a chance of explaining them to me. Like what, is someone else willing to do it instead and you're just not mentioning them?"

He grimaced. It seemed to be one of the few facial expressions he had mastered. "No, it's going to be me."

"You're useless! Ah, whatever. Things will happen as they happen, I suppose. You going to take me inside or what?"

"No, you won't be allowed in. They already know you're approaching, and that I'm with you, but they won't do anything unless you get too close."

"Like worker bees defending a nest."

"Please stop making any and all reference to hives and hive minds in relation to us."

"Not until you prove me wrong."

I couldn't tell much about Eden from the distance we were at when Fex decided it was time to split up. It did look like it was made entirely of cobweb, or perhaps yarn, and on its surface I could see little specks moving about—angels no doubt, for some reason crawling like ants.

Eden itself seemed to qualify as a nest by its composition, and certainly the way it formed a hive-like structure, but most of the angels were in the land around it. They were everywhere, and with great variety. The smallest ones I had ever seen—little bug-like creatures with many wings—flitted about in the air and trees. Rising like dead cedar trees were others, incredibly long, tall, and gray. Even the more familiar shapes of Watchers and Ophanim were odd, all the wrong size or color.

We split up far earlier than I had anticipated, but it was clear we had to. Two pale angels with thick, snakelike bodies were positioned, head against head, forming a sort of organic gate. I couldn't be certain if they were alive, but it wasn't them that forced us to part—it was another set of Ophanim, great floating bodies like old-fashioned dresses, that came up on either side of Fex and moved him forward.

Nothing was taking notice of me, but I decided not to risk it.

"Just take a different way in. There's probably one or two holes," Fex called out as he walked away, but he didn't look back. "Just don't follow me."

I walked off the road. It was mostly open land with a couple trees and shrubs, but I thought it would be enough to just be far away from the main road—not necessarily hidden. I followed Fex parallel from there.

A smaller angel of some sort—I couldn't identify its creed—took to following me. It had human arms, six of them in fact, but hooves instead of hands. Its head was that of a sphere, and its glassy eye stared at me with what seemed to me to be great worry.

I brushed it away—or really, the air next to it. I was not willing to touch its skin, which looked moist. There was no visible entrance to Eden, and Fex was stopped short of the outer wall. He must have been communicating with the Ophanim in some way, because after a silent break, he began to unwrap his bandages.

At first it went normally enough, layer after layer of white bandage coming undone. And then he continued and continued, and his shoulder began to shrink, and by the time he was done there was nothing more than an indent in his skin. It looked like his skin had been removed with a careful little shovel, or molded like it was made of clay. There were no signs of vein, muscle, or blood at all—not even on the bandages.

He had smaller chunks missing from his chest and sides as well. Every time he finished unwrapping, the two Ophanim would lean over and inspect his skin.

Finally he did his face—and indeed, parts of it were missing. But this time instead of a smooth cut, his skin looked like it had ruptured—bubbles of pure black had emerged from about where his left eye should have been, and seemed to have spread slowly from there.

He seemed as horrified as the Ophanim at this development. He lightly ran his hand along his skin, and the blackness caved slightly at his touch. Part of it came off, chalklike, on his fingertips.

The effect this had on the Ophanim was immediate: they attacked. They weren't quite meant for combat with their bulbous bodies, but one of them flared its wings—all those hundreds of wings and eyes—and charged at Fex. He toppled over onto the ground, and got up again to face it. The other one moved aside, perhaps aware that if it joined the fight it would likely cause more harm to its ally than good.

I would have liked to stay and watch—after all Fex had told me once before that he was of the most powerful class of angels. However, he didn't do anything in the way of defense. In fact, as he and the Ophan took another short break, I realized he might have intended this.

But I wasn't going to let him do that—die, or whatever. There was no way he was getting away from me like that. I needed him to stick around. How else was I going to find my way around Eden? Not to mention all the gooey and stupidly friendly feelings I had been developing of late.

I ran toward them. Fex stood slackly as the Ophan attacked again, this time using its five hands. The four outer ones gripped him like he was a toy, and the center one grasped his head.

The other Ophan, meanwhile, had taken notice of me. But it was light, and I easily pushed it aside, where it steadied itself slowly.

The Ophan holding Fex began to burn him. His skin didn't blister and melt like human skin; instead it just crumbled and cracked all the way across his face and down his back. Parts of his human shape began to go lopsided, and then finally slip away. A wing here and an eye there, all of them fading with the fire.

I had nothing but my bare fists, a backpack, and an overly warm coat, and I decided the best course of action was to just punch the Ophan.

And oddly enough, that seemed to be enough. Its body didn't feel like anything much, and though warm to touch, had no ill effect on me. It was like punching a sheet, and the Ophan toppled over pathetically. Its burning had been interrupted, but its grip kept tight.

While it was still struggling to get up, I ran to Fex. The right side of his face was still roughly intact, though pitch black cracks ran across it. His eye itself—as he really did have only one at this point—was a foggy black, one that almost seemed to be swirling.

The rest of his body was in a similar state of destruction. After a great deal of kicking and prying, I freed him from the Ophan's grasp and lifted him—his body was a lot lighter than it should have been, and it wasn't just because he was missing several hunks of flesh. He felt hollow, and I had no way of knowing if he was even alive.

The two Ophanim were apparently still too disorientated to resist as I walked off with him into the thinning woodland. I walked for a long time before deciding to rest, but I doubt it would have made a difference. He really wasn't slowing me down in the slightest.

I placed him down in a field of long grass, and waited for something to happen. I seemed to do that fairly often, waiting, but it was what had to be done. He was either going to wake up or he wasn't, and I didn't have much control over that.

And then there was the matter of Naomi and the radio. Wasn't she going to contact me again? Surely it had been long enough now.

A wind started up, and I huddled in my coat. I guess I never thought of it before, but Fex didn't feel cold at all, did he? The only reason he even wore clothes was probably some form of courtesy on his part, because it obviously didn't matter that he was wearing a T-shirt in whatever degree weather this was.

I waited for another couple of minutes. The Ophanim weren't coming, it seemed. The other angels hovering curiously about the field didn't seem to harbor any malice toward him, so I figured we were safe. Either way, I drew my handgun, grabbed a couple clips of ammunition and reluctantly shed one of my coats. Safety over comfort.

When it became clear nothing much was going to happen, I set out to see if I could change that. I couldn't stray far from Fex, but I felt oddly self-conscious near him, and ran off a couple yards to a position where I could still see his body.

"Ada? Is that your name? Or is it Orifiel?" I mumbled, feeling utterly ridiculous. There wasn't anything silly about this at all actually, and in fact it seemed like a quite viable method to contact the deer-angel, but I was unused to talking to what at least felt like myself.

Trees shook, but it wasn't because of my summons. Just the wind.

I tried whistling next, on a whim. Then I tried to meditate, and when I found my head impossible to empty, I just tried focusing really hard on thoughts of radios.

Thinking back to all my previous encounters with the deer-angel, it wasn't like there was a pattern to them. It had first lured me into the woods, where it had been shot—I realized now it must have been a very regular deer that Gavreel had killed and an angel had possessed the corpse. But why would it want to do that? And what did Gavreel stand to gain?

After that, it appeared again after Midori had killed Kasos, and again after Midori had left. The only connection there seemed to be was disaster, but even that seemed a frayed thread of hope. There wasn't that much disastrous about Gavreel shooting a deer, after all.

But it was all I had, and luckily involved my only real skill: destruction. I gripped my gun tightly and fired.

Not blindly, that wouldn't have made much sense. But at the angels—the tiny ones mostly, whose white bodies were destroyed when bullets pierced them, and left behind little blood and many feathers.

I shot them all. It was like a game of sorts, as they truly were everywhere, and it took them a long time to really fear me. Most of them died without conflict, and didn't even leave much for remains—but others did, and their bodies began to collect on the forest floor.

I only stopped when I ran out of ammo, though most of the angels had fled by then. I rolled one of the bodies with my foot idly. It was like cotton, and felt boneless and easy to crush. Like a stuffed animal.

"Well, that was terrible," said a voice, and my first instinct was to reply in a mocking voice. Then I remembered it made a lot more sense to look for the source.

"Well, you did come," I said, "so it did work." I didn't see the deer-angel anywhere, nor could I be sure that was who was speaking. But odds are it was, and that was good enough.

"It's not like I *left*." It had a decisively feminine voice, but one that didn't quite sound like Ada's.

"Show yourself." I gripped my gun tightly and held it up to aim, though I was out of bullets. It just made me feel safer. "Are you named Ada or Orifiel?"

"I don't see why I have to confirm one way or the other," the voice said lazily. I heard a sound behind me and turned around to see the deer-angel had jumped out of a tree—and wasn't in an animal shape anymore. She had taken on a human shape, and a relatively proper one at that, quite unlike Naomi's headless body. She had carried with her a pair of antlers and her single eye, but otherwise she appeared almost perfectly human. However, her skin did have a rather translucent and glassy look to it.

"Isn't that ever confusing for you? It's confusing for me." I lowered my gun, though I did keep a tight grip on it.

She sighed and did a weird thing with her head, moving it back and forth like some kind of snake. I wasn't sure if it was supposed to be, like, an emotional gesture or something. "Just use Orifiel. It's my proper name—"

"Just that? Not Orifieliaxion or whatever?"

"No. Obviously not." She looked severely offended. "Ada is my stage name for when I'm on air, okay? Naomi's too dull to do so, but me and Emil actually have the sense to hide our identities when broadcasting."

"Okay, seriously, what is up with the br—"

"Broadcasts? I can't tell you, sorry."

"Okay, you know what? No. Just no. I've been hearing that so often. Like what are you going to do, give me some cryptic yet slowly revealing information and then disappear for a few days? Because I am so sick of that. Don't tell me you're somehow working on the side of the angels, because Angel Radio pretty much only broadcasts information related to killing angels. You know what? I'm going to shoot you." I raised my gun again.

"Calm down," said Orifiel, looking neither scared nor particularly impressed. "Yes, of course we're on the side of the angels. We are angels. There is no other side. And while I can assure you we never said anything that hazardous to our own kind, we were ordered to say every word we did. Preapproved topics and everything. Don't freak out about it."

"Why would you do that? And why would you communicate to just me?"

"*Just* you? Don't be so presumptuous. We spoke to all. Only reason I've been hanging around you is because you're the closest human to where we were located. So maybe there's been a couple cases of exception regarding you, but trust me, we speak to all."

"Midori couldn't hear it, though," I said, and my heart sank as I realized the implications of that fact.

Orifiel didn't understand, however. "The other human didn't? It's not like we could pick and choose who heard us speak, you know. It was all at once, and very loud."

"Speaking of speaking—"

"Are you wondering how I can speak to you, when Naomi could not?"

"What, were you hiding out in the bushes that whole time? I probably suffered some severe hearing loss from that, you know." I had actually yet to notice any problems, but they were bound to be coming.

"I was around, yes. I don't exactly enjoy Naomi's presence. The difference between her and me is simple: I'm smarter. The only angels normally capable of speaking to you directly are those capable of taking your human shape, the Seraphim. The less blessed communicate with each other with frequencies far above your range of hearing, and indeed, entirely done without the use of mouths. In fact, most of us can barely change shapes without a great deal of pain or limitation on what we can become. Even the exceptions, those fake humans we planted in those camp sites, needed a constant flow of energy to keep themselves going."

"You seem free enough to change into whatever you like."

"I have a very diverse diet."

"Okay, I don't want to know what that means."

"It means that my true form is a lot larger than this, and when I consume something I can—"

"I said I don't want to know. Please don't tell me."

"I don't know how it works, but I can take the shape of most things I swallow whole—my true form is blobulous at best, and—"

I clapped my hands over my ears. "I don't actually want to know any of this."

"Oh! Are you hurt that I had to eat a human to even speak to you? Don't fear! She may not be fully dead. At least, I'd hope not. Who knows, actually?"

Since I could still hear her quite well, I removed my hands. "It's really gross, that's all." I sighed. "I saw a—carapace, I believe you call them—who was doing something fairly similar, though. When it died, all these animals were inside its body."

"Can't say I invented the technique." She shrugged. "Though I should note I'm not at risk for becoming something like that, so you don't have to fear me."

"Right, because the only reason I'd be scared of you is because you're *not* a demon."

"Are you going to kill us?" said Orifiel suddenly.

"What?"

"You're here, next to our Eden. Are you going to kill us?"

"All the angels? That does seem highly unlikely, doesn't it?"

"It's very possible, I'm sad to say, if you destroy Eden. Please don't do it."

"What do you want me to do?"

"Go."

"Without Midori?" I still wasn't sure what I was going to do about her, but I certainly wasn't going anywhere without a talk.

"It may be too late for her anyway."

"What do you mean? What is it that you're doing to her?"

Orifiel shook her head. "It may already be too late."

And with a particular sense for ending conversations on a mysteriously irritating note, she leapt into a tree and changed shape to a bird, flying off without another sound.

## 24

ORIFIEL HADN'T been useless, but she had been annoying, and I walked back to Fex's body in a bad mood.

I felt his chest, but there was no sign of a heartbeat or breathing. But I couldn't be sure if it was time to give up on him or not.

And it wasn't like there was much else for me to do; after all, with Orifiel gone, there wasn't anyone else I could turn to for help.

But I hated waiting around, and I soon found myself gazing over at Eden. Surely it wouldn't hurt to look around a little more? I could even bring Fex with me if I was careful; he weighed much less than my bag did.

I had run out of bullets, and it would be a long walk down to town to look for more. But I did have matches, and fire consistently seemed to be the most effective way of dealing with the angels.

Leaving my bag behind, I pocketed my matches and lighters, picked Fex up, slung him over my shoulder, and left. As long as I was observant, he probably wasn't at risk for attack. And even then, I could probably outrun any angel that might come after us.

Many angels did start to follow us as we came closer to Eden, but they all seemed too small to be a threat. The ones that dared to get close would investigate the black spots on Fex's face, and remembering the Ophanim's reactions to it, I covered them up with a scarf.

They mostly lost interest after that. A few seemed on edge as I got closer to the wall, and their forms bristled as I reached out to touch the great white expanse.

It was slightly sticky, leaving a faint residue on my fingertips. It was somewhat soft, putting up little resistance to my touch, and a bit springy. It was composed of many smaller strings, which in turn made up larger ones. With a bit of maneuvering, I found myself able to slip my hand inside, though I was entirely unwilling to go any farther.

There had to be a couple holes or something that the angels used to get in. I walked along the surface, hand trailing the wall, until I came upon what I was looking for: a large opening. However, it lay on the same route Fex had been using to get in, and was heavily guarded by various angels. The two largest ones were a twin pair that were partially lodged into the wall, just heads and arms extending outside. Their whole heads were nothing more than spheres covered in eyes, and I backed away from them very quickly.

There couldn't be only one entrance, right? After a good ten minutes of walking, however, I gave up on that thought and just decided I was going to have to make my own way in. It was a fairly soft wall.

Putting Fex down, I grabbed a section of the wall and pulled, and found it surprisingly easy to remove. It didn't break very easily, but it did separate enough for me to move it aside. I kept going like this—pulling strands, moving them aside, and often pressing on them to condense them a bit—until I had a hole about the size of my body. There was no sign of the other side yet.

It was a big structure, but how thick could the walls be? I itched to just burn my way through, though that would likely be too dangerous. Instead I continued to dig at the wall.

After what seemed like hours, the inside had been breached; the hot air that rushed out smelled like sweat and old leaves. And darkness too, if darkness could have a smell.

I went back for Fex and pulled a lighter out of my pocket. It didn't illuminate much, but made me feel a lot safer as I entered Eden.

As soon as I passed across the threshold and stood quite plainly in the pitch dark, there was a change in Fex. He started to move, really fussing about, and I dropped him in surprise.

He woke up quicker than I would have thought possible, and sounded very awake. "Why are you here? Why am I here?" His silhouetted self frantically looked around, until he spotted the entrance and ran outside.

I followed him. "Hey, Fex, wait up!" I called out.

Luckily he hadn't gone far—he just leaned against the outer wall. "I can't be in there," he said, looking at me with heavy eyes.

"Why not? Also, while I'm talking, way to make me freak out earlier. What, were you just going to let yourself die?"

"Yes, and you shouldn't have saved me. I'm sick, Erika. I can't be alive for much longer."

"You look...." To tell the truth, he did look very sick. It wasn't just the black veins and missing chunks of skin—his one eye was weary and red, and his skin had a certain baggy look to it. "You don't have to die, though. Don't angels have like, medicine?"

"We don't need that sort of thing. Do you know what's in there?"

"Uh, no? Because you never bothered to tell me, remember?"

"Okay, I was hoping you'd either give up on—whatever it is you think you're doing—or just walk in and confer with the Metatron, remove Midori, and then give up. And that was a hypothetical question either way. *Do you know what's in there?* No, you don't. Because you don't understand us in the slightest."

"Get to the point already."

"I'm not a person, Erika, any more than any of the other angels. I'm special in one way: I have been given extra power above the rest. But it's all temporary. I'm temporary."

"What?"

"Listen, do you know the difference between me and Gavreel? Technically nothing. I mean that. Nothing. We're the same person by any count of genetics."

"But you look and act—"

"Different, yes. But we're the same. Because the angels, all of us, are one. We are the Metatron, and we are many. I am nothing more than a facet of myself, temporarily dispatched for the old purpose of observation, ready at any time to be reabsorbed into my true body."

"So—"

"*Not* a hive mind." Fex grimaced again. "*A single mind.* When we remerge with our true body, all our gained thoughts and memories become part of the Metatron. When I said that I had limits on when I could use my powers, this was true too. I maintain a connection to the Metatron at all times, and my power is only on loan. But my memories are mine until I rejoin—meaning if I do something, the Metatron knows. But the details are lost to them until I myself become lost to them."

"That's weird as hell."

He gave a dazed half smile. "Hey, no offense, but I happen to think it's weird as hell that you're constantly alone. I'm constantly on the verge of mental unsoundness here, and I'm not even fully cut off from the Metatron's voice. How do you even manage?"

"We talk to other people, I guess? But if you're so desperate to become one with yourself again, why can't you go in there?"

"Because I'm sick." He placed a hand over the gap where his eye should have been. "What do you think this is? A choice? I'm sick, and I'm dying, and if I even get too close to the Metatron, we could all die. And don't give me that look—I will find a way to kill myself if you try to drag me in there."

"What happened, though? Where did you catch it?"

"Where do you think?" He sighed. "You dragged me out into the void, and one of the carapaces gave it to me."

"What, a demon gave an angel a disease?"

"I'm starting to get a feeling you've been misunderstanding something very crucial to all this: carapaces, or demons as you seem to insist on calling them, are angels. They're sick ones, and I'm going to become one if I don't get killed soon."

"Actually, that *was* a fact Gavreel had told me." I had forgotten it had been him who had told me about demons. Between all those visits and all that information, it could get hard to remember who had said what.

"Please disregard anything he's ever said to you. You should know that by now."

"Isn't he you, though? Or part of you? Why does he act so oddly?"

"As Seraphim, we are granted the most freedom in our actions. I don't know what's with him. I don't know what he knows. We are the same, yes, but different sides of the same."

"Is he around here, though? Do you think he'll talk to me again?"

"I definitely don't doubt it. He's probably not going to cause you any trouble, but I hope he stops by and kills me, since you evidently aren't planning to."

"Nope."

He swallowed. "Just get Midori out of there. There's a good chance she's sick too. And she absolutely cannot enter our system. If she synthesizes with us, we will die. She will die. It'll all be over."

I fidgeted my fingers. Everything being over sounded exactly like what I wanted from all this: the end. I would have to lose Midori, but she was nothing more than another angel, and a lying one at that. "What are you doing to her? Where is she?"

"She'll be in the core. And we are synthesizing her."

"Thanks for the details."

He gave a one-shoulder shrug. "There isn't much else to say."

"Right. Of course. You do know I can totally just pick you up and toss you in there, right? You're weak and surprisingly light."

"I'm this funny thing called a shape-shifter, it turns out, and I may or may not be able to just fly away from your grasp. I don't know. Let's find out."

"Shut up. Don't die. I'll be back in a few with Midori." I turned back to go into Eden once more.

"I am going to die, by the way, when you leave. Your words aren't going to stop me," Fex called after me.

I went back out and stared him down. "Yes. Stay. Live. Listen to me."

"Nope! In fact—" He paused, closing his eyes for a couple seconds. "Here come my executioners right now! I called them over; hope you don't mind."

Two Ophanim, different ones from before, rushed down from the sky. They were much larger too, and they each had a great and many-toothed mouth taking up half their abdomen.

"This is just another quick mess I have to clean up," I said to Fex. "You're not going anywhere."

"Watch out!" he said jovially. "They're rather specialized for combat, these two. Like guard cells."

Guards or not, they were still angels, and I prepped a lighter.

They ignored me, and moved to Fex. I tried to push one aside, but it was much too heavy for that. Its body swayed slightly, but it continued to advance. I flicked my lighter, and forced one of the Ophan's wings over the flame.

The Ophan caught fire fast, the flames soon spreading to the rest of the body. But the angel did not seem to suffer from this, and in the end it was I who was forced to move aside before my hand burned.

"Many Ophanim actually light themselves on fire, you know. You've basically just weaponized it before it could be bothered to do so itself," Fex said, lounging on the grass and waiting for the Ophanim to reach him.

The other one, conscious of the first's sudden status of being on fire, lit itself up as well.

This was a problem. I didn't have any other weapons, and I was not fireproof. The Ophanim moved very slowly, and that gave me time to think. They were probably going to crush Fex in their jaws, as it seemed that was their only viable method of attack. So at least I knew it was going to be another minute before their floating put them in range of Fex.

My bag way back in the field, and the only things I had on hand were my matches and lighters. But nature does provide some bounty—I grabbed a good-size rock and stood ready.

I dove under one of the Ophanim—there was maybe only a foot of space between its burning body and the ground, and my skin grew hot. It was no better when I stood up—I was instantly sweating like crazy, and my vision became blurry.

Under its body was not quite lit, but more like starlight. Some light was also let in its neck hole, through which I could see its ringed head.

I readied my rock—how hard could this be? I had a pretty good arm for tossing things, and it was pretty much a straight shot. Besides those interlocking rings, but I was wishing for the best of luck on that one.

I threw it as hard as I could, and it bounced right off and came flying straight down. I picked it up for another shot, and this time it bounced away, well out of my reach.

How far away was Fex now? The Ophan did not stop moving, but its head did start to descend—and I had the queasy sort of feeling that things were becoming the wrong size, because its head was much larger than it had looked from the ground. Its skull-adorned face lowered itself to my level, and its wings parted to show its humanlike face, eyes the size of my splayed hands.

I went ahead and just punched it. It didn't respond in any way, its wings flapping once or twice whenever its head got too close to the ground moving slowly forward.

It was too hot for me to keep up my pathetic punching for much longer. "Ugh," I grunted, falling red-faced and fevered to the ground. "Why won't you just die?" I moaned.

My breath was heavy, and colder than the air around it. I rolled onto the dirt, which felt like coal against my skin.

I was going to fall unconscious at this rate, and then Fex would die, and then I would die, or maybe I'd die first and then Fex would. Someone was going to die, though….

Music rang in my ears, a thousand choral voices, and I lost myself to blackness.

## 25

I AWOKE without much fanfare or recognition—I just suddenly was, and though my head was heavy, I sat up and shook it off.

I had been moved slightly to the side, but otherwise nothing had really changed. The sun was beginning to set with a rather boring-looking yellow hue, and Fex was standing quite unharmed across from me.

"You've been out for a while." He made no effort to help me up, and I stood up on my own.

"I gathered as much. Feeling less like suicide, then?"

"Please. I'm always going to be alive." He gestured to Eden. "Just not with this consciousness. Isn't it in your best interest anyway that I die? You know, so all my memories die with me?"

"You haven't even seen anything that scandalous. I'm not sweating. And besides, I need you alive. Probably. Hey, what did you do with those Ophanim anyway?" There wasn't a sign of a struggle, not even a couple strands of burnt grass.

"I called them off; what else? As long as I didn't show my face to them, they were all the willing to oblige. Besides, you really think I'd pointlessly kill my own just to save your life?"

"I'm under the impression you saved my life either way, so I don't really care."

"I still need you alive." He shrugged. "You know, to remove Midori before she kills us all. Also, don't you think you're forgetting something?"

His elaborate series of fanning hand gestures and wide grin made me sigh. "Thank you. It's not like I was putting off saying it to be mean to you, by the way. I mean that quite genuinely. Now don't die while I'm gone."

I was still feeling a bit woozy, but I figured that'd be gone by the time I found Midori. I dug for a lighter and prepared to depart.

"At the rate you handle things, I'm probably better off joining you. You know, so you don't burn to death."

I glared at him.

He backed off. "Hey, just making a joke here. I've seen the way you've killed things. You've got a real knack for survival."

"Wait—are you implying I'm going to have to kill Midori?"

"We'll see. Or, you'll see. But I trust you to make the truest judgment—or do you want me to 'hold your hand' throughout? I mean that in a sarcastic, expression-y way, to clarify, definitely not a literal one."

"Oh, you know just the things to say to a girl to make her heart flutter!" I said. "Are you, like, passive-aggressively asking me to ask you to come along? I thought you were going to explode into a demon at any second."

"I never said that. A more accurate guess would be any minute, and it's not like there'd be no warning signs. You should just kill me when I start to turn, and we'll be fine." His eyes lit up suddenly. "And if you really insist, of course I'll accompany you into Eden! It is rather dark and hard to navigate. Especially when you're heading right to the heart."

"Oh, shut up." He got up and stood next to me, waiting for me to enter. "Actually, I have one more thing to take care of. Probably shouldn't go in there unarmed, right?"

"Do you have a weapon in mind?"

"Fire has always worked. Almost always. But it still stands as my best bet. But—"

"Fire is hard to control. And you can't harm the Metatron."

"Yes. So I'm just going to skip down to the ski lodge. Be right back."

"Can't I join you for that?"

I paused. While I *was* considering bringing some sort of ski pole or fire safety axe back with me, I was really more interested in finding a radio to contact Ada or Naomi with.

Actually, Ada was likely hiding in the trees nearby. But it still wouldn't hurt to see if Angel Radio was on, and usually the only way to achieve that was with a radio.

I didn't want to explain it to Fex, though, fearful he might judge me for… what? It was a program that was evidently sponsored by him, or the Metatron, or whatever. Like he wouldn't already know about it. I just felt oddly ashamed to discuss it with him.

"Private reasons," I settled on saying.

"Nothing is private anymore. Come on. I know about weapons. I know what to expect in there."

"You can just tell me, for once."

"It's more fun this way."

I exhaled heavily. "Okay. But if I need alone time, promise to go away for a couple minutes."

"Do skis make you too emotional to function?" Fex wondered aloud. I didn't bother to answer.

I was honestly glad of Fex's presence—it beat being alone and mopey. But I didn't care to speak much along the way down the hill. The air was rapidly cooling off, and the sun disappeared in such a sudden fashion that by the time I realized it was dark I also realized I had no memory of seeing the sun set—it had just happened.

The ski lodge ended up being fairly close to the weblike mass of Eden, and it became apparent when I reached the bottom of the hill that it had been mostly swallowed by the white wall of the Metatron's exterior. I continued instead down the road a bit more and went into the nearest motel.

"This isn't a ski lodge," Fex observed. At least now I sort of understood how he knew things about human lives—if the Metatron was constantly reabsorbing and dispersing angels to collect information, they must have seen almost all the world by now. And Fex was tapped right into it all, likely receiving information without being truly aware of its flow.

All those thousands and millions of angels constantly observing everything must have learned to read a sign or two. Their knowledge could still best be described as laughable, but at least Fex seemed to have a very basic grip on what skiing was.

"This is a motel," I informed him. "Temporary housing for people on the move."

"I know that," Fex scolded. "I mean, it's not a ski lodge, which is where you said we were heading. A ski lodge can also be temporary housing for moving people, or people who were once moving on their skis but have since stopped for rest."

"Wow. You're really a font of information. It's almost like reading a book about ski lodges, or I guess, getting one read aloud to you."

"Skiing is a recreational sport that shares certain sacred mountains with snowboard practitioners. There are no snowboard lodges anywhere to be found, however."

"I'm really learning a lot," I said, doing my best to amp up the sarcasm in case he had missed it the first time.

He took no notice, and stared darkly into my eyes as he spoke, dead serious. "Skiers practice their art with certain aerodynamic planks that are attached to the feet and long arm-extending poles that direct their movement."

"Okay, Fex, I get it. You've... read a book or something on skiing. Or maybe made some guesses based on the pictures? Because I'm not sure you have your facts down one hundred percent."

"After a great game of ski, the artists will descend to their lodges for the ceremonial drinking of hot beverages," He said offhand, sounding offended. "This is to heat their cold and fragile bodies. If it is sunny out, it is meant to ward off evil spirits."

"This place is rather empty, isn't it?" I said in an attempt to distract him. It was true, however. It had been the off-season for winter sports, but surely a few of the rooms would be full? I was looking mostly for weapons, but I couldn't help notice how untouched the place was.

It was just a dinky motel, though, and not a place that should seem eerie if it looked abandoned. It just felt sad, though still carrying a twinge of creepiness. A sink sat full of water. A plate had been dropped on the floor. There was a dead dog chained up in the backyard.

But no corpses could be found in any of the rooms. The angels didn't eat humans, last time I checked—well, some obviously had, but most lacked anything resembling a mouth. But those bodies had to have gone somewhere.

I was so used to being left alone to solve these mysteries that I almost forgot I was in the company of one entirely capable of solving them all.

"Why are there so few bodies, anyway? Do you guys move them?"

"Move? Yes. In a way. We carried them away."

"Dead?"

"Of course." He spoke like he was scolding me. "What other way could we move them?"

"So, why do you do that?"

"Well, you'll find out, I guess, fairly soon. It will be a subject covered in our trek through Eden."

"I feel like you have some sort of thing about withholding information. Do you get off on it? Are you even capable of getting off, come to think of it?"

He raised and lowered his eyebrows without changing his expression from an unnaturally wide smile. "I don't know those terms. Are you armed and having private time yet?"

"No." I waved him off. "Go outside for like ten minutes. Shoo."

He obliged, and I quickly found what I needed: a knife from one of the rooms, another new lighter to keep in my pocket, and an AM radio. Then I settled onto one of the beds, and after I was done sneezing off the dust, I put the radio in front of me and turned it on.

Music played—it was a tune I knew, a pop song with lyrics that held long out over the vowels and featured a high number of cymbal crashes. I tuned it, each channel yielding an equally strong and familiar channel that struck me as comforting. An old commercial jingle played on one of the stations, and I listened with ardent intensity. For a moment I was on the verge of what felt like remembrance, of an autumn day spent in a cold car, watching the breeze sway the wilds....

I caught myself. An old memory sat on the brink of my mind. That long-ago day, and the next, spent listening to the radio while the policeman spoke outside. Someone brought me hot chocolate. Before my parents had died, I had listened to the radio every night. After those days of waiting in cars and lobbies, I had stopped.

I spun through the channels again. None led to Angel Radio.

How did the ghostly channel even work? It usually seemed to happen when I was using an actual radio, but it hadn't always... and surely it wasn't even related to the radio to start with. It was mass telepathy of some sort, and maybe it was rather silly of me to feel convinced the radio had ever been part of it—like a soccer player convinced what socks they wore affected the game's outcome.

But even as I thought it, the radio faded and crackled, and I was left with a message:

*"Hello. Welcome to Angel Radio. Today's weather is going to be dreadful, rain and fog as long as they can come. Perhaps school will be*

*canceled tomorrow. I do hope so. It's been so long since we've had a snow day—we didn't have one over the summer, not one at all."*

It was the voice of Emil, and it was not trying to hide itself in the static any longer. It was in my mind, all of it was at once, and I doubled over at first to try and contain it. I was overwhelmed with pain worse than a migraine, and by the time my brain was done bursting, I saw darkness and I was dizzyingly unsteady.

*"Hello again, and welcome to another day and another round of field notes—what is that? Where is it going? There? At this hour? Is that fire on its back? Are those eyes on its wings? What manner of peculiar is all this? And how, very much how, can I draw it?"*

And now it was the radio speaking to me, a booming and shaking apparition straight out of a cartoon—and even now it was changing further. The radio unfolded and extended and shifted until it resembled something I recalled having to doodle once in math class—a hypercube, a moving mechanism bordering on the fourth dimension. But the fourth dimension is time, isn't it? You can't just sit on the brink of time any more than you can sit on the brink of the second dimension. Physics just won't allow it.

The sight of this physics-breaking atrocity made me very uneasy, and my eyes itchy and dry. And then it finished its dance of intersecting and changing, and like a kernel of popcorn it exploded—just a little jump really, but it was enough to puff it up slightly and allow a black slime to swirl out.

*"It's cold out, but I'm not going to find myself a sweater. I could learn a skill by book reading, I suppose, but it's a lot of work. And nothing is quite how it looks in the books, is it? It's pointless. And those angels—"* The voice, Emil, was speaking as the radio continued to change. I wasn't sure if I could place the pronoun "he" on the voice at this point—it had a certain masculinity still, but as the black slime shaped itself into something with a human semblance, the voice changed too. It was lighter, and wholly familiar.

*"Those angels!"* it continued. *"Those angels! Those devils, those monsters, those demons, those foes! If I had a fist and a gun and a couple angels and a dark back alley, those angels would exist no more. Those angels, those angels, those angels!"* It kept its metallic nature, both in appearance and in voice—the body was perhaps more a shimmering onyx, and the voice still sounded like it was coming from

the speakers of the radio. Indeed, the body held the radio up to its chest and let its voice ring out. Each time it spoke it reused its old words, like the audio equivalent of a magazine-cutout hostage letter.

When it was done, it held the radio to its mouth and tilted its head, short hair tilting with it and falling in a certain painful way.

*"It is rather nice out here, without the cars and without the boats, without the train whistle at two and twelve every afternoon, and without the people. It is rather nice. And awfully, awfully boring—but that will never get to me unless I let it. The world is my—"* The voice shook, the body shook, and I shook. *"Those angels,"* it said like a broken record, the same sad tone each time. *"Those angels, those angels. Those angels, those angels, those angels."*

My eyes were burning, my mouth was dry, and I think somewhere in the mess I had begun to cry. An awfully overwhelming sensation of agitation rose from my stomach, and I stabbed the radio creature. I had to. I tore its body open and saw stars, not like those in the sky but more like the kind I saw when I closed my eyes very tightly and looked very closely—lines of negative space and spots of an invisible hue fell out like cotton stuffing and did not bother to collect on the bed. And when I had torn the odd thing open, the perfect mirrorlike body split and spilled and ripped like fabric, there was just the radio.

With a knife in it.

And the knife stuck out a bit, because with all my force I hadn't been able to pierce it very deeply.

I did not collect the knife—the lighter was going to have to be enough for today. And I had a feeling I wasn't going to be hearing from Ada or Naomi or Emil anytime soon, or very honestly, ever again.

Fex stood at the doorway and picked at his nails with his teeth. He bit, chewed, and spat them out onto the dusty red floor.

"A religious rite?" he asked with his ever-present vaguely curious air. But he did not look up from his hands. "A prayer?"

His grasp on humanity was never going to be perfect.

## 26

I DIDN'T want to talk to Fex, but he either didn't get my cue or had chosen to ignore it.

"You look ill. Not comparatively ill, of course, at least when compared to how much of a mess I currently am. But for your own standards, you seem quite ill."

"You sure have a way with words," I sang halfheartedly in a soft voice.

"Oh, see that is pleasant and all, but it is not like you." As he spoke he fell to singing his words as well, in a curious and awed way. He then experimented singing a variety of words. I stopped paying attention at "low streaked tenrec."

"We're going to now fight the—whatever it is," I reminded him, and he snapped out of his musical episode.

"We're not fighting anything. The only fighting will be in the case of you having to put me down before I infect Eden. We are going to remove Midori from the system, like a bloodsucking tick."

"Are there non-bloodsucking ticks?"

He rolled his head about. "Are you ready for this, though? I'm not sure you're feeling okay. You seem very stressed."

"You're asking if I'm okay? Not like, if I'm functioning at full emotional capacity?" I laughed far too hard and ended up gripping Fex's good shoulder for support.

He didn't seem confused by my actions. "I don't want to put this off, but I think you need to rest. You've had a long day, and a couple longer days in the past, and all in all I think it's time you take a rest."

"Isn't Midori going to mess you all up somehow, in whatever never-specified way?"

"Yes. And similarly, I'm at risk to succumb to my infections. But you can do this alone. I only desire to join you because I miss my home, true form, and body. If I sense I'm losing control while you sleep, I will kill myself duly, and you will continue with your mission. I have faith."

"Oi, look at you go!" I laughed again, but nothing he said was of particular humor, and I let it fade out before frowning. "I'm not tired, though. I'm just feeling sort of off-put, unsure, anxious, frightened, and in need of reassurance. Which I guess you can provide. Okay. Let's do this." I threw my stuff on the ground, then ran over to pick the lighter up again when it bounced under a car. I sat on the pavement of the motel's parking lot and invited Fex to sit across from me.

"I can't right-put you, or give you confidence or calm your nerves or make you brave," Fex told me, still standing. "And 'reassurance' is intentionally vague, isn't it?"

"It's exactly what you're good for. Come on, sit across from me already. Let's make this seem more official."

"What is official about sitting in a parking lot like this?"

"No, it's the whole across thing. So we can stare dramatically at each other while we speak." He finally obliged and sat across from me, mimicking my cross-legged position a few seconds later.

"Now?"

I sighed. I was actually rather tired, I decided, but my anxiety over what I had seen—or hadn't seen—in the motel room was keeping me too tense to even think about resting. "Has there, or is there, some sort of radio program run by angels?"

"No." He sounded rather unsure, so I tried again.

"Some sort of mind-linked system where you intentionally spread information about angels to all remaining human survivors, as some sort of test?"

"No." He was very sure about that one. In fact, he looked rather shocked I could even think up such an idea.

"Do you know of any angel by the name of Naomi?"

"No."

"Ada—or Orifiel, actually."

"No."

"Emil."

"No. None of those are particularly angelic names, you know. What are you so worried about?"

"The phrase 'Angel Radio,' does it mean anything at all?" I failed to put effort into my phrasing, and my words ended up coming out a bit slowly and with a higher-pitched squeak.

"No."

I didn't understand why I was upset. Nor why I was suddenly putting up a poor fight against my tears. I had known this for a long time now, hadn't I? Midori told it to me, and freaky angel-possessing-corpse girl or not, she hadn't seemed to be lying back then.

But it was so much worse this time—maybe it was the quizzical and thoroughly real look Fex was giving me, or the way I had felt my ears rumble under Naomi's deafening shouts. I stroked my shoulder. Her claws had left no marks, even when I imagined them bleeding. It had been real to me.

But the reality of the situation now seemed much different: I was a girl who heard voices in the static and got into arguments with myself. I was certainly some level of insane, right? But I didn't feel crazy. Aren't you not supposed to know when you are mentally unsound? Because I knew. And I just felt ashamed.

But mostly there was sobbing. My eyes were strained and squinted, and I told myself to stop. I didn't listen to myself, though. I just continued being a wreck.

Fex had some sort of slippery grip on what was going on, but I don't think angels are capable of empathy. But he did have some working knowledge of sympathy, and his hand hovered an inch from my shoulder, his eyes staring unblinkingly into mine.

I threw myself against him, not in the proper and perfectly romantic way, but in the sort of way you might try to fling yourself against a wall. And he was roughly equivalent to a wall too, very stiff, a little bit cold, and without much for breath. He tried to continue meeting my gaze, and when I curled my head against his chest, he took my head in his hands, almost like he was ready to lift it up again so he could continue his staring. But he didn't go through with the movement, and his fingernails dug into my skin.

At this point I was crying for my sake. I always had been, I suppose. When I found myself on the verge of calmness, I even tried to make myself distressed again, just so I could continue with my sobbing. I thought of everything I could, and everything made me sadder. Even the loss of terrible things made me viciously sad: death because I was never going to go to a relative's funeral; war because there were no more movies about it; long lines because I was never going to feel frustrated at another human being's presence ever again.

It was awful, just awful, but it came to pass whether I wished it to or not. And when I was done, I lifted my head and met Fex's unchanging and concerned gaze. His hands continued to grip my head in a most uncomfortable way.

"But what is this all about?"

"I've been hearing voices in my head for a long time now." My voice was still rather shaky.

"Oh," Fex said. "Me too."

"It's different for you, though. I'm walking around here talking with myself like a madwoman, hallucinating images and sounds and feelings... I even made up a story to help convince myself it was all real. How ridiculous is that? I wanted so badly to believe in my own mind that I constructed some bizarre narrative just to satisfy myself."

He pursed his lips but said nothing.

"Don't look at me like that! You only talk to yourself. You are yourself, and you're fine with it because it's what you're supposed to be. I'm not used to—I'm not *supposed to* imagine monsters, and frankly, I'm sort of left with the doubt that any of this is real! You could be just another imaginary companion—"

He interrupted my rant. "I'm not."

"Yeah, okay, but Orifiel seemed pretty real to me when she was hanging round too. So you know, I'm feeling a little like I'm leaning on the edge of a pit here. I'm on the brink, and my head hurts, and I want to eat some actually fresh food, and I really, really want to pet a dog right now."

"Sit calmly. If I could take on your pain for you, I would, because I would like nothing more than to not be alone in my mind anymore. But I understand why you're troubled. And I fear I can't help you with it—not once and not at all. But maybe you'll figure it out, eventually. So please, try to breathe and take a rest, and do your best to focus on the future instead of the past. I need to save Eden from Midori, and you need to save Midori from Eden, and together we share a simple and comforting goal."

I exhaled. His fingers were still rather tightly gripping my scalp, but he had eased up slightly. "Yeah, okay, whatever." I leaned forward and kissed him, but really it was more of a car crash with my lips, a rather desperate and ill-thought-out attempt at something I had no name for. Fex didn't seem to have a name for it either. Again he was best compared to a wall—though his fingers had loosened on my head and had slipped slightly down to my shoulders, it seemed more to have been a reactionary accident.

I backed off and found myself falling into a position that reflected my feelings about the kiss: well, that was awkward. Fex seemed mostly confused, but he permitted me to rather stupidly try to kiss him again. This time I placed my fingers lightly against his skull and tried a little bit harder, and Fex in turn copied me.

It was a slightly better kiss in the end, I guess, but I wasn't sure I liked it, or that I really liked him. I mean, liked him in any sort of sexual or romantic way. I felt very stupid about kissing him immediately after I had finished, and while his gaze suggested he was up for trying it out again, I knew there wasn't much point to it, and I shook his fingers off my skin and stood up again.

"What was that?" he asked, following me out of the parking lot. "I am aware of it, naturally, this kissing business, but it is always important to add more context and details to my memory."

"What, are you now trying to flirt with me?" I laughed. Despite everything, I was somehow in a much better mood. "Do you want to make out again?"

He had a bit of a giggle when he spoke as well, and a slight stammer. "Not really. But you know—I may be just one facet of a giant single-mind that's taken over your world and killed your species, but that doesn't mean that I can't feel anything at all. I mean that mostly in a physical sense, but maybe emotional."

"Oh, so you totally just got a boner for me now? I'm not really feeling it myself." I couldn't stop myself from laughing at my own joke, and though Fex was doing his best to sound calm, I suspected he was holding back his weird laughter too. As I crossed the streets of the town on my way back to Eden, I was again looking for a weapon—but now it was with a sort of light air that I searched, and I spun about and flung things every which way as I did so, humming.

"I'm not familiar with every word you say, though the use of it suggests something that is probably not true about myself—but uh, look, I'm just wondering what all this has been about? Don't leave a dying soul on the hook here, please."

"You're so clingy." I was talking to Fex mostly without looking, but I caught his eye when I spoke, and he looked at the ground, seeming rather embarrassed. I was joking, though, and he knew that, and I did another princess-worthy twirl as I tossed a heavy suitcase from the street through a store window.

"At least you're feeling better," he said, seeming resigned. "I'm glad about that." And he gave me a sort of fed up and affectionate smile.

"I just hope you're not expecting anything else from me."

"Expecting?"

"Love," I said idly.

"Ah," he said. "I'd just like to know where things stand. I mean, that was certainly an experience—any chance we'll do that again? Just asking."

"Oh, don't worry about trying to sound justified here—I don't care. But no." I found a bat, among other things, on an empty baseball diamond. I tossed it in my hands a few times. It was the perfect weight. "Definitely not. Simplicity is a virtue, you know."

Fex scoffed under his breath that it wasn't, but caught himself midway through, and joined in with my half-forced laughter.

## 27

EDEN WAS not pitch black in the dark. It glowed, with patches of teal light spread across the whole of its white wall. The angels never seemed to sleep, but they had gathered for the night in the trees and on top of Eden itself, and they too seemed to give off light. But it may have been a trick of the night sky—after all, many of them had a sort of prismatic quality to their bodies.

It took a while to find the entrance I had dug through the stringy wall. Fex had started to lag behind as we climbed the hill, and at the top he fell against Eden's wall to catch his breath.

"I'll last," he promised. "But I'll be dead before the next sunrise." He had wrapped the infected part of his face up again as we had ascended.

"How am I going to know when I have to kill you?" I asked. I did not want to kill Fex in the slightest, though I figured there probably wasn't another option. I was going to have to, or maybe he'd do it himself, but either way he was going to die. And it would help me now if I remembered that: there was no need to grieve him. It was going to happen. Best to appreciate him now while I could.

"Oh, I don't know. It's not like I've seen it happen. I'll probably start making some weird noises, and lose control of my shape-shifting," he said. "Hm."

"Hm?"

"Well, you know, it's not like I technically have to die when I become a carapace. In fact, we're not supposed to hurt them at all if we can help it. That's why I was holding back so much when we were in the void."

"That's convenient. So why do you keep telling me to kill you? You were about set to do it yourself, actually."

"The thing about carapaces is simple—they're just our corrupted bodies. Our consciousness—or rather the piece of the Metatron we were loaned when we were born—is still alive in there. It's just likewise corrupted, and acting mostly on instinct and who knows what else. But it can be cured—it's just not something you would want to hear about. Or would even consider."

"What is it, then?"

"It's exactly what we've been hoping to achieve this whole time: perfection. We were searching for the ideal human female for this very purpose—"

"Hold up." I narrowed my eyes. "You specifically need a *girl* to do this?"

"Yes. In fact, we only left women in our eradications. After the male population was removed, we began to narrow down the survivors in our efforts to find the perfect woman."

"I know this is a terrifying thought and millions of people died for it, but wow does it sound like some sort of dating show. *The search for the perfect woman*!" I laughed. "Okay. I'm done. Continue with your creepy plan."

"We needed a female," Fex explained. "Because last time we did this we needed a male. It's a balance. Next time we'll need a male, and so on, and so forth. When our chosen subject achieves perfection, they revive us and grant us—the Metatron us, I mean—the power needed to cure the carapaces and revitalize fully."

"Why do you even have the carapace demon creatures anyway? Why do you have to go through this process so many times?" I wasn't really thinking about the implications of it, either. Was Fex saying the angels were aliens of some sort, who traveled from planet to planet to do this? And how disappointing was it that other alien races also just had male and female? I was really hoping for some more exciting sexes.

Fex looked rather slyly at me, and I suspected he was proud of his kind, or himself, for this plan. "All things must die. It's in the cells—they can't replicate perfectly forever. No matter is infinite. But with this, we simply refresh. We renew. We recycle our selves. And all it takes is a proper genetic match and a bit of time."

"So you'd just… suck the life out of whoever you choose? Like a giant, more monstrous vampire?"

"Quite the contrary!" Fex said with glee. "Those we choose do not die—we become them. Only parts of our past selves remain—

the faintest of memories and instructions for what to do when the time for rebirth is at hand again. We are our chosen, and they become us."

"So that's what you'd do with Midori, then? Make her one of you?"

"Midori is dead, Erika. If I were to live—if you really wanted me to—you would have to be the one to attain perfection. There's no one else around—and the cloud of void and carapaces is growing ever closer." Fex grinned at me. "Though of course, once you did this, you wouldn't really be saving me anymore—you'd be saving yourself. I know you just want to save Midori and leave—and in fact, I encourage it. But if you really wanted to, you could take her place and become one with me."

I shivered—it was like a series of twitches and movements and a face being turned away, and it wasn't even cold out.

"What happens to the demons if I remove Midori and abandon you?"

"They seize hold of the Metatron. All angels become carapaces. The world becomes void and then rots away."

"You're not leaving me an option here, are you?" And he had seemed so helpful just an hour prior. I didn't want to die a bizarre death at the hands of some demon, but I really didn't want to fuse with a creepy omni-soul. Maybe if I just died at the end of the process—maybe that would have been okay.

"No, there's some hope. I don't want you to feel forced. If Midori forces herself into the Metatron, she'll have the same effect as the carapaces would have had. She must go as soon as possible. But once you remove her, there is a period of time where we'll be safe again, and the search can resume for another suitable candidate. I just hope we still have a couple left alive—the approach of the void is a rather consistent thing, I'm afraid. Considering how close it's gotten, we must have lost a number of our survivors." He glumly looked down. "It's okay, though. We can use someone less than ideal in dire emergencies."

"This is surreal." I shook my head, then laughed. "What a thing to say, huh? Like that's anything new. This whole thing is expected at this point."

"I'm sorry."

"Don't be." I helped him to his feet. "We still have work to do."

IT WAS dark inside Eden. The lights on the outside didn't even bleed through in the slightest, and my lighter didn't have enough light to let me see anything.

Luckily Fex knew exactly where we were. There didn't seem to be any walls around us, but he wove a twisty route in the darkness, leading me by a firm grip on my wrist. In my other hand I held my baseball bat ready, but nothing seemed to be stirring.

"You've placed us rather far from our destination," Fex said, before suddenly jerking me to the side.

"Ouch!" I said reflexively as I stumbled to catch my balance. "Why can't we just walk in a straight line? Is there even anything in here?"

"I'm opposed to this sort of thing," Fex said with a bit of a mumble. He let go of my wrist, and I couldn't see what he was doing. "But I'll be careful."

Then I could see—or at least, I could see what his hands were doing. From between them a light was growing. He nurtured it protectively, before finally tossing it about an inch above his outstretched hands, where it hovered.

It didn't provide much illumination, but I had a feeling he was holding his power back to prevent any harm from coming to Eden—and I could see why he might be wary. The space we were walking in was mostly empty, but slightly smaller than I had thought. To the right was another great mass of something, a sort of bluish-black and unidentifiable shape separate from the whiteness of everything else.

From the left wall, the one that led to the outside, there were strings. They were stiff, and I had a feeling it was a bad idea to touch them. They seemed to be pulsing with energy. They ran at all heights and angles, but always went from the wall to the inner structure.

"You would not enjoy the result of touching the supports. Though...." He looked wide-eyed at the nearest one, and seemed poised to grab it himself. He caught himself. "It would harm us," he reminded himself. He then reached up and grabbed the orb of light to extinguish it, and began leading me again.

"So what are they?"

"Supports. They connect the Metatron to the outer wall. They're extensions of ourself. While we must enter the inner sanctums to return back to the state of the Metatron, those that do not need to cease to be separate beings quite yet can simply rest on the wall and deposit their memories in that way."

"Does the Metatron have a physical form? I'm sort of imagining it as some sort of… giant ball of light at this point."

"Yes, very much. We have a single shape. We can't even change shape."

Light began to filter in through the darkness in a very organic manner. I didn't even notice it at first, but suddenly I was aware I could see my hands and the slightest outlines of Fex's face. I couldn't quite place where the light was coming from, though it seemed to be somewhere ahead of us.

It began to get brighter and brighter, but stopped when it was about as bright as an early winter's dawn.

The shape to the right was not quite consistent, nor was it quite as dark as I had thought. It was rough and bumpy, and as we walked it curved multiple times. It had a certain semblance to something, though I couldn't quite place what. It too seemed to be glowing, though, a sort of purple, sort of green, and sort of blue light that did little to illuminate.

"We're here," said Fex suddenly, though we seemed to be nowhere close to anywhere.

He had mostly loosened his grip on my wrist when it became bright enough that I could avoid the support strings on my own, but now he grabbed me tightly and pulled me to the inner shape, following its perimeter carefully.

"Is there a secret entrance?" I wondered aloud.

"There will be guards from here on out, and we'd best not alert them of our presence. As Midori has been placed in the Vask, all angels have ceased their search mode and have defaulted to protection of her. They will kill you."

"Or at least, try to." I tightened my grip on my bat and walked a bit more deliberately.

"No, they will kill you. In Eden, you are too close to the Metatron to stand a chance. Everything is alive and everything will attack you. You must remain unnoticed until we arrive at Midori's location."

We rounded what was sort of a corner and sort of a long curved structure. It was an outcropping of sorts, with a series of stonelike steps leading up to a tall and narrow opening. It seemed unguarded, but I let Fex walk ahead to check.

"No one is around," he said. "I'm on edge about this. There should be Seraphim this close to the Metatron."

"All the better, then." I jumped up and walked rather unsurely into the dark hole—it was again pitch black, and smelled odd. Fex knew exactly where to go, and he made me speed up.

"I'm worried about one thing—" he started, but a voice from behind me interrupted him.

"Me? I really hope you're not scared of me. That'd be a shame and rather odd."

Fex had stopped suddenly, but when he turned around to answer, he seemed to speak with more irritation than contempt. "I was referring to some sort of ambush. Afterward, I would have brought up the subject of you in this way—'also, wouldn't it be annoying if Gav showed up?' I don't fear you, obviously. I'm just rather annoyed that you were lying to Erika and feeding her a ton of false information. And generally acting bizarre."

"What, can't I have a little fun while I'm alive? My job's boring enough as is. No harm in screwing around a little. And besides—I found Midori! As in, our perfect match. That was all me."

"Technically *I* found her, thank you very much. I saw her first."

"I talked to her first."

"She liked me best."

"Definitely not!"

"Boys!" It was odd, on second thought, to break their quarreling to refer to them as something they were not in the slightest. "I think you're both forgetting that it doesn't matter who 'found' Midori—she's a threat to you either way."

"A threat?" Gavreel said, painfully confused.

"She's something like… an infected angel possessing a human corpse, bent on getting back into the Metatron. We're here to remove her."

"What? Really? That's wild. Uh, I guess I was going to ask what you were doing here, and possibly fight you over it, but I guess I really can't argue with that."

"That's good," said Fex. "Where are all the guards?"

"I already called them to assemble down in the Vask rooms. Intruder alert." Even in the darkness, I could make out the faint lines of Gavreel shrugging. "Called it right when I saw you enter. I'm not 'evil,'" he said with what seemed to be his attempt at air quotes. "Just doing my job."

Fex sighed. "Just go away already."

"Wait," I said before Gavreel could move. "I'm just remembering—when we first met, you shot a deer, right? Why didn't you want me to touch it?"

"Just messing with you." He shrugged again. I wondered where he even learned what a shrug was. "You moved slow during those first couple weeks. Me and a buddy were just experimenting with possession of dead animals, and you startled me. Had a good laugh about how confused you looked afterward."

"Oh. What was your friend's name?" It was weird to think angels could even have friends, honestly. Weren't they essentially friends with themselves, then? Fex and Gavreel didn't get along perfectly, essentially meaning they didn't get along with themselves. It was probably best not to overthink individuality in the context of angels.

"Mnyeph."

"That's a pretty cool name, I guess."

"Is it? Do you think my name is cool too?"

"Is it any longer than Gavreel?"

"No. Does that matter?"

"Are you guys going to stop making idle chitchat any time soon or am I going to have to physically lift Gavreel up and place him very far away?" Fex said.

"I can move very far away on my own, thank you," Gavreel said. "Do you want me to call off the guards or not?"

"Like I can't do that myself."

"What, in your state?" Gavreel leered. "Oh, like I can't smell it? You reek of disease. I ought to terminate you myself, you know. You're living on my blessing alone."

"And my protection," I said. In the dark it was hard to gauge his reaction, but he seemed to take a few steps back.

The cave, if that's what the structure was, had mostly taken shape as a very long and narrow tunnel. Its walls had a certain ribbed feeling to them, and the ceiling was only about a foot above my head. The floor was mostly curved, leading to a dire need to walk carefully or else stumble—which I ended up doing fairly often regardless.

It eventually opened up into a larger area with pale lights embedded in the walls, floors, and ceilings. The hard surface of the floor still felt slightly warped, but evened out until it was walkable. Nothing seemed to be here, however, besides a great deal more of the rounded tunnels we had arrived from.

Fex and Gavreel, of course, knew exactly where they were heading.

"Where is everything?" I asked. "Or is there just nothing here?"

"You're about correct," Fex said. "There is not much here that you can know. But we have a greater connection, and we can feel the Metatron all around us. We hear them. But you lack the link, so I suppose this place feels a bit like nothing."

"A bit less than nothing." We had entered another tunnel, and I was once again forced to find my way by feeling the walls and bumping into Fex repeatedly.

Luckily the tunnel was much shorter this time, and we stumbled into a small, circular, and red room.

"Here we are, then. Vask." Fex was still leading, and he stepped forward into the room. I noted how he had yet to touch anything—no doubt worried his infection might spread if he did.

There was a long period of silence. I wasn't sure if it was safe to enter, but Gavreel slipped by and stood next to Fex. They both stood in utter silence with blank looks on their faces. I was ready to ask what was happening when I realized: they probably were using telepathy to communicate with the Metatron, or at least the other deployed angels.

I nervously walked down to them. Neither of them was so much as blinking, and with a cautious sense of mind, I explored a bit. The room was very red; the sort of candy-colored shade most often found on the painted walls of dinky fast food joints. The walls were smooth too and had the faintest reflective quality to them. There were little paths leading between the odd shapes of the walls, to various other rooms.

The first room I dared to pop my head into was exactly the same as the one I was in, though with a more blue-gray color to it. But the next one was strikingly different. For one, I could see the angels clustered inside it—though to say they were inside it wasn't wholly correct. They *were* it, bodies sticking about halfway through on every surface and wings stretched out from the interior.

But far on the other end was another important, strange, and beautiful sight: Midori. She too was partially in the wall—and though my vision was obscured, I could make out how her body was coated in a weblike material that stuck her there. She was not sitting like I had imagined her to be—cross-legged, calm, and awake—but she looked rather like she had been thrown there, with her legs askew at odd angles and her head limp and facing the floor.

I wanted to run over and check out how she was doing, but I didn't feel safe trying to reach her with the angels in the way, and I returned back to Fex and Gavreel.

They hadn't budged. I sat on the floor and waited. It wasn't particularly cold or warm in the room. It wasn't particularly anything. The interior was unremarkable, the only sounds were ambient nothings, and there wasn't even a smell to the place. It was wholly boring, enough so that I found myself yawning.

What was keeping Fex and Gavreel? Were they arguing? If Gavreel had ordered the angels into Midori's room, surely they'd listen to him when he made them leave. And Fex was—well, at least he'd act as backup to whatever Gavreel was saying.

But it surely couldn't keep up for long. The black bubbling of his skin was starting to slip past his bandages, and if any angel saw him now he was dead.

I was considering hitting one of them to see if they reacted at this point. It had been at least twenty minutes before I had gotten fed up enough that I returned to the room Midori was in, took a good look at the feathery floor, and walked through it with great care.

The eyes of the angels did not turn to watch me. They looked vacantly ahead, distracted, and I made my way to where Midori was.

It was a little raised platform, and I sat across from her. I crossed my legs, and I lifted her head and looked into her glassy, dead eyes.

"Hello? Midori? Are you still in there?"

## 28

Midori did not answer me at first, or really, at all. She continued to lie there as unmoving and unbreathing as, well, a corpse.

But she couldn't be dead. Wasn't all of Eden supposed to die with her? Wasn't the whole world supposed to crumble with her death? I held her head in my hands and lightly shook her. I took her pulse. I checked her breathing.

There was nothing.

The room behind me was still full of angels, but they were still stuck in their obscure thoughts. I was the only thing stirring in the whole of Eden. But I wasn't going to give up. That had always been something I had been proud of, wasn't it? My tenacity? And to walk away from all this, to give up now—well, it certainly would achieve nothing, to say the least.

Most of Midori's body was covered in thin webbing, and it held her firmly against the wall. I regretted dropping my knife back at the motel—the web turned out to be very stretchy, but nearly impossible to break. It took a good minute to snap a single strand, and while I had time to spare, I couldn't be sure I had that much.

I settled on freeing her head and hands first, and then seeing if I could just drag her away. Her hands and arms came undone after a bit of work, but her head refused to unstick itself. When I leaned over to get a better grip on the web that was keeping her so firmly in place, I discovered why she wouldn't—and couldn't—budge: the back of her neck and bottom of her head were melded right into the wall.

I traced the area she was stuck on with my fingers. The wall behind her seemed to be pure rock—or at least, a very hard material with some resemblance to rock. It didn't seem capable of absorbing part of her head.

But of course, I had already seen the exact same thing on the angels. They were all stuck about halfway through solid surfaces too.

But somehow it seemed startlingly scary when the same thing was happening to a human—or at least, something in a human body.

I could free Midori's body as long as I cared to, but it wasn't going to free her mind. Fex had said that their chosen human was going to have to fuse minds with the Metatron. So Midori was alive. Just attempting to fuse with another consciousness that was technically already herself.

There was one other terrifying implication I had come to realize as well: if the angels and Midori could simply move through the walls, well, they definitely weren't just walls. They had to be organic. And they had to be alive.

The Metatron was in Eden, and Eden had simply been the white casting for this: a giant, hollow nest of angels.

I ran back to the small room where Fex and Gavreel still stood, still looking lifeless. Out of curiosity, I couldn't resist pushing gently on Gavreel, and found him light enough that he fell right to the ground. He didn't get up, and I hoped he wasn't going to have some way of remembering this.

Fex was looking worse, blacker and more hollow. I promised myself he would be fine for a little bit more.

The mere fact that I was likely inside some sort of giant organism freaked me out enough as I made my way outside—though it was unlikely it was truly alive, acting more or less like a storage unit for memories and energy of the angels. It was still just way too creepy.

It was a lot less time to get out than it had to get in. That was probably thanks to the lack of the boys slowing me down, and my sudden realization that it was faster to just run through the tunnels than carefully step it out.

The entrance to the Metatron was a curved and angular little outcropping, with the roof jutting at a sharp angle and the floor keeping almost flat. From the lightly shaded interior, I could make out a series of jagged rocks.

And when I stepped fully outside, I was on what was like a small pile of rocks, uneven and random, but when I took my lighter out and walked along their edge, they began to resemble something else entirely.

I took a few steps closer and raised my light ever so slightly, and found myself looking at a dark shape, one that was very hard to make out, so much so that I almost made myself pretend I couldn't recognize it—but I could, and I was done lying to myself.

It was a face, mouth open, eyes empty, and I was standing on its interlocking fingers. For a body of angels, it sure looked human—but never quite exactly, and it had a very uncanny resemblance to something much more animal or unknown than a true human.

But it sure freaked me out, and that was enough to make me want to flee, but there wasn't anywhere to go but out or in, and neither way seemed appealing. I ended up choosing the pathway that *didn't* involve going inside a giant body in the end, though I knew I couldn't exactly leave Midori on her own like that. I just needed a quick respite.

Or, I guess, I could figure out a new way to save her. The supports to the Metatron ran every which way, and what had Fex said again? That they were direct links to the Metatron? That sounded like it would be somewhat helpful.

I grabbed one of the strands with all my force, as I wanted to just get it over with already. It hurt as much as I expected it would, electric shocks coursing through my hand, but then came the second tier of pain: the mental sort.

I did not loosen my grip: if anything I tightened it. I did, however, fall to the ground. Far too many things were flashing before my eyes—or really, in my mind, because my eyes were squeezed shut. And nothing I saw could be understood. All I saw were colors and shapes and images, and sometimes I thought I saw something I knew, but a second later I would forget what it had been.

I continued to be bombarded with thoughts that cluttered my brain like static noise, but slowly they began to phase out, and I regained myself again. I wasn't quite melding minds with the Metatron, but I was acutely aware of its—or their, I realized—presence. I could also sense, in a similar way, Fex, Gavreel, and all the other angels out on Eden's outer shell. It wasn't that I could see them, but I knew of their location. There was a sort of input about them, based on their distance and whatever information they were currently feeding the Metatron.

The Metatron itself felt separate from this constant flow of data. I couldn't figure out a single thing about them. I just knew they were there. It was like they were breathing down my neck.

And watching. And listening. And then a word came to my mind. *Detach.*

The word came to me like I had thought it. I knew I hadn't.

*Remove yourself.*

The words were not really said, they were transmitted all at once. I knew I had heard them in the same way I knew I had heard any sound. But I had not *heard* them—I only had the memory of having done so, and the knowledge of what had been said. In this same way, the Metatron's voice was not truly a voice, and thus impossible to properly define.

*Be gone. Disconnect.*

I was unsure how to answer. Was I supposed to think back my answer?

*Go.*

The Metatron did not seem to have any trouble continuing to speak. In fact, their communication was continuous. They seemed rather irate, but this was simple interpretation from the words I heard. There was no tone to their voice.

I could also sense the other separated angels listening in on their voice. Somewhere, still sensed, Fex and Gavreel understood every word. But I doubted their ability to speak to me in the same way the Metatron could.

*You there, girl. Disappear.*

Where was Midori, though? Where was her mind?

"Where is Midori?" I asked aloud, but I doubted the Metatron's ability to hear without having one of their angels acting as a link. So I thought it very hard. *Where was Midori? Where was her mind stored?*

*The girl who is our ideal is attaining perfection. Leave her be.*

But why would I want to do that? I concentrated until my head spun on what I knew—Midori couldn't be alive, and she couldn't be ideal. She was never going to be perfect. She was toxic. She had to leave this place.

I wasn't sure if the Metatron got my message, for they were quiet.

*No,* they said at last.

That couldn't be right. Surely the Metatron would understand why I had to rescue Midori? Surely they had some sort of knowledge that something was wrong with Midori, and that it made perfect sense for me to take her and leave?

*She is our ideal. We have searched for her for a long time. She has the proper genetics. She has the proper attitude. She will become perfect when she becomes us. You may not remove her. We must complete the process. Leave.*

Why did attitude even factor in the decision process? But then again, I did remember the day I first met Midori, and how the angels were intent on testing our reactions to various events. I guess they were looking for someone compliant and even tempered, considering how Midori had reacted. After all, their chosen one was going to become the Metatron—it'd be a real shame if someone with the wrong sort of personality was granted all that power. And I guess when you accounted both for a certain type of personality and a specific sort of genetics, it really did narrow Earth's population down a bit. Though you'd still expect there to be some backups.

I tried to think these thoughts lightly, ever aware of the Metatron's constant listening in. It did not work.

*There is no other. She is our ideal. She will attain perfection. Leave us.*

The Metatron seemed fairly set on their choice, and I decided it might be time to give up on this strategy and try consulting with Fex on the matter. He was the one who had been so certain I could remove Midori anyway. He had to have an idea.

I let go of the support and made my way back to the Metatron's earthly body and entered its mouth.

*Cease and desist.*

I was not as surprised as I should have been that the Metatron's voice had followed me inside its body. I was just hoping our thoughts had disconnected.

*Go away.*

Their voice never seemed urgent, but the speed at which they repeated their words grew ever faster.

*Leave. Go. No. Remove yourself at once.*

As I came to the end of the first tunnel—which must have represented the throat in some way, though the anatomy was obviously very off—I came again to the large hollow room that stood in for some nonexistent organ. But it was no longer really empty; it was full of angels. More and more of them were filtering in from every surface, dragging themselves out from the walls, newly born. They had a certain spark-like glow as they adjusted to their new forms.

I readied my bat. There was no way I could take them all, certainly not while the Metatron continued to pump more and more into the room. But I could try to run past them, at least once I created myself a path.

Angels took a bat to the face in the same way I expected: they just sort of bounced away. Even the less gaseous-looking ones were light and empty. One of them, resembling a two-headed, six-legged white lion, was sent flying backward into the opposite wall, where it melted away.

Soon all of them melted back into the Metatron, which seemed aware of my every move, and knew it was pointless to continue the strategy of overwhelming me with numbers. Quality over quantity. I advanced only a few steps before a great violet shape fell from the ceiling and blocked my path. It rearranged itself into its true form—something I recognized to be a Seraph, though adjusted for the size of the room. The lower half of its body was still stuck to the Metatron, but its blank face, like a masquerade mask, and eight arms leaned over me.

It moved its head from side to side with motions like a snake. And the eyes that coated its body like pores, watched me and blinked. Its whole body was then on fire, one of its flaming paws darting suddenly in an attempt to crush me.

I stopped moving and dropped to the floor, rolling out of harm's way. I swung my bat at one of the Seraph's arms and found it as unresponsive as trying to hit a wall. At least my bat didn't break.

I dodged another assault by the Seraph—its moves were heavy and seemed likely to kill me in one strike, but were very slow. As long as I watched closely, its attacks weren't hard to dodge.

Its head was somewhat high up, but it wasn't exactly unreachable. It swept at me with three of its right arms, and I leapt into the air. Hot air from its burning limbs washed over my face, but I swung almost blindly at the Seraph's face before landing poorly on the ground. Luckily, the Seraph was in too much pain to take advantage of my temporary weakness, and I recovered before it could attempt another attack.

The white shell that protected its face had cracked open. Underneath was just blackness—perhaps it was just a glimpse of the inside of its body.

But at least I had damaged it, even if that damage was currently doing nothing to slow it down. In fact, a couple seconds after I had cracked its face, a new one fell off the ceiling and attached itself over the hole I had created. Right. It was literally going to be impossible to kill any of them, not without first killing the Metatron.

Which I wasn't allowed to do. Right.

I ran forward, skittering between the Seraph's limbs and barely made it through without burning my hair. The Seraph followed me across the room, moving its body along the ceiling like some sort of claw-machine. I ran into the first tunnel I could reach, though I had no idea if it was the one I was supposed to go in. At least the Seraph couldn't fit—

Oh wait. It totally could. It shed some of its size like old skin until it was almost exactly the size of the round tunnel and began to run after me. It propelled itself by its arms, and it grew many more so that it could continue to drag itself along. Its head rolled back, extending its neck so that the head could hide behind the body and out of the reach of my bat. After the head came the torso, and with it the great jaws of the stomach that reached impossibly around it.

The tunnel, too, began to change. I kept running and running, but the tunnel started to shake and quiver and shrink and grow in order to make me trip. I managed to keep my footing, barely, and luckily the Metatron seemed unable or unwilling to close the tunnel completely.

Every time the Seraph came close to me it exhaled a breath of hot air, and soon I was sweating in the sweltering sauna that the tunnel had become. I was out of energy, and I had been for a while now. It was with only the smallest dose of adrenaline that I continued to throw myself forward. I was so dizzy, I needed to almost fall over just to force my body forward.

But the end was in sight, and as I ran and panted my way forward, I became aware that the Seraph had ceased its pursuit. I stopped to look backward, and in my hazy vision I could see it there, waiting. It seemed like there was no reason for it to stop.

As much as I wanted to fall to the floor and catch my breath there, I made myself stumble forward into the next room, where I allowed myself to collapse on the cool floor.

The cool, wet floor. The floor itself was a pale teal, like a swimming pool, and a perfectly clear layer of water about two inches high covered it. As much as I wanted to investigate, I took a couple minutes to lie in the water and just breathe. I closed my eyes and watched the white colors cloud my vision and listened to my heart slow down again.

Only then did I get up, now feeling very sore and tired, and look around. And almost immediately I wished I hadn't, because one more mystery had just been solved.

Namely, where all the human bodies had gone. The room I was standing in was pale blue, and very, very high. I'd say impossibly high almost, because it didn't seem like a room this size could even fit in the Metatron. I could barely make out the top of it.

Along the walls were humans. Dead ones. Anything else would have been very unlikely. They were stuck to the wall in the same way that Midori was, though all of them had clearly been there much longer. The webbing that held them down covered most of their bodies, leaving just the top layer of their bodies exposed. Many of them had their entire heads covered, and just their stomachs or legs exposed.

It was like some sort of spiderweb—though surely there was a greater purpose to it than just a collection. Maybe the Metatron used them to gather information? Or to determine the needed genetics?

Out of morbid curiosity, I walked closer. They all looked so lifelike—the skin was perfectly preserved, and though some of them had had their eyes left open, many looked like they could have been asleep. Just resting in their beds of soft webbing, ready to wake one day, maybe.

It was this that prompted me to reach out and take one of the bodies' pulse—I just had to check. But of course, there was nothing to be felt. The dead are the dead, after all. And though these were all real people, with once real lives and once real places in the world.... Well, the world was a very different place now, and I was sure many of them were happier in death than they had been in life. No one wanted to wake up to the world now. So even if one of them ended up somehow being alive.... Well, I would be a humanitarian and just let them sleep. Surely anyone else would have done the same.

I walked on. There was another tunnel ahead, and while the Metatron was sure to spring something else on me the moment I left the company of the humans, I was going to have to deal with it one way or another. My socks were soaking wet from sweat and from the cool tide pool that was the floor, and I was really, really tired.

Oh well. All this was just another day. Just another problem to solve.

## 29

THE NEXT tunnel was identical to the first, though luckily a great deal shorter. The Metatron again tried to slow me down—shaking the floor and creating so many angels it became hard to move without tripping over one—but I kept my bat steady and my feet light, and I made it through tired but unscratched.

The room I came out into was just as large and hollow as every other one. The Metatron had planned ahead for my arrival, and a pair of fiery Seraphs blocked me from advancing. The two of them were obviously cut from the same mold, and were completely identical. Their actions mirrored each other too, and when I cautiously moved closer to get a better look, I saw they were connected at the back.

Despite having all the odds against me, I still wasn't feeling that worried about my prospects of survival. The angels were all terrifying, and I definitely did not enjoy having to jump around so much to avoid getting burned to a crisp, but I held true to my heart that I always had my last resort of fire.

The Seraphim's attack scope was fairly limited too. All they knew how to do was claw, crush, or burn, and it didn't take too long for me to learn the nuances of each of their attacks. As intimidating as they looked, they honestly weren't much of a threat. I didn't have a chance of harming them either, but at least I was capable of staying alive for a while.

I ducked past another blow by the Seraph on the right. It slammed its entire body on the ground in a move that must have hurt, but did keep me on my toes. Then, rather suddenly, the two Seraphim stopped moving entirely. The one that had fallen on the ground stayed there, while the other had simply frozen in place. Even its fire had ceased movement.

And then, with a fitting sound to match, the two of them were sucked into the ceiling, all at once losing their solid forms and becoming nothing more than a liquid for the Metatron to take back into themself.

The room was now empty, but there was an odd noise coming from somewhere out of sight. I kept my singed bat ready, but as I traversed the endless tunnels, nothing seemed to be moving. At last I came to a dead end, and then I decided I might as well turn completely around and see if I could make it back to Vask before the Metatron got back to trying to kill me.

I managed with relative ease to make my way back to the great hollow room near the entrance (or was it more appropriate to say mouth?) of the Metatron, and from there it was another round tunnel to Vask.

The warning signs began to appear before I could quite grasp what had happened. There was an odd smell, and a growing sound of squeaking and groaning. It was pitch black in the tunnel, but I could feel the floor was changing. It was taking my weight differently, and once I came into the light of the other room, I could see it was black and airy.

But I wasn't looking at the floor when I came out of the end of the tunnel. I was looking straight ahead. Gavreel was still, but Fex's body was moving and changing. His skin had begun to crumble, and black ooze replaced his missing limbs. In fact, he was almost wholly unrecognizable. The edge of the right side of his face was still intact, but now it looked like a mask—his eye was slowly dissolving from one side, melting and changing like wet paper.

Gavreel was still stuck, and didn't seem aware of what was happening. The black matter from Fex had caught onto his legs, and I could see it travel up his veins and spread rapidly.

The whole chamber had turned black, though it was still somehow illuminated. Was Midori safe? She was likely still susceptible to the disease, even if she was inhabiting a human corpse. But first I had to worry about Fex and Gavreel. If I didn't hurry up and kill them, the whole Metatron would collapse. Or was it maybe too late?

I realized I had been standing still for too long when I felt a layer of the black semisolid creep over my shoes. On impulse, I ran past the two dying angels and toward Midori's chamber.

The blackness was starting to spread here too but only gradually. The room of angels was not yet gone, but the first half of the room had already been infected. Many were only halfway turned, but these were small and weak angels, and the front line of them had already become carapaces. Weak ones, sure, but the moment I stepped past the threshold they began to gather and reform in the same way the shadows had back in the void lands—and indeed, they soon took the shape of a great black serpentlike thing. It had legs, tiny ones that were honestly more like thousands of little feet that emerged from the body's ooze for a few seconds whenever it wanted to move. The results were a spectacular bit of animal locomotion and a dizzying impression that the carapace was always moving.

But hey, I still had my bat, and I was in a hurry. I swung with all the force I could muster, aiming right for the head, and the head went flying. It reformed into a smaller ball of darkness, which crawled over to reform with the main body. A new head took its place.

Right. Creatures with no form were no fun. And surely impossible to really kill. I focused more on speed then, but the bat was a pretty hefty weapon to rapidly attack with. Even as I broke the carapace apart, its pieces either reformed or began to gnaw at my feet. I had to knock the ones that came close back into the main body, rather unfortunately.

The blackness of the walls was still moving—twisting and spreading with a sort of square and veinlike movement. In the second I took to scope Midori's safety, the carapace slashed at me with its tail, and I fell to the ground. I reactively grabbed the back of my ankle and found it to be bleeding. It had been cut who knows how deep, but it certainly had been cut. And it hurt like hell. I probably wasn't going to be able to stand up on my own, and certainly not walk.

The carapace circled me. From its depths a single yellow eye emerged to stare me down. And what seemed like minutes later, a large mouth that appeared to extend forever emerged too. Was it honestly going to eat me? How long did it take to suffocate again? A minute?

That seemed like far too long of a time to suffer. I dug in my pocket for my lighter, and lit a flame after a few frantic tries. The carapace backed off right away, aware of fire's potential damage. I still needed to kill it, but it had moved a couple feet back and was out of my floor-bound reach.

I threw the lighter. The flame went out as it fell, which probably shouldn't have been as much of a surprise as it was. I had spares, tons of them, so I dug another one out and crawled across the floor to try and get close enough to the carapace to burn it.

The carapace was still worried about the flame of my lighter, and it simply moved back a little bit more. Frustrated and still losing a lot of blood, I decided enough was enough, and I lit the floor on fire.

As someone currently bound to the floor, this was not a good or particularly clever move. Everything began to burn. The carapace disintegrated, but now I had the very real risk of burning to death. I crawled to the nearest not-on-fire section of wall and very uneasily got up on my one good foot. My other foot could not handle me putting any weight on it at all, and I hopped across the floor the best I could until I collapsed in front of Midori.

Her little raised platform was not on fire, and she had also successfully escaped risk of infection. But she was still unconscious. I traced the back of her head with my hands, and found it freed from the Metatron. But she was still not breathing—though this may have just been because she was an angel. Her body was warm enough.

I had no way to carry her out, though. In fact, if anything I would need her to help carry me out. But as the room burned behind us, she sat there, unmoving as a doll.

"This is ridiculous!" I said finally, getting very tired of having to do everything around here. I dug yet another lighter out of my pocket and lit it in front of her face.

It worked like smelling salts. Her eyes snapped open, and her pupils contracted at the sight of the fire. Then she blew it out.

"I'm trying to attain oneness here! What are you doing, Erika— trying to burn me to death?" Her voice was higher pitched than I remembered but still very welcome. She then looked around at the room behind us. "Oh, so you are. What exactly is going on here? Why are you in Eden?"

"To save you! From… yourself I guess. Look, you need to get out of here."

"The Metatron explained everything. I will save everything if I just focus hard enough. You need to get out, though—this place certainly isn't safe for you! I need to get back to sleep." She leaned back and banged her head against the wall. "What?"

Was it possible she didn't actually know? That she had forgotten she was an angel? Surely that sort of thing was impossible. But she definitely didn't seem to understand how dire our situation was.

"The Metatron is deteriorating from illness. We have to get out before they turn into a carapace."

"How did you get here? Or even find Eden? I'm supposed to be the chosen one...."

"I had Fex bring me here. Come on. We have to hurry." I couldn't help her to her feet, but I motioned for her to get up, and she did so. "I can't really walk anymore. Can you please help?"

"Of course." She still seemed rather unhappy at my presence, but she lifted me and let me lean on her shoulder. She was frowning all the while.

The floor was mostly burning in patches, and with a bit of painful hopping, we made our way to the "not yet but soon to be on fire" chamber where Fex and Gavreel were. But they were no longer stuck. Fex was mostly gone, writhing on the floor. Gavreel seemed too weak to really flee, but had backed as far away as he could.

"How could you let this happen?" yelled Gavreel as he caught sight of us. He looked particularly angry, especially since his true form was starting to leak past his human shape—and he had the sharp teeth to match.

"At least I got Midori." I tried to motion to her, but of course she was still holding me up. She had gone oddly blank as she took in the state of the other two angels and did not respond to my comment.

"Yeah, but that's rather pointless because you evidently forgot to off the *already infected* one!" I wasn't really sure what Fex was or what he was doing at this point, but he certainly was oozing a disgusting mush of goo from his body.

"I'm sorry you two got stuck standing still for like an hour. Obviously I wasn't going to wait around and watch."

"Waiting is—*was*—your job! If you had some patience, you might have had the sense to not let any of this happen. What were you doing anyway? We knew you, you know. We knew you were communing with the Metatron. So were we, in fact. Did you honestly scamper the whole way outside just to uselessly get information we could have told you?"

"You were just standing there—and, like, come on, multitasking is a virtue."

"It's not," Gavreel yelled. He seemed reluctant to do anything else. "Now finish Fex. And take the other girl's place, for our sake!"

"She's not taking my place. I earned that. I'm special," Midori said. She pointed weakly between us. "Erika isn't. There's specific guidelines and rules. She just wouldn't work. Only me."

"You're dead," said Gavreel. Midori didn't seem to interpret his words literally, however, and just looked offended. "Now do it already!" He pointed harshly to me.

I had dropped my bat in the fire room. But I always had more lighters. I motioned for Midori to lower me down, and she dropped me to the floor. I inched over to Fex and cautiously lit him on fire—his body was not catching, however, and I eventually found that only the fleshy parts of him were willing to burn. But it did make him stop thrashing about.

"Sorry," I said quietly, in case he was able to hear it. I mean, it wasn't like he had to die right away. He was probably going to live through the burning for a good couple minutes as long as he kept to his human shape.

There was a moment of silence as Fex combusted. Gavreel then let out a groan. "Hurry up and replace her!" He gestured angrily toward Midori, who backed off and looked ready to run back to her chamber.

"Midori, wait." She had yet to help me up, but I moved toward her feet and sat there. "You can't fuse with the Metatron. You don't fit."

"Fit? It was these two"—she gestured to the still burning Fex and the huddled over Gavreel—"who came to get me in the first place! And put me here! And they said that I was special, and then *they* said it too, in a voice like a million people, whispering in my ears. I was born for this."

"You're dead. Literally." I suppressed a very inappropriately timed laugh at how cliché this was sounding. But it was reality, I guess. "You've been dead the whole time. You'll cause more harm than good if the Metatron wastes all their energy on trying to fuse with you."

"What? That's outrageous!" she said. "You just want to be more than I am. You're jealous, and you don't want to be alone again either."

"No. I do think you're the best match for this. I really do. But I think you *were* the best—and now you're just an angel in the body of the best match for the Metatron, and you're very confused about it. Please pick me up before my feet catch fire."

She grumbled, and she looked down at her hands, and I had to wonder if she'd known all along. But she picked me up and rested me on her shoulder anyway.

"So you're going to do it? You're going to become the Metatron?" She had accepted defeat far quicker than I think I would have if I were in her shoes.

"No. I'd hate for that to happen. Besides, if I did that you'd be stuck out here alone again."

"So where are we going?"

"Out. This whole place is going down in a few minutes. Might as well start walking now before it's too late."

She smiled again, looking uneasy and unwell, and she wasn't really breathing. But her body was giving off heat, and when she caught my eye both of our smiles widened a bit more. I don't think either of us was really that angry at the other after all.

"Sounds like a plan."

I really had missed her.

# 30

"I HAVE no idea what you did to your ankle."

It was maybe ten minutes later, and we were outside. Though the narrow inner halls of the Metatron made it difficult for Midori to properly support me, that struggle was soon alleviated by the seeming collapse of the white shell that normally protected the Metatron. The walls were thin enough that we could walk right through them like cobweb, and we settled down in a nearby field.

"Didn't you stuff spiderweb into the last cut I had? That ended up healing fine." My ankle had already swelled up, and there seemed to be no way for me to hold it that didn't cause me to cringe.

"Sometimes the fastest way to heal from something is to believe you already have," Midori said. Then she paused. "But no prayer or crystal is going to fix this. There's a hospital in town and hopefully not all of the painkillers have expired. We can also grab you a cast, a crutch, a wheelchair—whatever you need."

She moved to pick me up, but I resisted her and stayed on the ground. She gave up right away and settled down next to me.

"What's up?"

"I'm not leaving here right now."

"Your foot is inflamed. You need some relief medication and proper bandaging to prevent infection."

"No. That can come later. Right now I need to fix this."

"Waiting?"

"Technically. Why don't we use this time wisely? Please, I want to know about you."

"I was a Seraph. And I am disgraced," she said heavily.

"Fex figured as much." I sighed. Was he really dead? It hadn't quite sunk in yet. I guess I was still clinging to the possibility that he, being a crazy supernatural slash extraterrestrial slash whatever, somehow had evaded death.

"When we Seraphim are born, we are blessed with an extraordinary amount of power from the Metatron. We can't eat or sleep, and thus have no way to create or preserve energy for ourselves. Instead the Metatron grants us a very finite amount. We use it not only to survive being temporarily separate from the Metatron, but also for any other problems we have to face—shape-shifting, for example, requires an immense amount of pure energy. We have to account for the transfer of mass and various whatevers that make up our chosen form."

"Where does the Metatron get their energy from, then?"

"The other lesser angels feed us. Many live purely for the purpose of feeding us. Should I stop referring to the Metatron as 'us'? It is proper, but it seems to be confusing you. We—the angels we—carry over any consumable matter to the Metatron, which they then absorb over however long. It's a slow process, so the Metatron requires a great deal of food to keep their energy levels high."

"Right. Back to your story. What does it mean to be disgraced? Fex refused to tell me."

Midori looked down. "I don't know. I can't remember."

"Is this one of those 'can't or won't' scenarios?"

"I mean it entirely. I can't remember what I did. The Metatron's consciousness is a singular one, and is built from the thoughts that we retrieve for it. I was one of the scouts. We were sent to Earth to essentially see what we could see—the Metatron was very weak at this point, and could only provide energy for maybe ten of us, and even that left them struggling and on the verge of death. But they had to do it. It was common for scouts to be disgraced, and they had to send as many as they could muster."

"Is this from space? You're from space, right? Like from another planet?"

"No. Not really, I think," she said slowly. "Anyway, one day I was depositing my mind back with the Metatron, and that was that—I never got my memories back. Normally, you see, the Metatron will basically copy our thoughts and return them so that we can further use them to survive. But I simply came to with nothing more than my basic inborn knowledge of what I was and the realization that I was disgraced. I can't even recall my time scouting. I'm just working off that assumption."

"And so you just killed a girl and took her place?"

"Not at first. The Metatron doesn't reabsorb us once we're disgraced. We're too corrupt for them. Instead they leave us to run out of energy and die. There are rehabilitation programs. Simple work that, if you prove yourself worthy enough, will earn you the right to move up the ranks until at last the Metatron will welcome you back to them. I didn't bother with this. I couldn't stand such lowly work. I killed Midori when I began to run low on energy. I knew she was a proper genetic match for the Metatron the moment I possessed her body—and I considered that a boon. It made it a lot easier to puppet her limbs around."

"Surely that isn't enough to survive on, though?"

"It's not. I didn't have enough to do anything special after that. I couldn't exactly shape-shift when I was possessing a body anyway, but then I used up all my spare energy when I had to fight off Kasos. She was going to kill you, and there was nothing else I could do. I've been running on empty for a long time now, and you know what? I'm scared of death. I don't want to die alone. That's why I'm doing this. That's why I've been so desperate—I thought that by pretending to be just a regular human and then striving to perfection, the Metatron would accidentally reabsorb me into themselves. Then we'd continue to look for a suitable human. It'd be fast and cause no harm. I didn't realize that process for perfection and reabsorption were so different."

I didn't have anything more to ask her about her past. But of course, the pressing matter of the future was still at hand.

"What are we supposed to do now?"

"Well, the Metatron's first and primary purpose is homeostasis, like with every living thing. All the angels are swarming back to help fight the infection, as well as replace damaged tissue with their own selves. They're in a full shutdown mode, and they won't be searching for a human cure until the current crisis is resolved."

"But isn't finding another human the only thing that will let them refresh themselves and actually remove the disease?"

"It's the ultimate, but brute force works too. This function is expected to only kick in for much minor infections. They weren't expecting for it to reach so far in or spread so fast. But their basic survival instincts don't differentiate these situations so well, and it comes down to whatever seems most pressing—and that's removing the pain."

"That doesn't sound too smart."

"Everyone makes bad decisions, Erika. We just want to live. Though...," said Midori with a quality of voice that suggested a sudden transition. "That reminds me. I want to apologize for how I've been acting. I don't want to give you the impression that I'm mad at you, or hate you. It's quite the opposite. I'm just... stressed."

"Please, it's me that should be apologizing. I've been remarkably rude to you too. You weren't really around to hear me say any of it—or think it, actually—but I think I've been holding you in a rather bitter part of my heart after you left. So I guess I don't quite have a reason to apologize, but I'd like to do it anyway. After all, you don't really need to say you're sorry either."

"I don't?"

"It's no skin off my back that you got a little grouchy. You were scared and you were dying, and you got a little irate as it started to go to your head. I've acted worse in my life. Not to spare the last few days—just a couple hours ago I was having a full-out emotional attack or whatever I'm supposed to call it. And before that I evidently hallucinated a whole slew of things. I think I might be crazy."

"You don't need to apologize for that. It's not your fault. And I mean, you're admitting it to me right now. Isn't admitting you have a problem the first step to solving it? I'm sure you'll figure yourself out one way or another, and I'll be standing beside you the whole time through. So don't feel so bad."

"Well, you shouldn't feel so bad about anything you've done either."

"Again, same to you."

"So I guess we're both agreeing... that we shouldn't hold ourselves so responsible?"

"I mean sometimes our problems are definitely our faults. But some things are innate and others can't be helped, so yeah, that's about right." The best way I could describe Midori's face was "welling up with emotion." It was an odd face on her, but not one particularly terrible. It just made me mimic her. "So I guess what I'm saying is this: I'm responsible for some of my problems, but not all, and you're saying that I shouldn't beat myself up about it. Right. Okay. And the same to you."

"We should move on."

"But to where? If the Metatron succumbs to their illness, the void lands will spread all over the planet. We will be unable to live anywhere."

That was a problem, wasn't it? "Can't you use your angel sense to, like, sniff out another human? I'm not above tricking someone into fusing with the Metatron, you know."

"That seems a bit morally low."

"I mean, if I'm doing it for your sake, it's still okay, right?"

"Uh... not morally. Sort of iffy. But I agree with you—I would much rather live with that on my conscience than be without you. The only problem is that I have no way to sense humans. We'd have to hope one or two of them are just nearby, which is a mix of incredible odds and statistically likely factors. The void is growing, and anyone still alive would be pushed by its spread in this direction."

"Oh man, I'm just realizing—if the void lands started around the opposite of here, that's like, southern Asia right? So everyone there has to be dead. I mean, there's a whole ocean in the way."

Midori expressed her thoughts through a shaky hand gesture that conveyed her mixed feelings. "We're not good with water. I can't say for certain anything much. You are correct in that we arrived there first. But I'd actually doubt that the carapaces even reached the islands. It's hard enough to convince an angel to cross a large body of water, and we're in possession of all our knowledge about the potential benefits."

"Then how did the disease even reach us here?"

"The same way it starts, I'd guess. We are very complex and yet very simple organisms. The Metatron, when they first decided to send out their angels and begin the renewal process, was not yet at risk of the disease. But we knew of it, and thus we were working in anticipation. The disease normally is born at the same time the Metatron is preparing to fight it, as they create a massive amount of angels, all at once, the risk of one of them being born wrong and infected grows higher and higher. If the Metatron has plenty of energy, infected angels are immediately culled. But one or more easily end up slipping past, and eventually succumb to their illness and become carapaces."

I had turned around at some point in her explanation—or really multiple points. I wasn't entirely happy with all this waiting around. Far off, but less so than before, the void was advancing and swirling like the living storm it was.

"Do you think I could just burn the void lands?"

"You'd burn everything underneath it too. And I'm not even sure that'd work."

"I don't know. When doesn't it?"

She paused. "Rarely. But it's still not a good idea."

"Yeah, yeah. Burning the world down might not be a good plan, whatever. But wow, we're really running through our options, huh? What's next? Do you think if you finished killing the Metatron, all the carapaces and angels would die?"

"Yes, but I'd die too, being an angel and all."

"Oh yeah. I still haven't committed that to memory. Ah, what else, then? You know, last time I was in the void lands, everything around me turned into a really cool dragon. What if I did that again but—wait for it—*lit it on fire!*"

"Fire is still never going to be a universal solution. That'd have the same effect as just regularly burning the void."

"Okay, well I'm out of ideas. And I'm not going to settle for waiting it out."

"Trust me, I don't want to either. I still have a weak biological link to the Metatron. I can sense the pain we are in. But I think right now the best we can do is just get you some pain killers and a crutch."

"But then what are we going to do after that?"

"I'm not exactly blessed with a creative mind. I share one with many others, and even my more apparent uniqueness is a side effect of inhabiting the mind of this dead girl. So I guess I'm waiting on you."

"What is your real name, then, if Midori is just your vessel?"

"I don't remember. It was removed from my knowledge along with the rest of me," she said, looking worried. "But! I believe it started with a T."

"All right, then. We can get going. But we're jogging really fast. Running, even."

"We can't do that in your condition."

"Then walk. Walk really, really fast."

A COUPLE pills, some painful lotion, and a couple poorly wrapped bandages later, we were back in the field, and I wasn't feeling nearly as woozy as I had expected to.

"I could still fall asleep at any moment," I warned.

"No way! No way." Midori giggled. "That's not possible."

"Modern medicine is amazing." I was not against joking around with her some more, but rather unfortunately returning to the field had ruined my mood for it. When we had left, Eden had been the worse for wear, with its white walls thinning. Now they were almost fully gone, and only the very top layer remained. Otherwise they were translucent, revealing the increasingly damaged body of the Metatron.

"What are you going to do?"

"I guess I'm going to run in there again."

"Is that really going to work?"

"I mean, there's more to the plan than just running in. There really isn't much choice in the matter about what I have to do."

"You're not going to go out there and try to fuse with the Metatron, right? You said you didn't want to. You hate angels."

"I don't know what I think. The hatred is still there, but I don't think it matters anymore. I can't trust myself, okay? That's been proven. I know who I am, and I know what I think, but it's like I've lost a veil of context. I can't make myself step back and reevaluate. I can only do things that I think I should do."

"You truly want to help us?"

"God, I don't know." I ran my fingers through my hair. "I've lost my mind, remember?"

"Yes. You'll be fine."

I exhaled sharply. "I was just thinking—oh, it sounds terrible. But what if I just did it for like, a minute? Just gave a little bit of myself away. Just enough for the Metatron to reboot themself."

"For the Metatron to refresh, they need all of you—mind and body."

"Okay, so just as little as I can give. But surely it'll help them fight off the infection, and then they can get back to looking for another human."

"You'll lose too much of everything."

"So, yeah, I was also thinking—you can't properly fuse with the Metatron because you share the same mind. But you're keeping the genetic flesh it needs. So what if we did it together? Maybe there'll be enough whatever to cure the Metatron."

"They don't let two people do it at once."

"Let's give it a shot. We have nothing else to do, or lose, for that matter."

"Our lives."

"Yeah, okay, besides that."

"I think our lives being at stake is a pretty notable risk, even if it's the only one."

"Yeah, but come on! Someone has to save the world or whatever. And sadly, I don't see anyone else stepping up. We'll be fine, though. Watch each other's backs. Live."

"If you're so confident...."

"I'm not *really*, but I am getting pretty good at faking it."

## 31

It was a lot easier to approach the Metatron the second time. The angels that normally held a fierce guard were too busy fighting off the disease that had taken over the great creature, and though some of them turned to stare, none made a move to attack.

"Maybe we should turn back, and real quick look for a weapon," I suggested. I still had my lighters, and while I guessed I always could burn everything to the ground, it would make escape a lot harder.

"There's not enough time for that!" Midori urged, though she looked utterly terrified. She was clinging to my arm while still supporting my weight, and carefully watching her step.

"Wouldn't it be nice to have some sort of backup, though? Like a gun or a bat or even like a broken glass bottle."

"Oh please! You know we can't harm the Metatron," Midori said, sounding righteously irritated at my suggestion. "They've suffered enough."

"I'm just saying."

The Metatron's body had actually shifted slightly since we left, and their long, almost human-shaped form had turned slightly on their side. Their handlike limbs had changed too and no longer provided easy access to the mouthlike aperture. Midori boosted me up, and then I pulled her up in turn.

"It smells putrid," she said sadly, and I guess that meant more to her than it did to me, because I couldn't smell a thing. "I've never seen them so ill."

The inside hadn't really changed as far as I could tell. Midori seemed heavily influenced by it, though, and sometimes she'd sigh or make little squeaky noises that I took to mean she was upset.

Only when we came to a room that was lit could I take in the damage: giant black lumps grew out of the walls, and things were definitely moving just below the surface of the floor—odd shapes that pulsated and looked sort of like large dogs under fleshy blankets.

With an athletic grace that I was unable to match, Midori leapt around them and the swollen veins that ran in every which way. After a much too long five minutes' worth of hesitation and poor jump planning, I made it to the other side and we set out for Vask.

"Everything already seems dead." I traced the walls with my hands, and they seemed much softer than before, and full of odd bumps and bruises. They reminded me of an open sore, and were indeed slightly wet to the touch. If I didn't need to feel the walls to navigate, I would definitely have kept my distance.

The heat began to seep in long before we came to Vask, and along with it came smoke. Midori paid little mind to it, though she did squint her eyes. I couldn't take more than a minute of breathing the heavy air, and I was forced to crawl. The air wasn't much better near the floor, however, and I had to stop to cough fairly often.

"You're slowing down," Midori said, but she said it with concern and wrapped her shawl around my face. It didn't really do much to block the smoke, but I appreciated the effort.

With the shawl still over my head, I didn't know we had reached the exit until I bumped into Midori's legs. I peeked through the fabric, and was utterly unsurprised at the level of damage the chamber had sustained. Fex lay on the floor, half melted and unmoving. Gavreel was almost entirely fused with the wall, and likewise had become very still. I still had to keep to the ground, but even if I could, I wouldn't have wanted to investigate them any further.

From there it was a short crawl to the room Midori had been in, which was luckily not on fire any longer but had been flooded. I stood up and waded across a knee-high pond of hot, yellowish liquid. It was thick, heavy, and not entirely translucent.

I took a moment to wipe it off my pants before climbing up to the platform, but regretted it immediately as some came off on my hands in disgusting goops.

"Shit. Please tell me this isn't pus because I feel like I might throw up."

"It's not, technically," Midori offered. "Very different biology at play here. But similar, I suppose. It certainly put out the fire."

"Ugh." I wrinkled my nose, but I couldn't really smell a thing. "Let's just become one with the terrible single-souled entity that has destroyed the world and get out of here."

"This isn't going to work," said Midori, but she followed suit as I knelt in front of the wall. I placed a hand lightly against it, before slowly increasing pressure. The wall didn't budge, not even a little bit.

"It's a state of mind." Midori sighed. She motioned for me to follow as she leaned forward and placed her head against the wall. "A deus ex machina." She closed her eyes as she spoke.

"You're using that phrase wrong."

"A machina ex deus, then."

"Still not right, and honestly I'm quite worried by whatever you're possibly trying to tell me. How am I supposed to enter some mystical state of mind with you worrying me like this?"

"They don't want two of us. They won't let us in."

"What, you're linked with the Metatron right now?"

"It's not like I can ever really stop. But can't you feel it? The vibrations in the wall? Can't you hear their voice?"

"I'm having difficulty concentrating."

"Oh, you don't have to concentrate. You just have to think." She placed her hand on my back and began to press lightly. "I'm sorry about this."

And she pushed me through the wall.

I WAS not entirely gone, nor was my existence suddenly one with the mind, as Midori had promised. I could still wiggle my toes on my right foot, and for some reason I found the sensation to be the most rewarding out of everything I was capable of, which wasn't much. Everything was rather hazy and closer to black than anything else. But it wasn't really that it was dark—it was more that my eyes had stopped working.

I couldn't tell if I could hear or not, because nothing was making a sound and I was entirely unable to open my mouth to make some myself. The only sensation I had was that of my own self, and my toes, which were still outside the wall.

It was awfully dark. I tried to retreat into my mind, as I figured I was supposed to, but something about this haze was making it hard for me to think. It really tore at my edges to exist in this place, immobile and confused.

There was an odd growing sensation along the tips of my unmoving fingertips, and it spread throughout my veins and nerves. I was acutely aware of it too. It wasn't just a shiver of skin, but of everything deeper than that. And then I looked down on myself and realized I had ceased to have a body. I was still aware, however, that I had a corporeal body. I just couldn't locate it.

This was bad. I still knew who I was, but this fog was making my previous state of mind look clear by comparison. If I lost myself in here, I'd be gone for good. I tried again to focus with all my mind on what had to be done, and I began to get a sort of sense of a voice. Maybe the Metatron's. Maybe not. But the words were so muffled, I only gathered the bare bones of thought.

*W*, the voice said. *L, K, M.*

Was that supposed to mean something? The voice's plea was so desperate and so quiet, I was struck with a sudden thought that caught fire through my mind like nothing else: this was pathetic. Absolutely weak. Why was I immobilized? I was the only one with power here. After all, I was the one who set the Metatron on fire. I was the one who brought the disease inside them. I was the only important factor in all of this, and all these angels, these angels of fire and eyes, they were pathetic.

And I was painfully stronger than them.

I began to run. I was able to do so quite easily, and the fog around me catered to my demands, clearing to reveal a space that was indeed dark, but the sort of dark you'd expect to find inside of a tree. And there, all around me and watching in a circle, were millions of faces and bodies and souls, the members of the Metatron. Some were dying, some were dead, and some were healthy. And the living looked at me with such fear that I simply had to laugh at them.

"You need me to live. I don't need you," I reminded them. But I was going to be true to myself and to Midori. I gave the Metatron my mind, some parts of it that I maybe never used, or never wanted to, and when all was said and done, I didn't feel any different. I wasn't even sure if I had done anything. All I had done was think, *Okay, I'm giving the worst parts of my mind to the Metatron.* Surely I didn't have to lose my conscious mind in the process?

I breathed for a moment, which was a feat considering I didn't actually need to. And then I thought for a moment. I tried my memories—boring ones at first, and then I stepped it up with the best of the best. The fire that had killed my parents. Funerals, both theirs and mine. The days I had spent living on my own, watching. But nothing was taken. And then I just tried anything I could. Algebra. Australian history. The plots of various mediocre books. Anything I knew—but still, nothing.

The Metatron was still trembling at my presence. No time had likely passed since I had last spoken. In fact, based on how this place worked, I had probably already spoken the moment I arrived here. There was no time in a lost mind.

I sighed, which was another task technically unneeded in this realm of existence. "What do you want from me?"

The Metatron leapt to life all at once. I did not have a real sense of many voices speaking at once, though many voices surely were. Instead there were simply the words, and maybe, an unimpressive voice.

*Lose yourself. You are not unworthy to us. We will do our best with you.*

"I will burn you," I reminded them. "I will turn you into nothing more than ash, and that ash will scatter into the wind and become nothing more than a mild irritant in my throat." As I spoke I summoned flames to my fingers until I was wreathed in them like a halo of pure energy.

*Lose yourself. We will take you away.*

Can a mind's confidence grow? They sure seemed to be getting bolder despite my threats. "Take me away? Don't be ridiculous. You will writhe before my feet hours before I'm done with you."

*Then lose yourself. We will free you. You may rest again.*

"I don't want to rest. You are the one who needs to lose yourself."

*No. You can lose yourself. You can leave. We will use you to the best of our ability. Let us handle it.*

It was such an alarming thought that it seemed to echo through my body. The fire faded. The room grew darker. And I was suddenly aware of how very alone and small I was. I was inside a mind, but it was nothing like mine. There were people here. And I was starting to think how maybe, perhaps, I wouldn't mind letting someone else do the work for me.

I nodded, and then I thought it, and then I spoke it—

"Okay."

A final word of acceptance. Because I was not a girl made of flame. I was a girl who wished to be fire—to burn and destroy and live without mercy or thought. But the world was full of thought, and I was full of thoughts, and maybe it was time I took a break from pretending I was responsible. Maybe it was time I let the world fix itself, and let things run their course. And maybe it was time I let myself rest, if only for a little while.

## 32

I LEAPT into the air, though there was no true air in the Metatron, nor was there any true anything, and from the air I did a flip, and I dove out into the realish world again.

That was putting everything in the simplest of terms, of course. There was a lot more to it than that. A lot more indescribable feelings and motions and happenings that tended to go along with phasing through semisolid matter and disconnecting from a grand supersoul.

Either way, I flew out of the wall like a bullet. And in my flight of maybe half a second, I was dimly aware that I had lost some part of my body. Then by the time I had landed, it was back again. I found my leg was better too.

Midori moved my head to her lap and cradled it in her hands while I waited for the dizziness to settle.

"Mido—am I missing any limbs?" It didn't feel like it, but I was still too dazed to be sure.

"Yes. But we replaced them for you. Do not fear. We just needed the flesh donation."

"Stop using 'we' as a singular pronoun. Shit, you're not, actually. Okay, please just stop using it. It's confusing. Just 'I,' please…." I was still too tired to really mind what I was saying.

"You talk a lot for someone who just lost a lot of yourself. But… it seems to have worked."

My vision was clearing, so I sat up and shook off the clouds of black that still pulsated in my vision. "So wait, what are my new limbs, then?" I looked my arms over. They seemed identical, and already the memory of having lost them was fading.

"The same matter as the angels. We—they needed human flesh, but it's not like they can't produce their own alternatives fairly easily. So it's not very hard to just create replacement limbs. It's not like they'd want to leave you high and dry and with minor difficulty living."

"Does this mean anything?"

"What, like you're an angel now? Obviously not. Your new limbs are not human, but unless you actually examine them at a molecular level, you won't be able to tell the difference. And they are susceptible to the infection, but they can't become carapaces since they lack minds."

"About my mind...."

"I don't know." She sighed. "I can pretty much tell you everything I know, and I still wouldn't be able to satisfy you. I have no way of knowing what was removed from you. I can see your limbs have changed, but I can't see your mind."

"And neither do I."

She shrugged. "Well, it's done now. The Metatron are already fixing themselves. It's going to be a difficult task, considering how little you gave up and how unsuited your genes are to them. But they're doing what they can."

"What do we do now?"

"Go outside."

There was a rumbling just then, and we both slid as the floor tilted. There was an aesthetic change in the Metatron, and I could feel the energy in the walls—they were healing. Almost on instinct Midori and I began to run with little regard for anything. We dashed right past the chamber that held Fex and Gavreel, and out of the corner of my eye, I swore they were both alive. But at once I found myself feeling very little about the situation that was their lives, and I continued running without another thought of them.

There was something in my mind now, a greater sense. Before I had heard the voice of the Metatron—but now, I did not. I just knew the voice. There were no words, anymore. Just feelings. A side effect, I suppose, of what I had given up.

By the time we had made it out, we were both exhausted. The fingerlike appendages had moved again, and with a series of poorly planned and fairly dangerous jumps we made it to the ground and fled through the ever-thinning walls of silk that coated the Metatron.

We didn't stop running until we were far away, out on a grassy knoll and looking down at the Metatron. They almost looked like some sort of maggot—a dark shape, lying in the folds of rotting white, helplessly stuck on the ground. On the other side, the darkness loomed.

"Will they be okay?" Angels from all over were still heading to protect the Metatron, and no matter where I looked there was movement. Midori seemed caught up in it too—she stared restlessly at the rivers of angels, perhaps wishing to join their numbers.

"Of course. The Metatron will not die. I simply won't stand for that."

"So what do we do?"

She looked at me and sighed, but it wasn't really a fed up sort of sigh, much more an affectionate one. "Nothing, Erika. The Metatron will care for themself."

"So what'll they do?" I still wasn't used to the idea of waiting and watching. I couldn't help but feel like I was supposed to have a greater part in all this: like ride an angel into battle and wield a shining sword. Not sit on a hill, among flowers.

"Fight. Sort of. You lost some mass. A little goes a long way. And some mind—again, a little goes a hell of a long way. The Metatron will use their new boon of energy to fight off the infection, and while they will probably not recover, it will certainly be progress."

Down below, far away enough that it looked like nothing more than a delusion, the Metatron was stirring. And snapping. And clacking and clicking and writhing and growing, and slowly, and carefully, they unfolded their body.

"So they'll fail? Will I have to lose another part of myself again, after which they'll fight and lose again, thus creating a cycle of loss? Was there any point to this at all?"

I couldn't be sure if the Metatron was bipedal or quadrupedal, but they seemed to have a lot of limbs. Arms, it appeared, and many of them. But they were not yet standing up, just shaking and scratching at their indigo skin.

"Don't be ridiculous. They won't and can't fail. They'll fight the infection as long as they can, and build up immunity. It won't be a cure-all. Maybe they'll just leave and sleep for a couple hundred years. Or maybe there's still another human out there, and they'll use them." Midori eyed me warily for a second. I had a feeling, like I usually did, that she knew more than she was letting on. "They know you've lost enough already."

But I didn't feel like I had lost anything. In fact, I felt quite content. Ironically, I couldn't remember the last time I had felt so at ease. There was still the nagging feeling I should be doing something, but it wasn't strong enough to drive me to action. As a matter of fact, I really only seemed to care about the ultimate fate of these things by principle alone, with very little having to do with my personal feelings. Was that what I had lost? My empathy? I could sense the Metatron in my veins, but something in my mind kept me disinterested. It was no longer a surreal existence, that angel soul. It was a new normality.

"I don't know. I bet I could go another round with the Metatron if they ever need me again."

"And again, and again, and again—I wouldn't let you, you know. You could keep going, and they could keep removing more and more of you, and you wouldn't mind a day. But as someone who is not you, I'd notice, and I doubt I'd care for the changes very much."

"So they decided to remove any malice? Figures, I guess." I cycled idly through my memories, trying to notice any gaps. But I couldn't. Everything seemed in order. I guess that was just another side effect of the process. I had an impression something was off with my memories, but I was unable to place what.

Down below, the Metatron peeled off its skin, shedding layer after layer until there was a simple shape of light. And then—arms and fingers and hands and some elbows, but mostly just arms. And then from its back, blossoming like flowers, wings erupted from the top section of its body. There were twelve pairs total, placed on the long serpentine body like segments of a spine. The hands quieted their movements. The body settled. The light looked like fur, and from every gap there were eyes, and while the body never stopped moving, it began to cycle from arms to eyes to light, over and over again.

But the wings stayed the same.

"They... look much stronger than I would have thought possible," said Midori, and she looked at me with great worry. I didn't share her concern. I was doing fine. Keeping and restoring the health of the Metatron had been my duty, after all.

It began to move—how, I do not know. But it was on its way, and I suppose it could have been flying. On the other side, the darkness was doing something, but it was too dark to discern what. And while all this was very odd to me, it was all at once also very familiar, and I realized

I didn't really care that much about it. They were going to fight. All right. What next.

Midori still seemed stuck on the Metatron, still longing. Her beautiful hair caught the wind in a way that deserved some sort of poetry to be written about it.

"What are you going to do when all this is over? Return?" I asked.

"Die."

"Are you, honestly?"

"In a long number of years. I have enough energy to sustain me for that long."

"Oh. In that case, me too."

"I'm sorry, by the way, for pushing you into the Metatron."

"Oh, you were right, though. They wouldn't take two of us at once. I don't mind."

"No really, I'm sorry." She seemed much more emotional than I was about it.

"Honestly, I'm thankful." I smiled despite myself, which felt like an inappropriate response. But Midori smiled back. And then I laughed, and then she laughed, and neither of us was sure what we were doing or why. But we were laughing and crying and smiling, and I fell back on the ground and held my stomach and looked at the sky, still covered in angels. And Midori fell down as well, but she misaimed and fell on my face, and we both laughed about that for ages.

And then I got up again, and I looked absentmindedly at the battle behind me, but I was not at all invested in it. I was really looking at Midori, and as she sat on her knees, I leaned over and kissed her forehead, and we laughed about it, and then I kissed her on the lips and neither of us could laugh about it, even if we tried very, very hard.

We fell over on the grass yet again, and I felt like I couldn't breathe. My ribs ached and my knuckles creaked. And far off, something was burning and something was growling.

Above us, the angels continued to fly. The sky was clear and chilly, and my eyes were watering. But then again, all of that, everything in the world, may have just been a result of our laughter. I curled up against Midori and held her in my arms, the grass bending beneath our bodies and nothing in the sky paying us any mind.

I kissed her again.

"Funny," she said. "Very truly funny." But she meant it in the way of peculiar, not humorous. I couldn't be sure what she was talking of—the Metatron or us?

We paused again. Or rather, I did.

"Like a movie."

Our laughter had never quite ceased, and I don't suppose it ever could. The only thing that could happen would be the intervals spacing out over hours and days and weeks. But it stopped there, and it paused as I did.

"What's a movie?" I had to ask.

And Midori paused too.

Friend to dogs, writer, cult fiend, and part-time wage slave to the illuminati, A. M. BLAUSHILD has an understandable lack of free time. With an attitude best described as "naively cheerful," A. M. has only recently been thrust toward the adult world, and her peaceful optimism is still going strong. Subsiding on possibly the world's worst diet, A. M. is driven to write more than most humans should—she has been accused more than once of being a robot. Though she desperately tries to write a diverse portfolio of subjects, but angels tend to get tangled in there fairly often. She seems to have some sort of weird thing for cults as well, and boy, nothing really pumps her up like a good old-fashioned angel cult. When she isn't off adding to her manuscript collection, A. M. enjoys long walks in the pitch black of night, the company of friends and cats, and wearing cute clothes.

E-mail: AmBlaushild@gmail.com
Tumblr: Hellisntreal.tumblr.com

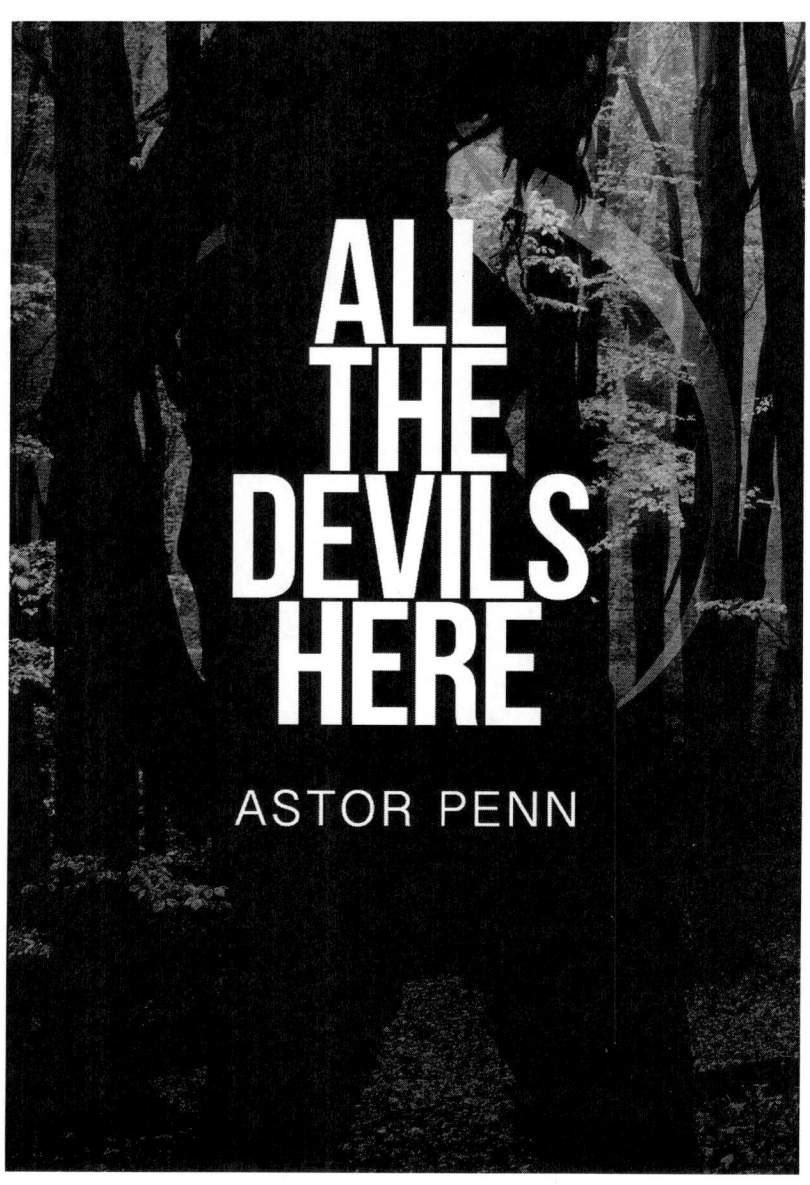

www.harmonyinkpress.com

www.harmonyinkpress.com

# THE LITTLE BLACK DRESS

## LINDA PALUND

www.harmonyinkpress.com

www.harmonyinkpress.com

Made in United States
North Haven, CT
10 October 2022